BOUND
TO THE
HIGHLANDER

The Highland Chiefs Series
By

Kate Robbins

Tirgearr Publishing

This book is a work of fiction. Names, characters, places,
and incidents either are products of the author's imagination or
are used fictitiously. Any resemblance to actual persons, living
or dead, events, or locales is entirely coincidental.

MacIntosh Clan Crest brooch depicted on this cover is used
with the kind permission of Gaelic Themes Ltd. Special thanks
to Licensed to Kilt. Photograph by Vanessa Noseworthy.

Published by Tirgearr Publishing
Ireland
www.tirgearrpublishing.com

ISBN 978-1-910234-01-3

A CIP catalogue record for this book is
available from the British Library.

10 9 8 7 6 5 4 3 2 1

DEDICATION

For my muse, Bridgie, and my man-beasts. Always there.

ACKNOWLEDGEMENTS

Thank you to Nancy and Lynn for enjoying PS I Love you so much that it inspired me to start writing Bound to the Highlander.

Thank you to my crit partner, Melanie, my number one butt-kicker.

Huge thanks to my editor, Maudeen, for holding my hand and talking me off the ledge many times.

Thanks to Kemberlee of Tirgearr Publishing for her guidance and encouragement, and for always finding the right thing to say to make me laugh.

Thanks to Paul Butler and Don McNair for their patience and fantabulous instruction.

Thanks to the awesome writers in the RWAC loop and to my Scribe Wenches for your support.

Thanks to the following for reading (sometimes more than once) and providing feedback: Nancy B, Melanie, Paul, Michelle O, Andrea, Karen D, Christine, Norma, Neil, Linda, Lynn, Amy, Karen E, Tina F, Jodi, Vanessa, Karen S, Kellie, Kelly Jean, Leona, Jean, Stephanie P, Vicki M, Diane, Nancy H, Myra, Jayla, Michelle H, Jenn, Sharon, Yolanda, Valerie, Vicki B, Lesleyanne, Rati, Libby, Necie, Jacqui, Steph, Maxine, and Earl.

Super-duper special thanks to my husband, Dave, and my two amazing boys, Nicholas and Daniel, for giving me the space and time I need to explore this writing habit I've acquired. Hey, it's healthier than smoking, right? You make me want to work hard every day.

If I've missed anyone, my sincerest apologies.

I hope you all enjoy reading Bound to the Highlander as much as I enjoyed writing it. There's something magical about Scotland. My recent travels there have only increased my fascination for the history and the culture.

CHAPTER ONE

Near Inverness, Scotland, April 1430

A horse's scream pierced the air sending a chill down her spine. *Brèagha.* Aileana Chattan quit pacing and dashed to the window. Thank God. They were home at last.

She strained toward the eerie quiet below just as the procession crested the hill beyond the gatehouse. She was right, it was her uncle's horse Brèagha, but the poor beast hobbled as three men grasped his leather reins and struggled to keep the distressed animal in check. Bile rose in her throat when she spied the body face down across its back.

She tore through the hallway, down the winding stairs, and raced out into the courtyard. Cold mud soaked her feet and her heart pummeled as the somber hunters approached. She looked to Andrews, her steward, to confirm her fear.

"I'm sorry, lass." He shifted his weight, but did not look up.

Her gaze returned to the body—his fiery red hair hung in tangles and his pale, limp hands were red-streaked. Shivers coursed through her as she beheld his unmoving form.

Her uncle, their chief, was dead.

A soundless 'No' faltered on her lips. Men and horses spun

around her, threatening her balance. She reached out to cling to something. Anything. Air slipped through her fingers as she stumbled forward. Andrews caught her the moment her knees buckled.

"I've got you, Lady Aileana. Come, we must get him inside." He placed one strong arm around her shoulder and kept her moving forward, her feet skimming the ground.

No one spoke as they entered the large stone and wooden stable. The huntsmen pulled her uncle's body from the horse and laid him at her feet. She dropped to the ground beside him. The foul stench of manure filled her nostrils and she fought the urge to retch.

"Why did you bring him in here?" The stable was no place for their chief.

"He ordered us. We had no other way to get the laird's body home and he wanted us to save Brèagha for you," Andrews said.

Her gaze shifted between her uncle's body and the horse's wild eyes. She swallowed the thick knot lodged in her throat.

"What happened?"

"We were tracking deer when something spooked him." Andrews's voice was low and grim. "Your uncle's sword was drawn. They were both injured when they fell."

The horse snorted and bobbed his head up and down. Aileana stood to view his injuries better. A deep gash oozed jagged crimson lines down his flank, pooling at his hoof. She moved to Brèagha's side and buried her fingers in his mane. His coat was covered with a sheen of sweat.

"Dear God, you won't see week's end." She must save him. "Andrews?"

"Get Argyle's surgeon," Andrews said. The stable boy fled to do his bidding.

There wasn't much she could do for the faithful beast, but

she had to try. Uncle Iain had wanted it. Aileana returned to kneel by her uncle's side and brushed a lock of red, matted hair from his brow. She gathered his limp hand into hers and searched for any remaining hint of life, but there was none. Aileana closed her eyes, tears spilling onto her cheeks.

She pictured the two of them walking through the glen with the heather—splashed mountains all around. She had loved his tales of legends and victories and could feel warm air caressing her skin and fluttering her skirts. He smiled, giving her all the comfort she needed.

Brèagha's grunt brought her back to the present and her eyes flew open. In this story, there was no victory. Her velvet gown was no protection from the cold, uncaring earth beneath her. The image of Uncle Iain and the colourful mountains faded to gray.

The men, *her men*, encircled her. They waited for her signal to move the body to his room for cleansing. Blood pounded in her ears as she struggled to do what she must, though she hated to release his hands. She cried out when she tried to fold them across his breast, but they slipped to the ground.

"Let me help, m'lady." Andrews' strong, weathered fingers covered hers and together they laid her uncle's hands across his chest. Andrews pulled her up and held her close. His strong arms tightened around her, reassuring her as she tried to contain her grief.

"Move him," Andrews said. "Now."

Thank God for Andrews. He didn't want his chief lying in filth any more than she did. The men nodded and encircled him.

"What's this?" The familiar voice boomed from the doorway. "What's happened?"

Gawain Chattan scanned the stable until his gaze landed on the body. His tall, thin frame was a silhouette against the gray sky and his expression was masked, even as he lifted his eyes to meet hers.

"The laird is dead," Andrews said.

His words pierced her. This was really happening.

"No!" Father Addison emerged from behind Gawain and rushed to Aileana's side. "No, it cannot be! When?" The priest smoothed Aileana's hair, tears forming in his crinkled eyes.

It all seemed like a hazy dream. Less than a sennight ago, they had spoken of travelling to France. Now he was a body deplete of life on the putrid stable floor.

"Yesterday," Andrews said.

Gawain turned to the men. "Deliver his body to his room and find the gravedigger."

She gasped. How could he be so unmoved? Cold seeped into her belly.

"For pity sake man, give the lass a moment." Andrews stepped forward, still holding her tight as if she needed protection from Gawain.

Their words echoed through her. She broke free from Andrews's embrace and moved to Gawain's side, her fingers itching to touch his. She hoped he would comfort her, as Andrews had, but Gawain never would. Instead, his brows knit as he examined her. Did it just occur to him she was present?

"Of course. Father Addison, please escort Lady Aileana to her room and see that her maids attend her. These distasteful details are not a lady's concern."

His voice was too calm, as if he was unaffected. She barely kept from collapsing, yet Gawain stood aloof with the countenance of someone reviewing the crofters' rents. She forced a weak smile, for inside he must be just as devastated as she. How she longed for some of his strength.

Father Addison ushered her from the stable. Above them, gloomy clouds parted and one brief shaft of sunlight shone

4

through, reminding her of a recent sermon on Christ's ascension. Aileana clutched her chest. Her uncle was gone forever.

Father Addison wrapped his arms around her and guided her up the stone steps to the castle keep. Her ever-faithful maid, Gwen, met them as they entered. Once in her chamber, Gwen draped a thick quilt over Aileana's legs while she stared into the hearth, lulled by the dancing flames.

"My lady, would you care for some heather mead?" Gwen asked.

Aileana stirred. "Thank you, no." Numbing emptiness nipped at her heart. Gwen produced a pouch of dried valerian and sprinkled some into the mead, passing it to her anyway.

Aileana held up her hand. "No, Gwen, I don't want anything to help me sleep."

"Come my lady, you will need this tonight."

Aileana placed the goblet on the side table. Her uncle's warm smile was the comfort she needed. "I fear nothing will help just yet." Her voice cracked. "So much must be done."

"There's nothing that cannot wait until the morn. And your uncle would want you to take care of yourself."

She sighed as fresh tears flowed, giving in to the ache in her chest.

Gwen placed loving arms around her. "'Twill be all right."

Aileana drew a deep breath. As much as she would like to bury herself in her grief, there were responsibilities which fell to her. Much would change with her uncle gone. For starters, she would have to marry. Was she ready for this? Her hands shook as she reached for the sweet draught. Perhaps it would help.

She sipped. The normally fragrant drink was tasteless.

She recognized the worry on Gwen's face. Aileana was fortunate to have such a woman for a lady's maid. Gwen should have had her own maid instead of serving others. Still, she endured her demotion in status with grace.

The maid squeezed her shoulders. "Please, my lady. Drink up, 'twill help."

"Thank you, no. I cannot drink it." She clattered the goblet onto the table and pushed it away.

"I wish there was something I could do for you," Gwen said.

"There is nothing anyone can do. I'm an orphan, one of means, but an orphan just the same."

The word conjured demons from the past as piercing as winter's north wind.

Aileana never knew her mother. Regarding her father, Uncle always said, "Do not seek revenge. Seek meaning." Despite these tragedies, she might not be the person she was today without them. Still, losing parents when one is so young is nothing compared to losing them when one is older with a lifetime of memories to lament. Uncle Iain was the one parent she'd had for most of her life.

"I feel helpless," Gwen said.

Aileana reached for her hand as more tears flowed. "I will come through this, Gwen. I just need some time to accept what has passed and what must occur."

"What do you mean?"

"Gawain and I will marry."

Gwen's jaw dropped a fraction. "My lady, your uncle—"

"Uncle and I never discussed it. Nevertheless, as he is my cousin, he is the most logical choice to keep the Chattan line going. A new chief must be established right away. As you know, these matters are never left to sit. For the clan's sake, the wedding will be arranged soon enough, but our betrothal must occur within the next few days."

Her insides fluttered. It was necessary, but her life was

changing faster than she ever thought possible. Entering into this new stage without her uncle to guide and encourage her was unfathomable, but it was her duty. "I shall marry Sir Gawain and he will be our new chief. I am certain 'tis what Uncle intended."

Gwen's grip on Aileana's hand tightened.

"Gwen, what is it? You realize that while he and I are not yet betrothed, the ceremony would no doubt have occurred after my birthday."

"But Gawain—"

"Must I always remind you? He is a knight and deserves our respect." Aileana retrieved her hand from Gwen's grasp. "We do so by addressing him as he is due. I'm uncertain why you find that impossible to remember." Why did Gwen react so? She trusted the woman's judgment under normal circumstances. On the subject of Gawain, their opinions differed.

Aileana had known Gawain most of her life and considered him a decent man, even if his thoughts and feelings were a mystery. Six months ago he'd arrived at Chattan Castle, newly knighted and, at her uncle's bidding, took up the constable's post. It was beneath his status as her intended, but they were shorthanded and Uncle Iain posted him because he required someone he could trust. Who better than family? Gawain had endured the post without complaint.

Since his return, Gwen had treated him with a bare minimum of respect to his face and expressed her dislike in private. Her primary objection was his reserved demeanour. Suspicious, she called it. Aileana had no clue how his countenance could be considered criminal.

Gwen inhaled through her nose and exhaled through her mouth. "My lady—" A soft knock at the door interrupted her. Gwen's expression was apologetic as she crossed the room. A moment later, Father Addison entered.

Despite his years at Chattan Castle, this marked the first occasion he'd ever entered Aileana's private domain. He scanned her room, almost bold in his perusal. She watched his gaze trail over the crimson velvet curtains accenting her canopied bed. Similar draperies hung above the shuttered windows, illuminating the winding staircase to the right. He lingered on this detail. It led to the east tower and overlooked the loch. Why would he care about that?

"Lady Aileana, how do you fare? Is there anything I may do for you?" Father Addison wrung his hands together. His brow was drawn tight and his gaze flicked around the room instead of looking at her. What did he seek?

"Has my uncle been blessed?"

"Aye, m'lady, he has. Andrews can speak with you about the arrangements if you wish."

"Can that not wait until the morn?" Gwen asked.

"Aye, of course." His gaze rested on Aileana at last. He smiled; his expression full of the warmth she was used to. Curious.

"Father, might I have a word with you?" Gwen asked. She crossed her arms and grazed her fingers along her sleeves.

"Is something amiss, Gwen?" Aileana asked.

"Not at all. Just a question I have about tomorrow's service, my lady."

Aileana was so tired and her bed held the promise of respite from the horrific day behind her. The one ahead would be no easier, but rest would help. "I'll see myself to bed, Gwen. You may leave with Father Addison."

She just had the words out when Gwen ushered the priest through the door.

Aileana removed her girdle, the one her uncle had ordered from Edinburgh last year. She folded the gold stitched piece and placed it on the edge of her bed. She untied the sleeves and sides of her gown and scooped the thick garment over her head, laying it across a chair.

Her limbs were heavy and her head pounded. She blew out the candles and crawled into her down-filled bed. The quilt's weight was more effective than Gwen's valerian, soothing her body and pulling her toward sweet slumber.

Aileana arose at sunrise the next morning, climbed the stairs to the tower, and gazed out beyond the palisades to the loch beyond. On a morning like this, Uncle Iain would point out the mirror image of the mountains and water. She closed her eyes and drank in the fresh air, willing her anguish to settle.

Many clansmen would come to mourn today. She must face these men her uncle was honour bound to protect for they were more than that to him—they were brothers. She linked her fingers together. Before this day was over, her grief would surely coil around her heart and consume her. She breathed in the cool air as deep as she could, as if that one act alone would give her the courage she needed.

After breaking her fast, she tried stitching bluebells onto a lace handkerchief while she waited for Andrews near the great hall's stone hearth. She'd welcome any task to refocus her mind for the next few hours. After she clipped the threads and reworked the pattern several times, she threw it down and reached for her manuscript.

She ignored surprised expressions from new servants regarding her ability. True, not many ladies of the gentry in the Highlands could read, but that was because not all were fortunate enough to have a doting parent whose fondest wish was to make them happy.

She would steal away whenever possible and had read and reread her uncle's humble collection many times. Her favourite was Christine de Pizan's *The Book of the City of Ladies*. It had been a gift from him the previous year.

"You've a clever mind, lass, keen on the written word I see," her uncle had said. "I've brought you something special from France." His grin had stretched wide.

"What's it about, Uncle?"

"Let's just say it's better to see all sides of a thing before judging it." He had placed the manuscript in her hands and kissed her forehead. "I'll let you decipher the rest."

He'd been right. The book detailed ridiculous falsehoods about women—written by men. Still, the broader topic of a woman's ability compared to a man's had sparked many lively discussions between them. She stroked the leather-bound script before laying it aside. Reading it would now never be the same.

Her thoughts turned to Gawain. He was a good man who would do his duty and marry her and little would change. It wasn't as if she were to marry someone who didn't understand how Chattan Castle operated or her role in it. She could rely on him.

She would prove to him he could rely on her as well. He would want to examine the estate's assets and his inheritance right away. Andrews would pull their records and she'd review them with Gawain the moment he was ready. While Chattan Castle wasn't large, they were comfortable enough and he would take charge of it all.

"M'lady?"

She looked up to see Andrews waiting. There was no turning away. She must face the task ahead because her uncle would expect no less. She squared her shoulders and followed him to the solar.

She was surprised to find Father Addison inside, pacing. And further surprised when Andrews closed the door behind her.

"Where is Sir Gawain?" Aileana asked.

"M'lady, 'tis unnecessary for the constable to attend matters related to your uncle's funeral," Andrews said.

She hadn't asked about the constable. She'd asked about her future husband.

"You see, my dear, Gawain—"

The door swung wide and the man in question stepped into the room, scowling straight away at Andrews.

Aileana stepped back a pace. His normal aloof demeanour was much preferable to the imposing figure before her. Dark circles rimmed his eyes. His face was red and a sheen of sweat marked his brow.

"What passes here?"

His voice was tight, as if he held his control by a thread.

"We were about to discuss the funeral service with her ladyship. Is there something we can do for you, Sir Gawain?" Father Addison asked.

"As I instructed yesterday, you may not burden Lady Aileana with these unpleasant details." Gawain clenched and unclenched his hands as he spoke.

Father Addison moved closer to Aileana and placed his arm around her shoulder, "Sir Gawain, 'tis natural for her ladyship to help plan the funeral service for her uncle. She will be better prepared for what is to come. After all, he was her only family."

She stiffened. Gawain was a distant cousin, but she still considered him kin.

"Please," Aileana said. "We're all grief-stricken. I thank you, Father, and you Andrews, for your consideration. It means a great deal to me, as it would have to my uncle." She turned to Gawain, "Your consideration for my well-being is much appreciated, Sir Gawain, but I am quite able to discuss the funeral. Your kindness does your clan great justice."

What else could she say to him? She hadn't spoken to him since they parted ways the day her uncle had been brought to the stable and they had not yet discussed any of that which consumed her thoughts.

His eyes narrowed and his lips formed a thin line, "As you wish, my lady."

Before she spoke another word, he turned on his heel and stalked out, slamming the door behind him. She closed her eyes. How on earth could she resolve anything with the man when he kept her at such arm's length?

The remainder of the day was a blur of faces and condolences. Aileana registered little of it. As the last shovel full of earth fell onto her past, her future, cloaked in black, mounted his horse and tore off toward the gatehouse and beyond. His grief must be overwhelming indeed.

* * *

James MacIntosh tried to reconcile his dilemma as he looked down upon the mourners from the crag above them. He'd indulged the old man last year by agreeing to his terms out of mutual respect, though he never intended to see it through. Now the man was dead and he was honour-bound to attach himself to a young, unsophisticated lass and an outdated way of life with no room for change. His destrier, Arion, fidgeted beneath him and he flexed his thighs to still the animal.

A moment later, a man broke from the group on horseback, tearing off with his black cloak flying behind him. He would expect they all return to Chattan Castle to commiserate. Whoever the rider was, it appeared he couldn't get away fast enough.

Courtesy dictated James join them and address the arrangement. Instead, he watched the remaining group retreat to the castle.

He scratched his day-old beard. There must be a way out. By tomorrow, if he hadn't shown up to pay his respects, it would be considered a slight. The last person disappeared through the gatehouse. James stared after them for several moments before turning in the opposite direction. He needed one more night to think it through. Tomorrow he would meet with Lady Aileana and defy the old man's wish.

Chapter Two

"Your absence was notable yesterday, m'lord."

James locked eyes with the grey-haired man seated across from him in his solar. His gut twisted. Normally, he would have entertained a guest in the great hall, but with so many servants bustling around, James preferred privacy for what he thought might be on the man's mind. Still, James didn't expect this sort of bold reproach for missing Chattan's funeral.

"I had pressing business at Inverness. You may pass along my condolences to the lass and tell her I will visit in person as soon as my schedule permits." James leaned back, folding his arms across his chest.

The visitor had arrived early and was afforded all the courtesy a clergyman should, but James was not about to be chastised. He need not answer to this man or anyone else except his king.

"M'lord, I am duty bound to provide my lady with the anticipated time of your arrival." Father Addison settled in his chair, hands folded in his lap.

Was this a standoff? Christ! The priest had more patience than Chattan and his father had two years prior. He didn't want this match then and he didn't want it now.

James crossed the room toward a side table topped with a

tankard of heather ale and goblets. Hanging above the table was one of numerous tapestries dotting the stone walls of Moy Hall. The exquisite weaving created a visual history of battles fought and won. This one depicted a conflict between his clan and the Camerons. MacIntosh longswords assaulted the brass-studded targe of the Cameron's defeated chief. The warrior used it to shield himself from the onslaught to no avail, and yet the man smiled. He had accepted defeat.

James poured the golden draught into two goblets, breathing deep and steady. This alliance represented everything he didn't want. Why in hell his father had insisted upon it, James couldn't say.

Chattan had approached them and persisted until the contract was signed. Not long after, James's father died. James had been too busy over the last two years leading his clan to give the arrangement much thought. In truth, he preferred to keep it as quiet as possible. The Chattans refused to support the king's progressive law on authoritative reform, so there was no way James could see the betrothal through—he being on the opposite end of the debate.

Now everything had changed.

The contract would be difficult to break since the girl had no ward. Chattan's steward and this priest knew about the agreement and it appeared they intended to hold him to it.

If James aligned with this clan, the king could very well remove his title, lands, or worse! James valued his neck too much to risk it for the likes of a woman.

James scrubbed his hand over his face. The priest wanted the betrothal to occur straight away, however, and James had no choice but refuse. It was an impossible time for him since Parliament would convene at Inverness in four days and he must be present. Now was not the time to topple the king's delicate balance of power.

He shook his head. Chattans were not just non-supporters; they were superstitious and incapable of change. He'd heard the child Aileana even kept a witch for a maid. Such wise-women, or healers as they liked to call themselves, had no place in a lady's chamber. How could this Father Addison, a so-called man of God, defy the Bishop and tolerate such heresy? They would not progress and James would be damned if he'd take one step backward.

He returned to his seat and passed a goblet to Father Addison. The man raised it in silent salute as he leafed through a bound copy of the Gospels on James's desk.

"I never took you for devout," the priest said and smiled.

"It belonged to my mother."

"She could read?"

"Aye, a little."

"Hmm. Lady Aileana as well, though more than a little. Her uncle devoted many hours to her education."

"To what end?" James asked.

"A good question. He said he wanted her to always understand what occurred around her." Father Addison replaced the wooden cover on top of the elegant scripture. He took a deep draught of the ale and leaned back with all the countenance of a man engaged in a most pleasant conversation.

James shifted in his seat, trying to ignore his persistence. This was ridiculous.

"Father—"

"She doesn't know about the arrangement." The priest's expression turned grim.

"How is that possible?" So much for knowing what happened around her. Perhaps the girl grew too headstrong for them. Though, that was unlikely considering she was just a waif. Yet, Chattan had claimed his greatest concern was her wellbeing, so why keep the arrangement from her? Whether she was strong or weak was irrelevant since her opinion was of no consequence in this matter.

"Because the laird never got around to it."

"To telling her she'd be engaged in a month? Cruel." *So much for her wellbeing.* "And to think, I agreed to this out of pity for the old man. Perhaps he had me fooled the whole time."

"No!" Addison slammed his goblet on the desk.

James leaned forward. "I should not have to remind you, Father, whose company you keep. If there's something else I need to know, be out with it and take your leave."

"I beg your pardon m'lord. I meant no offence. You see, the situation with Lady Aileana requires delicacy and swiftness."

James cocked his head to the side.

"You imply the lass carries a bastard?" This was too much. How dare he beg on the part of the loose wench? No wonder Chattan wouldn't give up until the contract was signed. Christ, the girl couldn't have been more than sixteen summers at the time.

"Father, I think it is time you leave here and beg for alms someplace else." James stood and pointed toward the door. "You may inform Lady Aileana she is under no obligation from me." Could it be this easy?

Father Addison deflated and looked like he was about to weep.

"Please m'lord, Lady Aileana is most chaste. She carries no bairn, yet her affliction has to do with another."

"Enough! I'll hear no more. You may expect me later today to discuss the contract." James strode toward the door and cast his eyes outward leaving no doubt in his meaning. Father Addison obliged and left the room, offering a curt nod as he passed.

James returned to his writing table, pausing before moving to the shelf. He opened a wooden box lined with red velvet.

Inside were papers his father had insisted must be kept separate from the account scrolls. One never knew when one might need things like land deeds and other written agreements in haste.

Among the documents was a folded, wax-sealed letter. He flipped it over several times before securing it inside his jerkin.

James returned to the writing table, downed the last of his ale, and slammed the goblet hard on the desk with a resounding thunk. He turned to stand at the open window resting his hands on the window ledge. The sky was a pale yellowish hue and the day would be bright, despite the gathering storm within.

He stood motionless for a long time, scanning the activity three stories below. Men trained with wooden swords, a market offered wagons full of produce, and many of his tenants had already arrived to barter their wares. He had everything he needed; enough men to defend his territory, more resources than he could deplete in two lifetimes, and plenty of women to bed when and where he chose.

His legacy to his clan would be ill served by adding a meager estate and a young, unsophisticated lass into the mix. His future success must include a union with another strong, noble family. Times had changed under a new monarchy and, in order to survive, he must change with them.

King James Stewart, first of his name, had already demonstrated just how far he was willing to go to impose his idea of progress. James and his younger brother, Calum, had travelled to Parliament at Inverness shortly after their father's death. The king had extended the invitation so that James, among thirty-nine other Highland chiefs, would accept new laws restricting their power. They listened in shock. The resulting uproar ended in three hangings and several imprisonments. James remembered it well.

He had learned much through his dealings with the king to date. This monarch cared little for how Highlanders resolved their issues in the past, and in order to prosper in King James's new Scotland, he would have to somewhat conform to the man's ways. That meant earning an earl's title and strong position at court. The simplest way to do that was to accept a marriage proposal from someone of the king's choosing. He'd inherited his baron's title and while that distinction allowed him many privileges, as the Earl of Moray he would be afforded a much stronger voice.

James watched Father Addison cross the bailey's threshold leaving Moy Hall. A great number of men greeted him as he passed. Despite his tolerance of the old ways, respect followed the priest.

Fulfilling Chattan's contract or any previous offers from among his neighbours meant he would forever remain stagnant. Constant bickering over tiny strips of land was by no means his idea of progress. His fingers gripped the stone window ledge.

As the priest disappeared past the gatehouse, a knock echoed through the door, interrupting his thoughts.

"Enter."

Calum MacIntosh swung the door wide and sauntered into the solar. His smirk implied he'd spoken to Father Addison on his way out.

"I hear congratulations are in order, Brother." His dark eyes twinkled.

James faced the man, younger by two years, and glared. Calum's grin broadened. He enjoyed this.

James shook his head. "Do not be absurd. I'm not marrying anyone, much less a waif who has yet to see her eighteenth year."

"Now, now. There's no need to be unkind. I hear Aileana

Kate Robbins

Chattan has grown into quite the beauty in the last couple of years." Calum helped himself to the remaining ale.

"I doubt that very much. Look, Calum, I have little interest in this subject, as you well know." James crossed his arms. "I have no intention of carrying out a contract with anyone's niece, daughter, or sister until I'm damn good and ready. While Chattan was our father's oldest friend, my respect for him will only stretch so far. The priest was just here telling me the girl was not virginal."

Calum relaxed into the seat Father Addison had occupied. He leaned back with his long legs outstretched as if they discussed nothing more than a tenant's sheep count.

"That may be so, Brother, but you have a responsibility to this clan and this family. You are its chief and are expected to produce its next one." Calum linked his hands and placed them behind his head. "In order to do that, you must stop trying to bed every loose woman in the country and marry. Wait." Calum released his hands, sat up straight and chuckled. "You're worried she's not virginal? When has that ever mattered to you before? You accepted this proposal and you are honour bound to see it through since the girl has no one to care for her." He re-linked his hands behind his head and leaned back once again. "You know if Father were here this would have already occurred."

James had heard enough. He didn't need a reminder of his duty. Before he died, their father had expressed his sincerest wish that his sons back the progressive Stewart. It hadn't been easy at first. The man was bent on unifying Scotland, which meant the chiefs and nobles must relinquish some of their power for the greater good. In theory this made perfect sense, but theory meant little in the real world of the Highlands where centuries of feuds had shaped a people who would not change without a damned good reason. His father might have been swayed by Chattan's proposal, but he would have seen more sense in James's intentions.

"Well, Father's not here, is he? I am Chief. And if I say I will refuse this match then that's the way it will be."

James refused to listen to any more of this nonsense. He would not bend, not to a priest and not to Calum. He passed his brother and crossed the room in three strides. He was almost in the hallway when Calum spoke again from over his shoulder.

"James, Clan Chattan needs your protection."

The comment stopped him at the threshold. Raiding in the shire had increased and the Chattan estate was small and vulnerable, meaning an alliance would benefit them. There were benefits to his clan as well. Clan Chattan was a confederation of smaller ones and some had stood in battle with him before. Their loyalty would not be an issue. The extra numbers they provided would assist with surprise attacks from those damned Camerons as well.

"James, you do realize you would control the estate that includes Chattan Castle and the farms Chattan oversaw?"

James's own lands stretched as far north as Inverness and as far east as the Cairngorm Mountains, and while these acquisitions were valuable, were they worth the personal sacrifice?

Why couldn't Calum see 'twas impossible? It would be easy to marry someone local and ignore the affairs of their nation, but he could not. His influence was great enough that if he were to back the Stewart, others would follow, yet it was a delicate operation which took time and patience.

"Aye, but at what cost?"

His exasperated retort was enough to quell Calum long enough to provide an opportunity for escape. He descended the winding staircase of the west tower and strode through the tapestry-covered hallway toward the main entrance. These hangings also depicted various individuals in their moment of defeat. He glared at them. Damn them all!

James strode toward the stables where Arion waited. Urging the great white horse from his stall, he mounted the beast and tore off across the barren expanse outside the thick walls of the bailey, his teeth bared and his jaw set. Before long, they were enveloped in dense forest.

He rode hard for about an hour along the beaten road passing verdant, rolling farmland until he stopped near a small loch. The sun broke through the clouds and daytime stars twinkled on its flat surface. Shady trees clung together on one side while the other spread out into a green carpet forming a large field. These lush surroundings weren't far from Chattan lands. He dismounted and walked Arion over to a small babbling stream for a well-deserved drink, patting the horse's thick neck.

The cool air helped. Refusing Chattan's proposal should have been easy, yet he couldn't without revealing his larger plan. His neighbours would never support him outright. No, he must stay the course and allow them to follow his lead over time. If Scotland were to survive as a thriving, independent state, she must unify, in every sense of the word, and the one man who had the drive and intelligence to make that happen was the Stewart king.

James remounted Arion and headed to Chattan Castle where he would put an end to this ridiculous arrangement once and for all.

Aileana paced. Something was wrong with Gawain and wondering about it was exhausting. He'd disappeared straight after the burial and she hadn't seen him since. Normally, he greeted her each morning without fail, but today he was nowhere to be found.

Since her uncle's death, Gawain had been short tempered with many servants, including this morning at sunrise when he'd pitched into Andrews for questioning him on his whereabouts the previous evening. When Andrews reported this to her she was quick to defend, but did Gawain deserve her faith?

She jumped when Gwen cleared her throat from the doorway of the great hall.

"What!" Aileana hadn't meant to snap.

Gwen smiled. "I apologize for interrupting you, my lady, but I was wondering if you would care to break your fast?"

"Oh Gwen, I am so sorry. Please forgive my rudeness."

"No need to apologize, my lady," Gwen smiled. "You've been through a great ordeal. Would you like some bread and mead?"

Gwen didn't deserve Aileana's frustration, she was ever the comforter. The woman could ease tension out of stone with one of those smiles. What Aileana needed wasn't nourishment or to remain cooped up inside the cheerless walls of the castle.

"Thank you, no. I believe I shall walk for a time and collect wildflowers." She drew in a deep breath. "I'm overdue for fresh air and I see the cowslip are wilting. Heaven knows we need all the peace and tranquility we can acquire from their energy these days." Aileana walked past Gwen and squeezed her hand.

"An excellent choice, my lady," Gwen grinned.

"You have taught me well." Aileana smiled back. Gwen was a practicing pagan as were many others at the castle. Aileana herself was a Catholic Christian, however, under the kind-hearted guidance of Father Addison, she'd been taught tolerance. There were times, she feared, she and he were in the minority in this world.

Gwen fetched Aileana's blue cloak and draped it over her

shoulders. The air was warm enough to leave her hair uncovered so she let her long blonde curls hang loose across her back. She replaced her soft-soled slippers with hard, leather shoes better suited for the outdoors and left Chattan Castle.

The early morning mist was refreshing as she walked along the well-beaten road leading north toward Inverness. The fog lifted just enough to expose the stunning landscape. Out here, with the rolling green hills and explosions of colour, she could spread her arms wide and feel free from the pain gripping her. The tightness in her chest eased. In the distance, the sharp mountain peaks protruded from the crawling mist towards the blue sky. The day would be lovely when the fog burned off.

Aileana reached the crossroads and turned right, following a smaller path leading east. Thick brush and oak trees framed the path, often giving way to vast farmlands that lay beyond. Littered here and there were bluebells, lady fingers, and cowslip. She knelt to collect some, pausing to inhale their sweet scent.

The flowers brought back memories of the many times her uncle had brought them to her. Widowed and with no children of his own, he took guardianship of Aileana after her father's death and came to love and treat her as if she were his own. All these years, they had only each other and she was lost without him.

Her hair prickled at her nape. She stepped onto the road and looked both ways, her arms full of flowers. The thunder of hooves reached her ears at about the same time her peripheral vision caught a flash of something white and very large coming around the bend just ahead. She leapt out of the way to avoid being trampled, landing on her backside. She strained her neck and viewed the largest horse she'd ever seen. The dense fog had prevented her from seeing the horse or its rider approaching at top speed. She was lucky to have avoided serious injury.

Aileana's heart raced. She should have known better than to walk alone, considering all the recent raids. Was the rider friend or foe? She recognized a small path across the road. If she could get around the giant beast before the rider saw her, she could slip through the trees undetected.

Within a split second, however, the rider dismounted and held out his large hand. His deep chuckle made her cheeks burn.

"I'm sorry, lass. I didn't expect to see anyone out at this hour, nor this far from any dwelling."

The tall man took in her appearance, his sweeping glance resting on the embroidered stitching of her low neckline. His gaze lingered there before travelling up her throat. She held her breath as his eyes trailed over her body.

"You can ride with me if you like." His husky voice conjured images of silk sweeping across her flesh.

She was entranced by the sight of him. Thick muscles flexed beneath a dark leather jerkin which ended just above his knee and was secured at his waist with a broad belt. In his current position, she could see his thigh muscle tense and her face grew hotter. His plaid covered one shoulder and ran underneath his sword arm secured by a large silver brooch offset with rubies and centred with a wildcat.

MacIntosh.

They supported the king. It wasn't well known, but Uncle had speculated to those he trusted. Anyone who supported a man who pawned his people like cattle for his personal gain was no friend of hers.

It was clear from his inappropriate suggestion, she was better off not knowing him. He was no gentleman, despite his expensive accessory and giant horse. No decent man would speak that way to a lady. Couldn't he tell by the way she was dressed that she was no common wench? Then again, it would not matter to this base sort of man. Either way, without a chaperone, she was not about to remain in his company for one more second. His hand hung in mid-air, but she ignored it, hoisting herself instead off the cold ground.

She mustered the most authoritative voice she could. "No thank you." Aileana lifted her chin and walked away.

"Wait lass. I'm sorry to have startled you. What are you called?"

Aileana turned on her heel intent to put this rogue in his place and ran into his chest. She gasped. The thick, rich scent of leather enveloped her, sending an unexpected shiver down her spine. She stumbled, but he was quick enough to catch her by the arms before she fell. Her hands splayed flat against his chest. Bulging muscles underneath his jerkin begged her fingers to stroke their curve.

His bright green eyes bore into hers. While his long brown hair was tied at his nape, a few strands had broken free and fell loose across his face. She fought the irresistible urge to reach up and tuck them behind his ear.

"Who are you?"

His deep voice was warm honey on her flesh. He smelled of sweet ale and she was transfixed by his mouth which curved in all the right ways.

"Perhaps you're a faerie come to steal me away."

His raspy voice made her skin tingle.

"Good sir—"

"I bet you taste as delicious as you smell."

Aileana pushed against his chest. He pushed back. The stranger pulled her forward, his mouth now no more than an inch from hers. His hard body pressed against hers, spreading heat to her very core.

His fingers brushed the side of her mouth and his lips parted. Her knees trembled. His intent was clear and their

26

proximity was inappropriate.

Panic hit her hard.

She twisted free from his grasp and dashed through the brush. She didn't look back until she was sure he wasn't following. Scanning her surroundings, she spied a more defined trail that would lead her to Chattan Castle without having to cross the main road again.

Aileana slowed her pace and drew a steadying breath. Who was that man and why had she let him hold her? She should have backed off upon his approach. Had he really meant to kiss her? A few more deep breaths slowed her heartbeat enough so that when she turned towards the main lane, leading up to Chattan grounds, she was calmer. But only a little. Her home was a welcome sight.

Chapter Three

Chattan Castle was small, but many considered it one of the most beautiful in the shire and Aileana took great pride in overseeing its upkeep. The path to the castle's entrance was bordered with beautiful flowers and shrubs of all sizes and colours. She bent low to inspect the budding azaleas and remembered the lost bounty of wild flowers still scattered along the road.

She should go back to collect them. Then again, she would not risk running into that rascal again.

"Damned MacIntosh." Aileana was not one to mutter under her breath, but the man had unraveled her.

"M'lady? I'm sorry, I didn't see you there." Hurst, her gardener, poked his head up from the brush.

Aileana jumped.

"Hurst. I'm sorry. I did not see you either." Her voice squeaked. She smoothed her skirts. "Tell me, will our garden reach its usual potential this year?"

"Ahh, m'lady, you'll be pleased when the azaleas are in full bloom. The bluebells and hawthorn are coming along and I believe your new roses will be in fine form before long."

Her uncle had no time for planning combinations of colours and style of flowers, but Hurst was just as enthusiastic as she.

When she was but eight summers, she and Hurst had designed the entire front garden and many travellers to this part of the country often stopped by to view the acclaimed Chattan grounds. It gave her something to focus on after her father's death. Aileana's responsibilities within the walls of the castle kept her from spending much time in her garden in recent years; however, she loved the brief visits she managed.

"Thank you."

"It's my pleasure, m'lady. Agnes and I are broken-hearted over the laird. You'll call on us if you need anything."

She could call on them and countless others at any time. She needed to reassure them they could rely on her for the same. Without knowing it, he'd reminded her of her purpose - them. Whether clansmen from the village or former nobility like Gwen, they all needed her protection. No matter what became of her, she would not let them down. She must find Gawain and set their betrothal in motion.

Aileana nodded and continued on to the castle. The smell of cooking meat met her as she entered the keep, sparking her hunger for the first time in days. Gwen met her in the great hall and took her cloak as Aileana sat near the hearth. The maid stared at her for a moment before she left the room. Gwen returned a short time later with a trencher of cheese, meats, and bread which she placed on a side table.

Gwen's brow was knit and she chewed on her bottom lip. "Are you certain you won't take your meal in the dining hall?"

"Not today." It was the same response she'd given every day since Uncle Iain had died. They shared their meals in that room and she could not yet bring herself to do so alone.

Aileana ate in silence while Gwen stared at her.

"Is something wrong?" Aileana asked.

"Your cheeks have more colour. You look well this morn."

Aileana remembered the man on the road and her face grew

warm. There was no way Gwen could know of her encounter. "I had an invigorating walk."

"Aye. Walking can do that." Gwen didn't leave or change her curious expression.

"Was there anything else, Gwen?"

"Nothing else, my lady."

Yet, she didn't move from her spot. The maid was lying through her teeth, but Aileana was too hungry to care. Gwen never did or said anything without reason and was too sharp for her own good.

"Pardon me, m'lady, but you are requested in the solar." Colleen, the newest maid, wrung her hands. Gawain must be there and ready to talk. She stood while Gwen smoothed her dress and raked expert fingers through her wind kissed tresses.

"May I be of assistance?" Gwen asked, her expression full of concern.

"Aye, please bring refreshments to the solar. I'm certain Gawain will appreciate the offering, considering his early rise this morning."

Gwen pursed her lips, but she did not say anything. Good. This was nerve-racking enough without anyone adding to her trepidation. Though she had no reason to be nervous, Gwen's frown unsettled her.

Aileana took a deep breath and squared her shoulders as she walked through the stone hallway to the solar. Her uncle had loved this room and furnished it to include the cushioned bench beside the fireplace. She frowned, realizing she would never spend another evening there reading to him. Aileana put the dismal thought away as she reached out to grasp the flat metal latch on the door. Her future lay behind it.

She hesitated and smoothed her pale blue dress again; hoping Gawain would be pleased by her appearance. Regardless of his reserved ways, they needed to address this marriage and his usual tight-lipped manner would not do. Perhaps with no one else around, he would engage in an actual conversation for once. Her life would be much easier if he would just tell her what he wanted instead of shutting her out.

Picturing him, she lifted the latch. She pushed on the door with a smile on her face and an appropriate greeting ready.

The heavy door arced across the floor quieter than a whisper. Aileana scanned the room. At first it looked empty, but she soon saw him sitting in her uncle's chair behind his writing desk with his back to the door. He twirled what looked like a letter between his fingers. One leg was half slung over the other and the sight of a thick calf muscle surprised her. Didn't Gawain pad his leg irons?

He seemed quite relaxed. Something wasn't right.

Her heart beat a little faster as she crossed the threshold and crept further into the room to catch a better view of the lower half of his body. Woollen plaid covered a dark leather jerkin. A wave of nausea washed over her as she inched closer. Her eyes trailed up his torso where the plaid swept over a thick shoulder then disappeared behind brown hair.

She tripped on a chair, out of place in the centre of the room, and cursed to herself when the sound alerted him to her presence. She froze as his head turned and green eyes met hers. Her mouth dropped. It was not possible! What was he doing here?

The man pushed back the chair. The sharp scrape of wood across stone echoed and sent a hundred butterflies loose in her gut. He turned toward her and stepped around the writing desk. She should flee, but could not uproot herself. His intent gaze pinned her. When he was near enough that she could have reached out to touch him, he held out a piece of folded parchment. She wanted to hide from him, from herself, from anything that would remind her how unhinged he made her.

31

He placed the letter in her hand and she looked down. Her clan crest was stamped in red wax. The seal was unmistakable. She placed her thumbs on either side of it and pressed, the soft crack echoing in the silent room. He stood so close, sending every nerve in her body on end. His leather scent filled her senses again, feeding her urge to slip into his arms.

She must get a hold of her scattered wits.

Her hands shook as she unfolded the letter and recognized her uncle's scripted hand. A stabbing pain tore into her chest. How many letters had he sent her over the years when travelling? This would be the last one she ever read. She registered the stranger guiding her to a chair.

Through misty eyes she began. The first words were of a formal nature listing her uncle's full title, properties and other assets, none of which were a surprise, but the last paragraph forced her breath to catch in her throat.

Upon her eighteenth birthday, my niece, Aileana Chattan, shall enter into a three month betrothal contract with James MacIntosh, Chief of the MacIntosh Clan of Inverness-shire. Upon their marriage, the Chattan Clan will fall under the protection of that Chief. In the event of my death before her eighteenth birthday, their betrothal must occur without delay.

Aileana's breath hissed through her teeth. James MacIntosh? Her head throbbed as she absorbed the enormity of her uncle's wishes.

Uncle Iain wanted a union between her clan and those who backed the Stewart king and would encourage others to follow. How could he do this to her? She never imagined he would marry her to anyone but Gawain, and never considered he would contemplate a permanent link between the Chattans and another clan. And on whom did he settle? The most arrogant, insufferable, womanizer this side of the green. She had no time for him or his traitorous clan.

Aileana re-read the letter again. There must be some mistake. Uncle would not force her to marry the chief of *that* clan.

The MacIntosh had visited the estate over the years, since his lands bordered her uncle's. During those times she would observe, with mortification, the castle's female servants bending over backwards to gain even one brief glance from him. Well, she was not some gushing maid about to throw herself at his feet.

"Lady Aileana?"

She had not seen him in about three years.

"It is my pleasure to reacquaint with you after so long." His deep voice interrupted her inner rant. "I believe you've blossomed since our last meeting. I mean, it has been quite some time since we last met."

Her guts lurched as realization dawned. Her eyes snapped up to lock with his. When they'd met on the road, he was coming here. May a hole open up and swallow her now. She'd acted like a smitten kitchen maid. She dropped her chin to her chest, fighting the burning sensation behind her eyes. She would not cry in front of him, no matter how embarrassed.

"I believe the letter you're holding contains business we must discuss concerning your uncle's wishes. I knew him well. He was an honourable man and I respected him. I'm very sorry for your loss."

She tilted her head to look up at him. He appeared sincere. She should be gracious and thank the MacIntosh for his kindness toward her uncle, however, no words would come. How could the man expect her to forget what happened with her father? And who was responsible?

"Lady Aileana, are you unwell? Shall I fetch a maid?"

This was absurd. She wasn't a child unable to control her emotions. *Speak!*

"I am well, my lord, thank you," she said, straightening her back.

"I understand this is a shock. The reason for my visit today was to speak with you in private on the subject to avoid any discomfort which could be viewed by the servants." His expression darkened. "I am aware this arrangement was not shared with you until now."

She had not recognized him earlier, no doubt because she had never given him much attention in the past. So annoyed was she by everyone else's reaction to him, she always avoided him. Now for the first time, she saw him.

Strong jaw, straight nose, firm lips and those damned eyes. Aye, the maids were right, he was handsome. Maybe too handsome, and she had no idea how to handle him or this confounding letter.

Nothing made any sense. Uncle had always treated everyone from the grandest lord to the lowliest servant with respect and honour. He must have felt a powerful connection to this man to entrust him with his estate—and her!

Gawain. He expected to inherit the estate. What would he think?

Aileana cleared her throat. "Lord MacIntosh, I appreciate your consideration. Your thoughtfulness does you great justice, to be sure. I believe before we proceed further you must know another expects to gain these lands and my hand."

Aileana watched the muscle in his jaw flex.

"Please allow me to explain," she said. "My cousin Gawain is entitled to this estate since Uncle's passing and, in truth, when I entered this room earlier expected him seated where you were. Just as I assumed he was next in line, I am certain he does as well."

"You are sure of this?" He leaned towards her. Too close.

She couldn't think straight.

"I—I mean, who else knew of yours and Uncle's arrangement?" How long had it been in place? Why had no one told her?

"My brother Calum, your steward, and your priest knew of this agreement. If what you say is true, and while it is unfortunate, your uncle changed his mind at some point."

She gasped. He presumed to know her uncle's mind? How dare he?

"I will speak to your cousin," he said.

"No need, my lord. He's my cousin and I will speak for my uncle's wishes." Her retort was a little harsher than intended, but no one would speak for Iain Chattan except her.

"Very well then. How do you wish to proceed?"

She didn't know that or anything anymore. Still, he needed an answer.

"We will receive you three days hence. I expect that will provide me with enough time to speak with Gawain and prepare." Her mouth seemed separated from her mind.

"For the betrothal ceremony?" His jaw slacked. Wasn't that why he was here?

"It shall occur at the same time," Aileana said. Regret stabbed her as soon as the words were past her lips.

"In three days then."

She raised her hand to him on instinct when he stood. He held her fingers and placed a warm kiss on the back of her hand sparking tiny sensations up her arm. A moment later he was gone.

Someone, two people in fact, had a lot of explaining to do. But what if others knew as well. Gwen? That might explain her odd behaviour earlier. Gawain? That could explain his avoidance. Did everyone in the castle know about this except her?

She'd probe them soon enough. For now, she had to wrap

her head around the letter. Her uncle must have left an accompanying one just for her explaining his request. She placed the letter on the desk and rummaged through it. An hour later, her hands were as empty as when she started.

* * *

James threw Arion's leather reins at the stable hand and strode toward Moy Hall, muttering curses all the way. When in hell had a woman ever gotten under his skin like that? He knew when, but at least then he could blame youth and inexperience. Now, he had no excuse.

James was about to become attached in a very permanent way. He must be out of his wits to allow the situation to get this far. To say he had been surprised by her beauty was a gross understatement. Calum said she'd blossomed and he wasn't mistaken. Far from it. Long flowing golden curls framed her flawless face offset by deep blue eyes and a pouty little mouth he wanted to taste. From his first vision of her, seated on the ground with dozens of wildflowers scattered about, he wanted her. He didn't want to help her up, rather join her there and taste her sweetness.

Standing above her, he was drawn to the deep cleavage her square neckline revealed. His loins had tightened at the sight. Oh aye, he would have taken her right there on the roadside had she not walked away from him. Had she actually dismissed him? He was unused to that kind of reaction from anyone, much less a woman. Woman or no, he was in it deep enough now and he had no idea what to do about her.

Chapter Four

Aileana drew in a deep breath and returned to the great hall to reason out this latest troubling development. What logical motive could her uncle have for this union? Money? Power? True, the MacIntosh was far wealthier than she, not to mention the most influential nobleman in the shire. Still, it was unlike her uncle to put much weight on such things regarding her happiness. Did he lack faith in Gawain's ability to manage the estate and protect their tenants? If so, it made little sense. Her more immediate concern was how she'd break this news to him.

"Gaw—Sir Gawain awaits you in the solar, my lady," Gwen said from just inside the hall. Aileana hadn't even heard her enter. Was there caution in Gwen's tone? Or perhaps it was her own trepidation causing cold tentacles of dread to creep up her spine. As she approached the solar, she braced herself for the difficult task of explaining the latest development. She scarce understood it herself.

As she reached for the latch, Gawain swung the door wide. He held a letter in his hand and his whole body seethed. His lips were drawn back revealing uneven teeth and he sneered like a wild cat about to strike. Her throat dried.

She had left the letter on her uncle's desk. Cheeks burning

from her mistake, she opened her mouth to speak, but the words caught in her throat.

"What is this?" Gawain asked.

Aileana straightened her shoulders. What was done was done. "'Tis a document the MacIntosh delivered earlier today. Gawain—"

He stepped towards her so she had to tilt her head up to look into his stormy gray eyes flashing lightning at her.

"How long did you wait after my cousin died to whore yourself to a rich man?"

Her stomach dropped. "What? Gawain. Please. It's not like that." How could he think she'd arranged this?

"Then tell me how it is. I'm surprised you'd cast me aside with so little regard. All this time, you waited to find an opportunity to be rid of me." His fists were clenched at his sides and his jaw was rigid. "All your pleasant greetings and your fake smiles. You're quite the little player, aren't you?"

Her breath came out in short pants while she wrung her hands. She has so little family left and she couldn't bear his anger when she was not to blame.

"Gawain, please let me explain."

"Enough. Your words are like poison." He emphasized the word by spitting on the hem of her gown. "I hope you rot in hell choking on MacIntosh banners, you spoiled, deceitful little whore!"

She gasped.

His hate-filled eyes scanned her with a look of pure and unmistakable disgust before shoving the letter at her. He then stormed away from her uncle's solar leaving her with an unspoken apology.

Her blood ran cold. She slipped into the solar and secured the letter inside a hidden compartment in the desk. She had forgotten to put it away earlier and Gawain must think her insensitive enough to leave it lying about on purpose. A cowardice act indeed if it had been true. Her eyes burned. This was far from how she envisioned breaking the news to him.

She should run after him and apologize for his discovery. She should tell him her uncle's intent was as much a surprise to her as it was to him. If he would only listen, she could salvage some kind of relationship with Gawain. He was family after all. Wouldn't he commiserate with her? She closed her eyes, spilling tears onto her cheeks.

"M'lady, a visitor," Colleen said. The maid stood in the doorway, face flushed and wearing a silly grin.

From behind her, the MacIntosh stepped into view. The maid peeped up at him then disappeared around the corner.

For a few heartbeats they stared at one another. She was distraught over what had just happened with Gawain and in no mood to exchange pleasantries with anyone—he of all people.

"My lord, is there something you require?"

"Who was the man I saw leaving just now?" His voice was deep; his words slow and deliberate.

"That was Gawain Chattan," she said, unable to stop a traitorous tear from spilling.

He frowned. She had neither the strength nor the desire to pretend interest in what could be bothering him. Couldn't he give her a moment to process?

"My lord, to what do I owe the pleasure of this second visit today? May I offer you a seat or refreshments?" Her patience wore thin, yet he kept on staring at her. Her insides might soon scatter in all directions if he didn't soon do something.

"There is nothing I require, Lady Aileana," he said. "Good day to you."

In the next instant, he too was gone, leaving her alone and too confused to see straight. Why would the MacIntosh return so soon after their previous meeting and then leave with such haste? She now didn't have time to catch up with Gawain to offer an explanation. Frustration grew inside her like a pestilence.

She paced the room to steady her inner turmoil and formed two conclusions. First, there was nothing she could do about Gawain tonight. Tomorrow, she would track him down and explain everything. She knew he was an early riser, and so was she. She'd await him outside his chamber if that's what it took and make him listen to her explanation. Second, she would receive the MacIntosh in three days and she must prepare everyone. She could do neither if she did not pull herself together.

How in heaven's name had this impossible turn of events come about?

She returned to the hall to find supper waiting. She picked at the warm bread and rabbit stew, but could not force herself to eat a morsel. Instead, she pushed the trencher away and sought refuge in her room to sort through the day's events. One hand on her hip, she raised the other to her mouth and paced. Aileana longed for her uncle's counsel.

She stopped at the staircase leading to the tower. No one else ever used it so she could enjoy some much needed peace and quiet up there. As she contemplated the climb, she heard Gwen humming.

The chamber was large enough for her wooden tub to remain in an inner dressing room. This pleased her since she had often felt a twinge of pity for the men who had to carry her uncle's tub to and from his room. Gwen was there waiting with a bath drawn and a fire crackling. Aileana eyed the steaming rose scented water. Bath first, maybe then a climb to the tower.

"Did you have a nice walk this morning?" Gwen asked.

Heat rose to her cheeks as Gwen helped remove her clothing. "Yes, I did thank you, a very refreshing one at that."

Aileana had forgotten the walk with everything else which had happened since. She offered nothing else and hoped the subject would be dropped. Aileana slipped as she stepped over the tub's edge and stumbled into it. Just thinking of the MacIntosh made her fluttery.

"My dear Lady," Gwen said, smiling. "I believe you returned from your walk more disturbed than refreshed. Did something happen?"

"Of course not. I walked and I returned." Why was Gwen concerned about her walk more than her meeting with Gawain?

"You walked and you returned." Gwen raised a single brow and crossed her arms. "Did you meet anyone on your walk?"

Aileana blinked at her. Was the woman a seer as well as a healer? "I have nothing interesting to report on that count."

"No chance encounter?"

"Chance encounter? Gwen, what makes you think that?"

"You were blushing when you returned. I don't think it was from over-exertion, at least not from walking."

Aileana gasped. Gwen thought she had a tryst with someone? How could she make such a leap? As a lady, Aileana was expected to bring all aspects of virginity to the marriage bed. Gwen, on the other hand, often boasted her experience would be welcomed by her future husband and thus had a fine list of conquests herself. Did the woman think of nothing else?

"You're mistaken, I have nothing of the sort to share with you," Aileana said. She was still coming to grips with her first encounter with the MacIntosh and had other, more pressing, matters requiring her attention than his damned looks and how she'd reacted to him.

"Do tell, who was he? The blacksmith's son? Oooh, he's ripe that one." Gwen grinned from ear to ear.

"It is you who enjoys such affairs, not I," Aileana said, the corner of her mouth pulling a little.

"Oh wait, I know, the new ferrier in the stable! I hear he's very good with his hands and I don't mean for shoeing horses either. No wonder you were flushed when you returned. Tell me, did he show you the new stallion?"

Aileana gasped again. "You're incorrigible! I did not have an encounter with any boy!"

She picked up her washcloth and lathered soap onto it with vigor as she glanced at Gwen from the corner of her eye. Gwen's eyes showed all the signs of teasing. Aileana sighed and faced her.

"Well, if you must know, I did meet someone on my walk this morning. It was the MacIntosh. He caught me off guard and I almost fell. I didn't know it was him until he arrived later with Uncle Iain's letter. He was on his way to stake his claim for Uncle's assets."

Gwen gasped. "He was coming here to do what?"

"Aye, I'm to be paired with the MacIntosh, Gwen. Don't ask me for any details because at this point I don't wish to discuss it."

Her eyes lit as though this was the best news she'd ever heard. "This is surprising, but that doesn't explain why you were flushed when you returned earlier." Gwen's smile stretched across her face.

Aileana didn't reply. She held her breath as Gwen searched her expression. The woman was far too calculating and far too pleased at the moment.

Gwen raised her eyebrows. "He's very handsome, isn't he?" Her hazel eyes sparkled with mischief.

"I have to admit, his looks escaped my notice. He was very proper and quite gentlemanlike in his address considering the delicate nature of our encounter." Aileana lied. As she spoke, she rubbed her arms.

"And you didn't happen to notice his eyes? His lips? Those powerful legs of his?"

With each question, Aileana blushed deeper and said nothing. She slipped further into the tub and continued to wash herself. Gwen didn't ask any more questions, but maintained a hint of her previous grin.

She tried to relax in the luxurious water, but just couldn't remain still. Her skin tingled everywhere she touched it, so she washed, rinsed then stepped out of the tub to be wrapped into linen sheets and guided to the fire to dry. Gwen beckoned two maids who removed all the bathwater, threw it out the window and wiped the tub down. They helped Aileana into her linen night shift and left the room.

Gwen brushed Aileana's hair until it was almost dry. The effect was soothing and eased some of her tension.

When she was finished, Gwen paused at the door. "I wish you pleasant dreams tonight, my lady. You deserve them." With that, she smiled and closed the door behind her.

A climb to the tower required energy she didn't have. Aileana crawled beneath the thick layers of quilts on her bed, curled on her side, and awaited sleep; but it would not come. Instead, she considered the ceremony that would take place three days hence.

A great number of visitors would arrive once the celebrations began. Every nobleman and his Lady within a day's ride, not to mention their tenants, would grace the doors of Chattan Castle and the feasting would continue for three days. That was the tradition. Some would be dear old friends she'd be very happy to see, but most would be curiosity seekers wanting to see how she and the great Laird MacIntosh appear together.

News was bound to spread fast of her uncle's wishes. Everyone would expect a feast to celebrate Aileana's new engagement after the funeral, but no doubt there'd be surprise and shock over the identity of the groom. Rumours grew over the years that many opportunistic mothers and fathers alike had set their sights on him for their daughters, but he had declined them all. Some even speculated his dutiful younger brother might have to provide a MacIntosh heir. Her uncle's legacy would prove them wrong.

Aileana sighed and turned onto her back, staring up at the crimson velvet encasing her canopy.

Too often these days, funerals and weddings followed one another. New alliances were forged in this way and without the consent of the unfortunate couple in question. Too often she sympathized with the sacrificial bride. Now it was her turn.

For the first time in her life, her future was unclear. What could she expect from this man and why hadn't her uncle spoken of the arrangement? Sure she wouldn't be of age for another month, but could this have been his idea of a birthday surprise? If that were the case, he had succeeded in surprising her, but she found no pleasure in it. And why were Father Addison and Andrews sworn to such secrecy on the matter? It made no sense at all. There was a piece to this mystery she couldn't see and both men had made themselves scarce today so she couldn't find an opportunity to challenge them. Of course, two visits from the MacIntosh and Gawain's return had prevented her from seeking anyone to question either.

And what about her father? All her life she was led to believe the king was responsible for her father's death and now she had to marry one of the monarch's biggest supporters. Something must have happened to change her uncle's mind in favour of James MacIntosh, but she couldn't for the life of her figure out what that could be.

She understood the restrictions preventing him from passing on his estate to her. The only way to secure her future at Chattan Castle was through marriage, yet he had treated her like the son who would have inherited it all. He taught her the business of the estate and how to account for and manage everything right down to the last blade of grass. To her knowledge, Gawain had received the same training. Wasn't that preparation so they could run the estate together? Why else would he have exposed Gawain to the essentials of management if he were not expected to use those skills?

Aileana turned onto her other side and the quilts tangled around her feet. She kicked them into submission and tried lying on her stomach.

She always enjoyed an enormous amount of freedom with her uncle and assumed she would have had much the same with Gawain. Would she have any now? How her uncle had concluded she would be better off partnered with a man who went through women like a hungry sheep in new spring pasture, she could not guess. A man like that wouldn't consider his wife's needs and feelings.

Aileana turned over again and fluffed the pillow before tossing her head upon it.

How could her uncle do this to her? How could he do this to Gawain? And why hadn't he shared this decision with her at any point after he'd finalized it? The arrangement had been in place long enough.

Maybe he cared less for her opinion than she always thought. That notion brought a strange, uncomfortable feeling to the pit of her stomach.

Poor Gawain. Where was he tonight? Where had he been since her uncle's death for that matter? It must have been a crushing blow to learn he wouldn't inherit the estate. It wasn't fair to either of them to find out like this, and she couldn't bear for him to think ill of her.

And how was she supposed to shelve years of dislike towards a womanizing Stewart supporter just because a secret letter told her she must? The notion was more than unreasonable. Beyond that, it was unfair, unrealistic, and impossible!

James MacIntosh. Her first impression of him was that of a rogue, yet in her uncle's solar he was considerate when he offered to assist with the situation regarding Gawain. His second visit was confounding. He'd come and gone so quickly she could see no purpose in it.

If she were honest with herself, she'd admit it wasn't his thoughtfulness or his strange behaviour that had her reeling—it was him—all of him! From his thick hair, to his unusual green eyes, and the sensual curl of his lips that never seemed to go away, James MacIntosh was the most attractive man she had ever seen. How could she have missed that before?

* * *

James emptied the last few drops of ale from the pitcher. He contemplated the situation and his conclusion one more time. In three days he would betroth himself to a woman to whom he was attracted, but whose connection could provide him with no political advance.

Three days.

He must go through with it, regardless of how difficult it might be to break it afterward. Once done, there would be only one ugly way out of it.

Chapter Five

"Will one of you please, once and for all, tell me what prompted my uncle to pair me with the likes of James MacIntosh? And if either of you 'there, there' me one more time I will put you in the stocks myself!" She never would, but her patience thinned with each passing moment. Her two most trusted advisors danced around her questions, treating her as though she were ten again. Enough was enough.

"M'lady—"

"No! No more 'm'lady'! I want a straight answer from you, Andrews. And I want it now!"

The priest and the steward exchanged an unsure glance, prompting her to place her hands on her hips. Father Addison deflated and collapsed onto the bench with his head in his hands.

"We thought we could protect you from the truth. Believe me when I say, your uncle did not make this decision lightly or without counsel. He was troubled during the time leading up to his visit with the elder MacIntosh and as I recall, it took two attempts to convince the man to accept the arrangement." Father Addison paused.

"Go on."

"He wasn't trying to hurt you, lass," Andrews said. "As to

his reasons, well they died with him." He crossed his arms over his chest.

"I don't believe you."

"You must my La—. You must." He glanced and Father Addison.

She turned to the priest again. "What truth were you protecting me from? What could be so important to destroy my life and Gawain's?"

Andrews' harrumph was the last straw. "What John? What is it about Gawain that makes you so cynical? I trust you would never voice any objection about the man in front of my uncle? So why do me the discourtesy?"

Father Addison reached for her but she swatted him away. "I do not need consoling like a fragile child. I need answers. You hold information which may have led to a complete change of heart from my uncle concerning my future."

How could they not realize she should have been told?

"What was the cause? Which of the three people involved did it concern most? The MacIntosh, a Stewart supporter? No? Maybe it was about Gawain, a man who served my uncle with faithful dedication. No?" Her voice cracked. "Then it must have something to do with me."

"Lady Aileana," Father Addison said. "Your uncle had no issue with your ability or loyalty. I understand your concern over MacIntosh involvement here. They are Stewart supporters. Your uncle was certain of it. I remember the night the Guard came to collect your father. Despite assurances he would be compensated, the Laird and he both knew 'twas unlikely. He went anyway, Aileana. He went because his king bade him. Why MacIntosh, or any other clan, would support James Stewart is beyond me, but your uncle thought long and hard about this decision before he made it. You must trust that."

His tone and his demeanour were sincere, but they were asking her to leap too far. "Trust in that? Well, Father, trust is a wonderful thing when it is expressed both ways. I'm to accept this decision without any rhyme or reason as to how it came about. For all I know, my uncle was blackmailed into this arrangement somehow by the same man who will soon be my husband!"

"That would be true if he needed anything we possess."

Damn Andrews and his logic.

"What then? He is doing us a favour to save us from crushing when the great King James sweeps the Highlands clear of non-supporters?" She waited for either of them to react. Nothing. "No. If it were something like that we, all four of us, would have spoken of it months ago. There's another reason. What is it?"

"Is it not enough for you to know your uncle agonized over this decision?" Andrews asked. His brows furrowed and he shifted.

"No. And your refusal to share information with me is an even greater indicator that there's a secret to uncover, and I will uncover it, Andrews." She pointed her index finger at his chest. "And I will also remember that you're still more loyal to a man in his grave than the heir he left behind." She stormed out of the great hall.

Never in her short life had she ever been so sure she was being lied to. There was something serious at play here and she could not let it go. Her uncle's secrecy, and his supposed agonizing, proof enough. By default, their lie would become hers. She would not let them forget it.

One thing was clear. Her sentiments regarding the MacIntosh were not shared among the masses. The men considered him honourable, convinced he'd continue the estate's success well into the next several generations. They would swear fealty to him as liege lord, believing the merger of the two clans would bring wealth, prosperity, and protection. A larger estate was not an ideal target for roaming clans who raided more and more these days.

They were all wrong. The clan could achieve all those things without James MacIntosh at the helm.

She had a great deal of love and respect for the people who worked and lived at Chattan Castle, but she could not concur with the excitement around her at the impending arrival of their future chief. The women were another irritating lot and admired the physical side of him. Gushed, more like. Everywhere she turned, the maids whispered about his body, his face and his gorgeous eyes. She had just about had enough when one of the kitchen staff mentioned his firm buttocks. Her reaction was swift and direct—she roared her disapproval and forbade anyone to discuss such an inappropriate topic. Even if there was at least a shred of truth to the last part.

Desperate for distraction, she immersed herself in celebration preparations by ensuring her guests had the utmost in comfort and hospitality when they arrived. She oversaw meal planning, flower arrangements, garlands hangings, fresh linens for the guest bedrooms, and table settings. Everything must be perfect. She fell heavy into her bed on the night before her betrothal ceremony in eager anticipation of a solid night sleep.

Gwen rapped on her chamber door early the next morning. The night, like the one before, was filled with tormenting dreams of her intended. In some, he locked her into a small, windowless room, his maniacal laughter filling her ears. In others, he loomed over her for a moment before bending toward her naked body. His smouldering kisses left a trail of molten heat in their wake. Her difficulty was determining which was more disturbing.

"Rise and shine, sleeping beauty. Today is the day your

dreams come true. My lady? My lady?"

Aileana's head was buried under three pillows and her quilts were all askew.

"Go away," she muttered.

"Did you not sleep well? Dreaming about a certain gentleman who will be here in a few short hours perhaps?"

Aileana erupted from the pillows.

"Aye I did, thanks to you! I hadn't given the MacIntosh's looks a second thought until you the put idea in my head."

Gwen paled and dropped her gaze to her feet. "I'm sorry if I'm to blame for your sleepless night, my lady and when you're expecting guests. It was thoughtless of me and I apologize. I understand if you wish someone else to attend you this morning."

Was Gwen teasing again? She often enjoyed the maid's playful nature, but there was no humour in it today. Still, it wasn't her fault Aileana's world had turned on its ear.

"Shall I call for Colleen?" Gwen asked.

Aileana sighed.

"My dearest Gwen, 'tis I who should apologize to you. I don't know what has put me in such a foul mood this morning. Yet, as you say, we have guests arriving soon and we shall not allow them to witness any tirades on my part, shall we? I wish you alone to attend me as usual." Acting like a spoiled child would not make her day go any easier. She must face this head on. "I've decided to wear the crimson gown today. What do you think?"

Gwen let out a huge breath and smiled. "I think it's perfect."

Perhaps focusing on her attire would still her fluttering belly. Her gown had just arrived from Edinburgh. It was made of crimson velvet with gold thread and ribbon woven in a knotted design framing the edges. Gwen insisted its square neckline enhanced Aileana's figure. Long, draping sleeves hung almost to the floor revealing her full-sleeved silk chemise angled at her wrists. Similar ribbons were weaved into her plaited hair.

Just before the eleventh hour, Gwen clasped her hands together and declared, "Oh, you are perfect! Do you not feel the power of rebirth today? Of all the days you could have chosen, Beltane is the most appropriate. And do you see? 'Tis raining this morn: a true sign of fertility and good luck."

Aileana scrunched her nose. "Gwen you know I don't believe in the old ways."

"I also know you don't look down upon those of us who still do. When the Beltane fires are lit tonight, what will your betrothed think? I've heard he supports the Bishop's opinion on heresy and that we're being labelled witches."

Though she kept her tone light, Gwen's worry shone through her eyes. Their usual twinkle dimmed.

"Nonsense. Our Bishop has no such opinion. That's a load of fear mongering spread about to pressure more people to attend mass. If I thought for a second you, or anyone else here, were in actual danger from James MacIntosh or any of his ilk, I'd never let him over the bridge."

Gwen laughed. "And what about you? Are you in any danger?"

Aileana's eyebrows shot up. "Me? Of course not. I will have as little to do with that man as possible. And speaking of which, I've learned Father Addison and Andrews both knew about this arrangement from its birth. Tell me Gwen, and tell me true, did you know anything about any of this?"

Silence followed for far too many heartbeats. Gwen's brow furrowed. Aileana couldn't bear it if her most trusted friend had also kept such a huge and important piece of information from her.

"My lady, I understand how shocked you must be to learn

trusted others knew of the arrangement, but let me assure you, I was not a member of that secret coven. My concern is only for your happiness and that does not involve keeping secrets from you."

"Yet, you dislike Gawain."

"My lady, you have reminded me on several occasions to be respectful towards him. I shall do so by remaining silent on that subject."

"So you didn't know about the arrangement but your dislike of Gawain holds true."

Silence.

"You don't have to berate the man to tell me what's on your mind."

"Very well, my lady. I do not think he is worthy. You deserve someone who will cherish you. I do not believe him capable of that."

"Knowing you as I do, I can accept that. Thank you, Gwen, for your honesty and your counsel. You are more dear to me than ever." It was true. Who else could she trust? Gwen would probably not find anyone worthy and it was nice to have someone so devoted to her happiness.

"Lady Aileana, your words make my heart swell. I have a gift for you." She lifted a wreath of colourful dried flowers onto Aileana's head, "Roses for love, carnations for health, lavender for luck, and daisies for innocence. Beltane flowers given from the heart, and blessed with love and this *witch's* art."

Aileana placed her hand over her heart. The gift and the declaration filled her with peace. "My deepest gratitude." Her words were but a whisper.

Gwen's watery smile was no doubt a mirror of Aileana's own. Such a sentiment was a reminder of the kind of love which had always surrounded her. What would her future hold?

"It's time, m'lady." Andrew's voice followed a soft rapping at the door.

The room spun around her for a moment. Aileana swayed until Gwen helped her into a chair. She was about to make a permanent commitment to James MacIntosh. Was there no way out of this?

"My lady, are you unwell?" Gwen asked. "I can see that you are not. We shall get you through this with great haste." Gwen gaze darted around the room. "Flowers! You need to think of flowers. Try this, start with 'A' and think about all the flowers beginning with that letter. When you're done with 'A', do the same for 'B' and so forth."

Aileana was quiet for a moment or two before nodding. If it took something like listing flowers to calm her frayed nerves, so be it. A second ago she was fine, now she was stupefied. What Gwen suggested took determined concentration, but after a few minutes her shoulders relaxed a little.

She took a deep steadying breath and glanced at Gwen. "I can do this."

"Yes you can. You've endured much over the past few days. It's natural for you to feel nervous about receiving guests without your uncle. This is the first time you will have to do it alone."

Her words were the truth. The funeral itself had been open to clansmen alone and other visitors were never in the form of a large crowd. This was the first time she would appear on her own so it was no wonder she struggled with composure. Gwen was right, it had everything to do with all her guests and not just one man.

She straightened her back and approached her bedchamber door.

"Wait! You can't go without your necklace," Gwen said.

It was a final reminder of who she was. A double string of

freshwater pearls was fastened at the front by a polished oval, amber pendant, set in gold. The piece had been in her family for many years, yet she'd never had the opportunity to see anyone wear it. Now it was hers.

She squared her shoulders and opened the door to find Andrews pacing. He did not smile, but offered his elbow to her. She curled her fingers around his arm and looked straight ahead, away from his apologetic gaze.

"Lady Aileana, please let me say—"

Her back straightened. "No, Andrews. You know what I want to hear from you and until you're ready to disclose everything, I'll only hear estate business. Right now, I have a duty to perform."

"Yes, m'lady," Andrews bowed his head low.

They walked down the back stairs and around the side courtyard to the family entrance of the chapel where Father Addison waited.

"Ah, there you are my child. You are quite the lady of the castle today. Your elegance is unmatched m'dear."

She was in no mood for his smooth words. "Do not pretend with me, Father. We both know I am playing into a lie here today. Must we give voice to it as well? Sinners we are, the lot of us." She almost found his shocked expression amusing. Almost.

"M'lady!"

She raised her chin. "Does it not say in Matthew, '...you must give an account on judgment day of every idle word you speak. The words you say reflect your fate; either you will be justified by them or you will be condemned." Let him stew on that one.

"M'lady, I assure you, we commit no sin here today." Father Addison's voice was low.

"You expect me to stand before God and vow to honour

this arrangement, knowing I do not believe in it. How is that not a sin?" She placed her fists on her hips. "And if we meet our end in the next moment? Are you prepared to face the consequences of your actions?"

"Lady Aileana, my soul is secure, as is yours. You have no cause for concern in that regard or any other that I'm aware of. Now, we should get started. We may begin post haste if you wish."

"Is his Lordship here already?" That couldn't be. 'Twas quite unlike a man of his elevation in the world. Her pulse picked up a notch.

Father Addison drew in a breath and smiled. "Why yes, he's been here for quite some time."

Gwen and Aileana exchanged a brief, but meaningful look. Her anxiousness was not about one man. That was all she needed to remember.

"Azalea, amaryllis, aster…"

Gwen's words spoken low in Aileana's ear served to calm her a little as she entered the small chapel. Several voices were audible from out in the sanctuary, but the rich timbre of James MacIntosh was unmistakable. The skin at her nape tingled.

The moment they entered, all eyes fell on her. Hers locked with his. She followed Father Addison to the chancel and turned to wait for James while the guests located their seats. A younger looking and grinning version of James jabbed him in the ribs prompting him to move up to where Aileana waited. The brother. Gwen gasped somewhere behind her.

The sight of James threatened to knock her on her behind again. He wore a red velvet brocade tunic with draped sleeves. His black hose was barely visible between the skirted garment and knee length leather boots. The crest on his chest was quartered with lion, ship, heart, and boar. His hair was tied and bound with leather straps which served to accent the strong lines of his face. She couldn't tear her eyes away from him even for a second. Her insides seemed to scatter in all directions at once.

He sauntered toward her like a predator stalking its prey. With every step her heart pounded faster as he focused all his attention on her. His stare seemed to hold such purpose that she wanted to shield herself from its scrutiny. He did not look pleased at all. That questioning, almost angry, expression was difficult to understand; still, her heart drummed.

Father Addison said something about commitment and honour. Aileana concentrated hard on the priest's words to little avail.

She placed her left hand on the bound scriptures as prompted. James covered it with his and squeezed. The resulting jolt from the strength and heat of his hand set her pulse racing. His gaze burned into her. Hellfire was not as hot as that man's stare.

Father Addison prompted her to repeat his words. They flowed from her with little comprehension as James's gaze traced the complete outline of her face and settle on her mouth. His eyes glowed like the day he had almost kissed her on the road. She leaned forward as though an invisible rope tugged her toward him. Gwen had asked her earlier if she was in danger. Perhaps she was after all.

In the next moment, the ceremony was over and she was walking down the aisle with James to form a receiving line for their guests. Her hand tingled where he had touched it, a lingering heat warming her. As they stood at the entrance -way, waiting for the first guests to reach them, he leaned in close. His warm breath excited the sensitive skin just below her ear, his voice rich and low.

"You are lovely, Lady Aileana."

He gave her a deep penetrating look before accepting the

good wishes bestowed upon them. Her lower belly coiled. She couldn't think when he looked at her like that.

She smiled with grace, but inside she trembled. Her senses were filled with his rich unbearable masculinity. His scent, still leather though he wore less of it today, drew her towards him to inhale more. While her mind told her to keep him at a distance, her body wanted him to devour her much like his eyes did. She was all a-flutter from only standing next to him. She tried to envision him like any other man she knew, but each time he said 'Thank you,' or 'We're glad you are here,' she was drawn closer. She tried to remain unaffected because if she didn't check herself, she could become swept up in his charms, like every other woman in the room. The ladies approached him like puffed up hens, making their way to the coop's most appealing cock. Well she wasn't anyone's silly hen.

Her cheeks warmed and her ears were hot all of a sudden. She would not act like them. She wouldn't need to. Maybe their marriage would be in name only with limited interaction between them.

Of course!

It made so much sense she almost laughed out loud. They needn't live together. Each could remain at their own home and perform duties as necessary. It was a marriage of convenience, that's all. This must have been what her uncle had intended all along.

The freedom such an arrangement provided made her smile. Over the past few days, control over her life slipped away like a selkie into the deep waters of the sea and she mourning on the shore. That was before. Now she was filled with renewed strength and purpose. She would not mourn her freedom, she'd still have it. Aileana smiled somewhat to herself. Anyone paying close attention would have thought her the blushing bride-to-be.

Still, the crowd that followed them from the chapel to the castle was far too pleased for her liking. Their cheers coupled with the piper's lively and playful march might have been infectious at another time. Tears stung her eyes. They acted on tradition, yet a celebration did not seem fitting, and there were three days of this unnatural gaiety to endure yet.

And still no Gawain. She'd seen neither hide nor hair of him since his awful discovery. She'd worked hard to push him from her thoughts over the past days, focusing on anything else to avoid her shame.

Her silent partner walking next to her didn't help. She should say something to him—but what? 'Have you supported any black-hearted monarchs lately, my lord?' Or maybe, 'Help a rotten king destroy anyone's family yet today Lord MacIntosh?' Gwen would tell her she was better than that and under normal circumstances she would agree. These events didn't bring out the best in her, that much was certain.

In the dining hall, James sat at the head of the table which made matters worse. How could she continue this pretence? Her irritation spiked again.

"The meal looks delicious, Lady Aileana."

Her head snapped up. The MacIntosh was staring at her. Agony was suffering through this situation in silence—torture was a forced idle conversation with him.

"You make your uncle proud with the lusciousness of this spread: smoked salmon, kippers, devilled eggs, and wild pheasant. Did you know these are all my favourites?"

"My uncle—"

"Would have been honoured by your compliment, m'lord," Father Addison said.

Later she might thank the priest for his interference, but he was on thinner ice than ever. She pushed her food around on her plate and kept her gaze downcast.

"Iain Chattan was an honourable man and a gracious host," someone further down the table said.

If they started toasting her uncle, she would explode.

"He loved to hold feasts like this one."

She needed saving from this madness.

"His favourite part was always dessert!"

Did they wish to break her?

"Lady Aileana, you must have many wonderful stories of your uncle to share."

Oh God.

She couldn't take one more comment and pushed her chair back, rising to her feet. Sheena Fraser entered the dining room at the same time; she had a saviour, after all.

"Lady Aileana, how wonderful it is to see you my dear." Aileana rushed toward the woman, her warm embrace a much needed crutch. She wiped away the few tears that had managed to escape from her eyes.

"Shhhhh, love." Sheena could read her so well. "We must be brave." The words were just the right ones to help her put her emotions in check and she returned to her seat. Aileana motioned for Father Addison to move to make room for Sheena. Aileana didn't care who she'd need to displace to have her aunt by marriage sit next to her.

"Aunt Sheena, I expect you remember Father Addison?" Introductions would provide a nice distraction from the causes of her discomfort—the discussion around the table and the man at the head of it. "And I believe you're acquainted with most of the other people around the table since you would have known them long before me."

"Long before indeed, child, but not that long." The jest was an expected retort from her favourite remaining relative.

"And finally, Aunt, I'd like to introduce you to Laird MacIntosh and his brother Calum. My lords, this is Lady

Sheena Fraser. Her husband was my uncle's brother."

"I am pleased to make your acquaintance, Lady Fraser. Am I to understand you are from this region? Not the Fraser estate on the other side of the loch?"

Sheena smiled. "Yes my lord. My husband was William Fraser. Were you acquainted with him?" Uncle William had died two years ago and Aileana never heard much about the particulars at the time, though there was something she could never quite reconcile about it all. The few bits and pieces she'd gleaned suggested William had been murdered, but there was never anything done about it despite pleas for assistance to King James. After all, it was his new law which prevented their clan from seeking justice from Baron MacIntosh, James's father. Sheena still wore mourning clothes and refused to talk of the ordeal except to repeat Uncle's famous line about seeking meaning.

"He was acquainted with my father who spoke well of him. I am sorry for your loss," James offered.

"I thank you my lord. Your father was an excellent man whom I recall meeting on occasion with your mother, a lovely woman. Please accept my respects for them both. Their deaths were a great shock."

"You honour me Lady Fraser. Your husband, died under mysterious circumstances if I recall."

Aileana stiffened as did Sheena beside her. Did the man have any decency? She glanced at James, his expression was curious. Was he daft? Would he not realize a conversation in that direction would upset her?

"Yes my lord, he did." Sheena's tone was cool.

She had to stop this before it got out of hand.

"Were you ever satisfied with the king's investigation?"

Aileana stood, placing her hands flat on the table. "Laird MacIntosh, I do not believe this is the time or the occasion to dredge up such unpleasant events from the past," Aileana said. Although keeping an even tone was difficult, she ensured the full impact of her words was not overshadowed by emotion. She was crossing a line of appropriate behaviour, but she didn't care. His eyebrows shot up and his jaw slacked.

"Not all of us have the ability to treat our losses in such a casual manner," she said. "Your king—"

"Aileana," Sheena said, her tone full of warning.

"—may or may not have actually conducted—"

Sheena was on her feet, but swaying with the back of her hand pressed against her forehead. "My lords, please forgive me. The excitement of the day has toyed with my delicate sensitivities. I must retire for a short respite, but I shall rejoin you for an afternoon tour of the grounds, if you will permit me. Lady Aileana, will you please accompany me?"

James arose. "Lady Fraser, please forgive me if I have upset you."

Aileana glared at him. His jaw clenched as his gaze darted between her and her aunt. Yes, it was a good thing she wouldn't have to spend much time with this man and his boar-like manners.

"You have not upset me, my lord. Rest assured, you will know if you do." It may have sounded like teasing to anyone else, but Sheena was dead serious. The escape Aileana sought earlier was at hand. She ushered Sheena out of the dining hall issuing apologies along the way. One thing was certain - she and the MacIntosh were not off to a good start.

Chapter Six

"Surely, brother, you realize, the lass was irritated with *you*."

Calum had been tight to James's heels as soon as the meal had ended. James headed toward the solar seeking a moment to clear his head and Calum wasn't going to let him have it.

"With me? I do not see that at all. She was concerned for her Aunt's welfare."

Turning from him wasn't working so James faced Calum.

"Aye, you continue to think that if it gives you comfort, however, I am not blinded by vanity or my throbbing loins. You caused the aunt's discomfort, James. You commit to this arrangement with Lady Aileana and then offend her family? I don't understand your actions."

James tensed. "Enough! The aunt was tired from her travels and you know nothing of my reasons for seeing this arrangement through."

"You're right, I don't understand. You are all contradiction, Brother. You say this is temporary, yet you sit in a dead man's dining hall as if it were your own. You regard his heir as though she were dessert. I caution you, for your looks betray your words whenever she is within your line of sight." The corner of Calum's mouth twitched.

"She is nothing to me, nor are Chattan's belongings. I resent your implication that I do this for selfish purposes. What would you have had me do? Refuse the agreement and dishonour us both?"

Calum shook his head. "I would have you see this through to the end. It's the right thing to do and you know it."

Calum crossed his arms and smirked. Damn him. Would he never cease his meddling? "I know nothing of the sort. I was a fool to agree to any of this."

"A fool indeed to protect a clan who will not survive without the strength of a larger one. Would you rather have them take up with the Camerons?"

"The Chattans are my neighbours and as such will always have my protection. How dare you imply I would not come to their aid!"

"Coming to their aid is one thing, but what you are doing is leaving them vulnerable to all manner of prey. You may as well tie the lass to a tree naked and yell, 'here she is! Come and get her!'"

James clenched his fists. Calum had gone too far with his wistful imaginings of his reaction to the lass and his purpose. "You cross a dangerous line," he said. "Consider yourself lucky I don't insult so easily. Leave me."

Calum's face dropped. "I'll leave, but you must consider one thing. If you will not marry Aileana, make sure you find her someone who is strong enough to care for her."

Calum turned and stalked away. James was unsure if his words or hurt expression weighed heavier in his wake. The day had not turned out at all like he'd imagined. He wouldn't admit it out loud, but Calum was right about his reaction to the lass. He didn't think it was possible for her loveliness to grow. Yet, in the chapel, all he could think about was unbraiding her hair and having it fall all around them as he buried himself within her.

She was not easy to draw out so he couldn't tell if she felt anything of the same sort for him. A grim expression settled over her face from the moment she entered the chapel to the time she left the dining hall with the aunt. He wanted to kiss it away. There was no doubt he would have to get control over the fire she ignited in him when she was near. No good could come of it.

As for protecting the clan, he had no intention of letting them fall under any fealty but his. He wouldn't speak of it yet to Calum because he wasn't quite sure how it would work. One thing was certain: he would have to make Aileana his ward. A new marriage contract would not need to include the clan and for that matter, he could pluck a young man of worth and means from the region. There was a particular thane who would benefit from the match. Even Calum might be persuaded to consider her. His arguments of late contained some manner of her welfare, yet he insisted James marry her. Everything his brother suggested could be satisfied in one form or another and didn't need to involve his future. He'd received an invitation from Queen Joan to visit Linlithgow Palace in a fortnight. Between now and then he would determine his intentions and present them to King James. This madness would all end.

He paced. The most worrisome aspect of this situation, though, was the cousin. Why had the man not shown up for the ceremony? He was the constable after all and therefore should have ensured the event's security. Could he have been the reason for the lass's demeanour? She'd been crying the day he saw the cousin leave. Were they lovers? Was that the *affliction* Father Addison had referred to on the day after Chattan's death?

He raked his fingers through his hair. None of it mattered anyway. He wouldn't be around long enough to watch her mourn a lost love. He stopped pacing and gazed out across the gardens. The object of his torment had just entered the rear courtyard from a side door and was making her way toward the garden. She looked back over her shoulder several times.

Well now, where was she going? The temptation was too great, he must follow her. He almost could hear Calum mocking him. *I thought you said you didn't want her.*

James located a route to the rear courtyard. Away from the castle, he entered a small maze. Although it was only May, there was no doubt the area was well tended and worth the praise he'd heard over the years. He listened for her, but no sound met his ears so he crept further along the path. Crunching stone just ahead caught his attention.

He followed as quietly as he could to avoid detection and continued along in this way for a while until he caught sight, not of Aileana, but a man. He was dark haired and tall wearing a black padded jerkin and common plaid. The man peeked around the tall hedge. James positioned himself to better glean what was in the man's line of view and his hair prickled. There, sitting on a flat rock near a pond was Aileana. He stepped forward to get a better view of her and alerted the man to his presence. Their gazes locked.

The cousin.

The man scowled and dashed through the brush. When James turned back to Aileana, she was staring at him.

Her eyes were wide and her cheeks red as flame. "Did you follow me, my lord?"

Aye, and now I know your true purpose.

"I sought some fresh air and was curious about the famed Chattan gardens. I heard a noise and followed it here." Would she admit to the tryst she had planned with her constable?

"Well you've located its source, although I did not know my step was so heavy."

"I should think not. Though yours was not the step I heard, was it?" He held his breath while he waited for her response. Would she admit it? He did not relish the revelation of her relationship with another, but this was his best way out. Still, her deceit left a sour taste in his mouth.

"I beg your pardon, my lord. I do not know what you mean."

So she would lie. How dare she deceive him. His jaw clenched. He would not indulge her. "How does your aunt fare?"

Her chin raised and her back straightened. "She is recovered and will be pleased by your inquiry." Her demeanour was far too cool.

"I am pleased to hear it. Will you return to the castle with me? I believe our guests may form the wrong conclusion should we remain without a chaperone for much longer." He was curious to learn what her reaction would be to that comment. Or perhaps she didn't care about appearances.

"Aye, my lord I will accompany you. Thank you for your consideration for my reputation. Most of the guests have retired to their rooms for a light rest before the evening feast."

He held out his arm to her and watched her cross the garden. When she reached him, her brow was furrowed, yet when their gazes met, he saw a flicker of a smile and found himself staring at her mouth again. Her lips parted and it was a great effort to tear his thoughts from the surge of desire shooting straight to his loins. He despised his body's response to her.

What a fool she would make of him.

Well, two could play that game. He would show her that stoking his fire would burn, white hot. Did she think she could smile at him and he would become blinded to her loose ways? Perhaps that was why she kept a witch, to drug those who would stand between her and what she wanted. Oh, he'd teach her a lesson all right. She'd find out he was a master at this game. Now, at least, he could have her in whatever manner he chose and feel no guilt for seducing an innocent. In the end, she would beg him to take her but he could prolong her torture for as long as possible. Tonight, he'd have her admit her guilt. Then he would have her.

* * *

Aileana and James walked together toward their chambers. When she turned to pass a parting comment, he surprised her by taking her hand and pressed it to his lips. His mouth was soft and warm against her skin. Raw heat moved through her. She opened her mouth to speak, but no words would come as he kissed her hand and stroked her palm with his fingers.

"Rest well, we have a long night ahead of us yet," he said. She watched his lips curl around his words. Her heart fluttered wild.

Before she could gather her thoughts, he gave her a devastating smile and disappeared around the corner and into his own chamber. Aileana entered hers and closed the door before collapsing in her chair near the open window. She didn't know what to make of him. He was as arrogant as the day was long and infuriating to boot. Who did the man think he was provoking poor Aunt Sheena like that? Did he think a kiss on her hand, albeit a nice one, forgave his behaviour?

Why Sheena had brushed off the incident once back in her room was a mystery. She dumped Aileana at her door and begged for Gwen's assistance. Aileana's respite in the garden was interrupted by the same man who'd frustrated her to begin with. Would she ever know peace again?

She was attracted to him, of that she had no doubt, but it did not help her cause. He had agreed to honour her uncle's wishes and that would make him her husband. Were they to live together, she would expect fidelity, though his reputation concerned her for she had no reason to disbelieve the stories. What if he was the kind of man who could never be satisfied by one woman? What if any affair he was engaged in continued after the wedding? And should that matter to her if they were to live apart? She would have to see him on occasion, considering she would bear his children. An image of their wedding night set her stomach fluttering again and unwanted heat to her cheeks.

An unexpected knock at the door made her jump. James's deep timbre on the other side was unmistakable. When she opened the door she discovered he and Father Addison.

"My child, are you unwell?" Father Addison asked, his tone full of concern.

"We're sorry to interrupt your respite my lady, however, we request your immediate presence in the solar to discuss an urgent message I just received," James said, saving her the trouble of explaining her flushed skin. His gaze was intense. If she didn't know better, she'd say he was well aware of the direction her thoughts had taken. He couldn't though. This missive must be serious.

"I am well I assure you, thank you, Father. Please lead the way."

After the older man moved ahead of them, James reached for Aileana's elbow to guide her along. His expression turned hard as soon as his hand touched her arm. His jaw clenched and his lips formed a straight line. His fingers applied hard pressure on her arm. Something was terribly wrong, she could sense it in him.

Aileana followed the men into her uncle's solar and James closed the door behind her. Before she could question, James motioned for her to sit down.

"My lord, if the news is so dire, I would prefer to stand. Please proceed."

"Very well," he said. "As I mentioned, I just received an urgent message. It was from my steward. He provided a report from the scouts I have positioned at strategic locations throughout this region for precautionary measures. I've had them there since the raid on the MacKenzie clan last year."

She remembered it well, homes burned, women violated. It wasn't just for looting purposes, these raiders were barbaric. She swallowed hard and bit the inside of her cheek as James continued.

"He said one of my scouts just returned to Moy Hall like the devil himself lay chase. He saw a raiding party about ten miles north of here. He couldn't be sure of their destination and tracked back to alert us." The news was not easy to digest. "I realize the impact of my next statement, but I feel it best if we cut the festivities short."

She tried to make no outward appearance of the disarm tugging at her.

When she did not speak, James continued. "I see no harm in continuing with the events planned for the rest of the day, but I suggest on the morrow, this residence as well as my own and others in the area prepare for possible attack."

Her guts lurched.

Aileana shook her head. "That cannot be. Surely this small pack of raiders is not bold enough to attack a property as large as yours or mine? I agree we should be cautious. We shall send reinforcements to any small residences in the area and provide shelter to any who would wish to have it. However, I'm sorry, but I cannot believe Chattan Castle would ever be attacked."

James turned his attention to Father Addison as if he knew she wouldn't agree.

"Father Addison, you visited the families who were attacked last year. What is your opinion of the level of brutality to which these men will descend?"

Father Addison was quiet for several long moments. The concern in his eyes was almost convincing enough. "My child, I have known you all your life. You are an intelligent woman, capable of heading this entire clan with no help from anyone. On this topic, however, I must agree with his Lordship. I can only hope the brutality I witnessed last year will never reach you. Unfortunately, hope won't keep them from arriving here with flaming arrows and an appetite for murder and mayhem that has been unmatched in my lifetime."

"And one small raiding party has you both this concerned?" she asked.

She looked at each man in turn. Father Addison led her by the hand to the bench to sit next to him. He drew a deep breath and patted her palms.

"As I'm sure you've heard, the MacKay's banner was found hanging in the village on the night of the attack. Their battle flag was unmistakable and there is no doubt these men are responsible for this horrific crime. Their disappearance has secured their guilt."

James turned from them towards the window, his arms crossed. She wished he'd show her his face. As Father Addison spoke, James remained silent.

"They are a large, territorial clan with many fertile lands who've increased their claim well into Sutherland and boast ownership of a great deal of the north. Their systematic raiding of nearby farms and estates has been a source of much hatred stemming from the neighbouring Sinclair, Sutherland, and Mackenzie clans, but the MacKays do not care, their greed is immeasurable."

She swallowed hard. This information was well known. "Father, I know who the MacKay are. Why are you giving me a history lesson?"

"'Tis important, Lady Aileana," James said without turning.

His voice was like a soothing caress on the back of her neck.

Father Addison continued. "Past confrontations to negotiate peaceful terms have not gone well and have ended in bloodshed. Up until last fall, MacKay attacks were restricted to those select clans in the north. The one on the MacKenzie clan was much farther south than any previous. These raiders are on the move - everyone knows it but no one knows why."

He squeezed her hand. For her comfort, or his own, she could not tell.

"Fergus McKay, the current chief, is a hulk of a man. 'Tis said that the attack was prompted by a simple insult between a MacKenzie clansman and the McKay over a pitcher of ale. 'Tis also said he planned the attack on them last fall including how the pain and suffering was to be inflicted. This man is capable of great torment to his victims.

"Having inherited a clan that had declared war on all in the north so many years ago, he has known murder and madness his whole life. The MacKay is said to have begun his own battle training at ten years of age and has developed the rigor his soldiers must endure to serve him. His twelve best fighters move like phantoms on the wind. They're dangerous beyond imagination, my dear, to be so bold as to post their own colours after such an attack, well 'tis like nothing I've seen."

Aileana left her seated position and made her way behind her uncle's desk to gaze at the portrait of her uncle. Father Addison was known to exaggerate anything he'd heard. However, if even half of this story was true, it could already be too late to get everyone to safety. How often had her uncle faced such dangers and kept it from her? She must face this as he would have. James could make the decision for her, yet here she was in the solar, asked to contribute her thoughts and opinion. Wasn't that what she wanted? Did that mean her betrothed was willing to make her his full partner or was he merely trying to curry favour to impress the other gentleman present? Either way, she must make a decision.

Her voice was steady when she spoke despite her trembling inside. "We will prepare for attack. I'll order all residents in outer areas to move inside the keep for protection, have every able bodied man on this estate prepared, and send away my guests first thing in the morn. I will do all of this, but I have one remaining question. What then? How long do we board ourselves up and stand with our swords drawn, ready to strike? Why aren't we planning to do something once and for all about these barbarians?"

James moved in front of her and stared hard into her eyes. He held her shoulders in his strong hands while he searched her face. She saw great strength in his. This was not the flirtatious cad she'd met on the road, nor gallant nobleman she'd committed to earlier that day, nor even the arrogant boar with whom she'd shared the noon meal. All other versions were gone. The man before her gave her a new impression. She was safe with this man.

"We *are* going to do something," he said. "And I intend to make sure of it." With that he left.

Aileana returned to her chamber alone. If they were all in such mortal danger, shouldn't the guests leave straight away? The orange-yellow light cast from the sun onto the tapestries in the hallway reminded her that by the time anyone prepared themselves to leave, darkness would have fallen. When she entered her chamber, it was to find Gwen and Sheena pacing and waiting for her.

"Oh Aileana, please tell us what's happened. Some of the guests said they saw you and the MacIntosh go into the solar with Father Addison. They said his Lordship came out a short time later with the look of death on him."

Sheena's pleading struck a chord. They relied on decisions

made by her and James and they deserved to know everything. Indeed, the rest of the castle would be just as anxious for news.

I must go and see to the guests. Gwen, please gather everyone in the great hall, tell them I shall explain everything there."

As soon as Gwen was gone, Aileana turned to her aunt. "We're sending everyone away on the morn. There's risk of an attack and I fear you are not safe here."

Aileana held her breath as she waited for her aunt's response. She didn't want her to leave though it was safest.

Sheena smiled and tilted her head up. "My dear, if this be the end, we shall face it together. I have every confidence in the security of this keep as well as the strength of his lordship's resolve. I trust with your intended near we shall be well protected here."

Sheena gave Aileana a gentle hug and a kiss on both cheeks. She pulled back, holding Aileana at arm's length. "I am sorry to see these celebrations ruined for you, but I'm certain of one thing; the MacIntosh is quite taken with you."

The comment was more than untimely. He was the last thing on her mind and she had little remorse for the interrupted celebrations either.

"Aunt Sheena, you defend the man after his insult earlier."

"He paid me no insult, Aileana. I blame neither the MacIntosh nor King James for my husband's death and neither should you. 'Tis a subject I do not wish to explore further." She chuckled. "I see from your clenched fists you would strike them both down to protect me and avenge your uncle, but it is not necessary. Iain's lesson to seek meaning has stayed with me these last two years and has provided me with great comfort."

"And you do not think the MacIntosh harbors blind faith in his king?"

Sheena's tone softened. "Your words put you in danger,

love. And besides, what my eyes viewed was that charming man never looked away from you during our brief encounter at the noon meal. I could see his intent. He's attracted to you. Best keep him at arm's length if you want to save your maidenhead for your wedding night."

With that, Sheena winked and floated out the door. How could she think like *that* at a time like *this*? Aileana wouldn't entertain any wantonness with that man. She had more important issues to attend to, the first being how she was going to make it into her dinner gown on her own? This was ridiculous. She could make decisions to benefit hundreds of people, but she couldn't dress herself. Although, in light of the news she had just received, her guests would forgive her for not changing her gown.

Lord, give me strength. She left her chamber and proceeded toward the great hall. She was just a few doors from her own when she ran into James.

"Are you ready? Your maid has gathered all the guests together and sent me to collect you." The confidence he portrayed had her yearning for more of her own yet she showed him none of her anxiety.

"Aye, I'm quite ready, thank you. I've gathered everyone together so they may all hear the same story."

Aileana watched James search her face. Light tingles began at the base of her neck as his gaze lingered on her mouth. Her stomach tightened and she took a deep breath.

"You are enchanting," he whispered. He took her hands into his and stroked with his thumbs. She didn't want to have any discussion of the sort with him at that moment. When he touched her, she couldn't think and she needed her wits.

"You showed great strength today. Chattan would have been proud of you, lass. I'm proud of you."

Could he know the impact such words had on her? Would it

encourage him to consult with her in the future when other serious concerns arose? Before she could question him, he reached around to the small of her back and drew her close. The full body contact sent her pulse racing, he was so hard - everywhere. His other hand came up to graze her lips. His fingers curled and stroked her cheek as he leaned down to brush his lips against hers. The heat she saw in his eyes stirred and terrified her at the same time.

James slid his hand from her cheek to underneath her hair, caressing the back of her neck while his mouth closed over hers. He flicked his tongue across her lips, coaxing her to open up to him. Her breasts strained against her gown's fabric and her hands slid up his chest of their own accord. His lips were warm and gentle, driving heat from the pit of her stomach to her limbs. His rich leather scent and his ragged breath robbed her wits. She was powerless to move, powerless to do anything but stand there and let him kiss her. His body pressed against hers provided the support she needed, for if he let her go in that moment she would surely crumble to the floor.

James consumed her in the most pleasant way. She wanted to taste him as well and stroked her tongue over his. He withdrew and gazed into her eyes with a furrowed brow.

Escaping his stare was as impossible as moving her limbs. Her body and her mind wanted two different things from this man. When he was near, she wanted him closer and when he kissed her, she yearned for something more. The problem was, when he touched her, thinking was impossible. She would gain no ground with this man while stirred like this. The fog parted from her brain as the noise from the gathered guests below broke through.

"I think we've kept our guests waiting long enough," he said with surprising calm as he stepped away from her. She took in his expression. There was no flush to his skin as she suspected hers betrayed. The earlier heat in his eyes was replaced with a narrowed gaze. Threads of disappointment weaved into her heart. He wasn't affected as she was. In fact, he seemed almost annoyed.

If that's the way he would behave, then she would too. "Aye, my lord, I believe we have." She raised her chin and walked away from him. Her disappointment increased when he did not take her elbow, instead fell into step behind her.

The distance to the hall was just long enough for her to compose herself, she'd taken in a lot today and it wasn't over yet. She clenched her fists open and closed at her sides as she pushed the MacIntosh's skilled lips from her mind.

Entering from the side, they moved to the large fireplace and hearth that was the focal point of the room. The guests had all gathered and the room fell quiet as she turned to face the greatest responsibility in her short life. She drew a deep breath.

"Thank you for joining us here. I'll come straight to the point. Raiders are on the move. We've no idea if they're the same ones from last harvest or not, but we've decided to break the festivities early.

"Dinner will be served this evening as planned although inside instead of out in the back gardens. If any of you wish to return to your homes this evening, we understand, however, I advise against travel after dark. The choice is yours, but know you are safe here. These walls have always provided adequate protection from raiders. His lordship and I both feel it best to err on the side of caution. If these are the same men as before....well, I don't need to remind anyone of the brutality to which they are capable."

She waited. At any moment the outburst would come. Men and women facing them rumbled among themselves and before long, the pitch arose and the din in the room became almost unbearable. James stepped in at the perfect time.

"Ladies and gentlemen, please." His voice carried over everyone else's and did wild things to her insides once again. "If you've any questions, please ask, but one at a time. I received an urgent message this afternoon from my steward. The raiders were spotted by one of my scouts. As we speak, a larger party is on their way to track them. I've also sent word to the King's Guard who are encamped not far from here and I'm sure will join the search as soon as word reaches them. For tonight, unless you must, I suggest you stay here. This is where you are safest."

His encouragement was enough for everyone except three couples who opted to leave straight away. Their journey was a short one and they agreed to travel together. One by one the guests left the hall leaving her and James alone. She drew a steadying breath.

"Thank you." She was grateful to him for keeping everyone calm. She didn't know what she'd have done if people had panicked and become hysterical. "Do you believe we're safe here?"

James turned her to face him.

"I do, or else I wouldn't leave."

He was leaving?

"Calum and I will intercept my scouts on their way to report to the Guard."

She would be damned if she'd let herself feel any more disappointment. She swallowed the lump rising in her throat. She wanted his arms around her again.

"If they're determined enough, they could do considerable harm here, couldn't they?" Perhaps she could steer her traitorous thoughts to a more necessary topic.

"I'm leaving some of my men here to assist with security. You will be perfectly safe as long as you remain within the castle keep." Here was her protector again.

She didn't know if she was grateful to him or not for evading her question. She drew another deep breath. She opened her mouth to say something, anything to him, but his fingers stroked her palm again and she couldn't think.

"I'm sorry I cannot join you for dinner. I expect you'll be even more ravishing than you have all day. Then again, it's best if you don't tempt me further." He drew his brows together. "I'll return by midday tomorrow, I promise."

His scent, along with the memory of his body pressed against her remained long after he left. Despising him grew more difficult by the hour.

Chapter Seven

"Ah, there you are. Are you ready?" James asked.

Calum was in the stable with the horses prepared. Father Addison stood beside him, both looked grave. "I think we should stay here, James. I have a bad feeling. Something isn't right."

Calum had been having *bad feelings* his entire life. Sometimes they were legitimate, but more often than not they amounted to nothing. Still, on this occasion, he would have to concur; a great deal did not add up at the moment.

"I have a feeling too, Brother. If someone doesn't challenge these raiders they'll have us hiding under our beds before long. I'll not yield without a fight. Are you coming with me or not?" James removed his short dagger from his boot and shoved it in his belt. Calum followed suit and mounted his horse.

"I'm coming. Father, be safe."

"Godspeed your swift return," Father Addison said. "The horses sense an evil presence this night m'lords."

The man looked mortified, yet James could not tell him how little danger he was in if MacKay and his clansmen risked their cover for some reason. Still, the sun had set and dusk approached like a dark omen. Silvery twilight cast an eerie impression over the horizon and Arion fidgeted beneath him.

"Father, surely God is on our side," Calum said.

"I have blessed you and will pray for you, m'lords. Now I must see to Lady Aileana, for I am certain she is as worried as I."

The priest scurried off before James could offer even a little reassurance.

"What are your thoughts?" Calum asked. "Can Fergus be this daft?"

"I can't imagine even an oaf like Fergus MacKay would expose himself now. My fear is the others have come back and are working a larger radius. Pray brother, pray Fergus is merely idle," James said.

Of the two options he posed, he'd take a bored Fergus MacKay any day.

Gwen entered the stable with two satchels of provisions. Her smile lingered on Calum. Interesting.

"You may have to play heroes tonight, but you don't have to do so on an empty stomach," she said and passed one to James first. "For you, my lord. My lady insists upon it."

James nodded, and left the stable. Calum followed moments later. They ate the roast pheasant and bread in silence and he was grateful for the momentary respite to gather his thoughts. Try as he might, they reverted back to a yellow-haired lass whose hold on him grew with each passing second. The scene in the garden still sent dark thoughts into his already rattled frame of mind.

She'd planned a rendezvous right under his nose and played innocent about it. She let him kiss her, and kissed him back. Those were not the actions of a young woman in love with someone else. She was either well skilled in the art of seduction or—well the alternative wasn't likely considering her actions regarding the cousin to date. The kiss should have revealed her true feelings, instead, it left him with more questions. In any case, his scout's report provided an escape from the woman and her confounding behaviour.

He tried hard to shake her from his thoughts, but her desire-hazed eyes kept intruding. God how he loved feeling her body pressed against him when she yielded. The stirring in his loins, when their tongues touched, told him he had better retreat else he'd have carried her off to his bed. This woman would have him on his knees, and as weak as a boy, if he weren't careful. He had to regain his wits over this lass, and soon too if he were to get the information he needed regarding the cousin. God help them both if he were to surrender to his growing desire.

She was all contradiction. Virgin. Seductress. Leader, too? She did what Chattan said she would - effectively handle the affairs of the estate - and he couldn't have been more surprised. In no time she had determined the correct course of action. He'd not seen any fear in her eyes. She was all strength and confidence. This young woman operated as though she'd been chief all along. James shook his head. Too many questions and no answers.

With a grimace he shoved the empty satchel back into the saddle's side pouch and steeled himself to the immediate task of locating the raiders. The rising full moon allowed them to find the main road leading toward Moy Hall with ease. The road was wide and he knew it well.

"May I make an observation?" Calum asked.

"No." He was in no mood for idle chit chat.

Calum laughed. "Well, I'll damned well make it anyway."

"Of course you will."

"I've been speaking with the lady's maid—"

"The heretic?"

"She's not what you think, Brother. She's a wise-woman, a healer."

"You may want to take what that woman says lightly. I

82

expect she's as superstitious as the priest."

"Regardless, they both have the lady's best interest at heart. I've learned some interesting things about them"

James stopped his horse. "Was this before or after you lay with her?"

"What?"

"Did she bewitch you into her bed so she could fill your head with nonsense?"

Calum stopped his horse. "You are way out of line! I have not bedded her and I believe she offers genuine concern regarding her lady's feelings toward the cousin."

"The cousin? What did she say about him?" Perhaps the woman would serve useful after all.

"Oh so now I have your attention?" Calum chuckled. "I wonder if you feel more for Lady Aileana than you care to admit. I've seen the way you look at her, like she is some extraordinary delight meant for you alone."

James shrugged, not willing to let Calum see the full extent of his musings regarding the lady. "You may share your information or we ride in silence. It is of no matter to me."

James waited. His brother's jesting was tiresome.

"The cousin is ill-favoured by the maid, the priest, the steward and—"

"And?"

"— especially by Iain Chattan."

"And the maid is certain of this?" Ill-favoured? That would explain Father Addison's visit and his plea.

"Quite. The lady would never hear any caution offered against the man and so the maid suffered her concerns in silence. She admits she protects Lady Aileana in her own way based on her beliefs that power lies in nature versus one almighty God."

"That kind of talk could land you both in the stocks, you realize."

"Aye, I do."

"Speak of it to no one, and keep your head."

This information was intriguing. Why would the lady hold the cousin in such high regard if everyone around her did not? Did they think they protected her? Why not warn her and arm her against foolish passion?

"Did the maid know why the man was so ill-favoured?"

"She said he is cruel, but did not expand on it."

"Cruel? Many men can appear cruel when their actions are misunderstood. And you accept this at face value?"

"She was convincing," he said, grinning.

Perhaps this was why Chattan wanted the arrangement solidified in writing including both their seals. Did the cousin pose some threat? Was it not cruel to blind the lass from such intentions? Who was more cruel? There were only two possibilities. Either Chattan wanted a more lucrative match for his niece, or the cousin was as bad as the maid thought. In both scenarios, Chattan made a choice for her benefit. And either way, James was the favoured solution. Perhaps he should feel honoured by the faith placed in him. Perhaps. While this information was enlightening, it still did not speak to the true nature of Aileana's feelings for Gawain Chattan.

About an hour into their journey, he caught sight of movement up ahead. He signaled Calum to dismount and they moved to the side of the road. They pulled their horses into the dense brush. He froze when a blade bit into his back.

"Make a move and you die." A gravelly voice growled into his ear.

"What do you want?" James asked.

"Don't ask questions and you may live longer."

He couldn't see his attacker, but he could tell that he was matched in strength. Cooperating was his best option—for now.

James calculated the man behind him was taller than he; the arm reaching around him, holding a blade to his throat, reached down instead of up. James's wrists were twisted and secured behind his back and a sack was placed over his head. The man shoved him back onto the road. Another pair of hands removed James's weapons: his short dagger tucked into his belt, a longer dagger strapped to his calf, and his broad sword sheathed at his hip.

His blood rose to the surface fuelling his outrage, but if he were to find an advantage he must keep his wits. Many footsteps shuffled around him. Some grunting indicated Calum's struggle.

Christ, don't fight back, Brother.

He replayed his abductor's voice in his head. Not one he recognized, but the man could have masked it. At least his throat hadn't been slit outright. Highwaymen then. They could be bargained with. A simple ransom request would do it, yet the men did nothing to rid him of his purse.

Instead, he was bound and gagged and thrown into a cart which was towed along the rugged, bumpy road. He couldn't be certain, but they seemed to have turned around and so in that case would be travelling back toward Chattan Castle. He made an attempt to loosen his bindings with no success. These men knew what they were about. During the attack, no one except his abductor spoke. There was no hesitation—this was no random act.

Soon afterward, the horse and cart came to a halt. The canvases were thrown off and they were hauled out, dragged a few feet, and thrust forward.

The sacks covering their heads were removed just before a wooden frame of a door slammed shut, clanging chains arranged, and a padlock clicked into place. James squinted to identify his captors but to no avail. He focused on his surroundings and the predicament they found themselves in. They were in a makeshift wooden prison. The posts were about twelve feet high and lashed together with rope and the door well secured. The cage was well built.

James moved to Calum to remove his ropes and gag. They turned back to back and fingered the ropes at their wrists. Though tied tight, they took little time to release. James shoved the ropes aside and pulled off his gag.

"They must have confidence in this structure," he whispered. "They had to know we'd help each other with our bindings. Although, even if we could get out of here, I have no idea where we are. Except—"

He surveyed every inch of their outdoor cell. It was solid with four corner posts, which were about two feet in diameter, and appeared secured underground making them immovable.

"Calum, there's hope. Look at the crofter's dwelling they entered." He watched Calum's face in the moonlight as he squinted until realization dawned. "It's where we left Fergus. We're still on our own land."

He watched some men come back out, but he couldn't make out if Fergus was among them. Where were they headed? What the hell was going on?

He deduced there were more than four men inside based on the number who came out over the next few hours to relieve themselves.

As he and Calum sat as prisoners, it gave him a chance to rationalize their predicament. He was still on his own damned land and the cottage he was imprisoned near was the same one he'd given to Fergus Mackay and his men as a safe haven the previous winter. Fergus's involvement made him seethe. His guts burned. What the hell did the man think he was doing?

"James, why did Fergus abduct us?" Calum asked. "After risking our neck for him, this is his repayment?"

"I'm as baffled as you are," James said.

He recalled how they'd met. Both had been tracking the beasts responsible for the MacKenzie attack. James and Calum learned that the MacKay and his clan were framed that day. With a bounty on their heads and the king away from Linlithgow for the winter months, Fergus was safer out of sight until James could address his Majesty in person. Only then could he convince King James of Fergus's innocence. Thus far, everything had gone rather smooth. He would address the matter during his upcoming visit to Linlithgow Palace.

"Why now, with a possible pardon so close, would that daft oaf pull a stunt like this? Did the man court death for sport?" Calum asked.

From what James knew of him, he was an honourable sort, if somewhat unrefined, but loyal nonetheless. He couldn't believe Fergus would repay his protection all these months with such lunacy. No, there had to be some other explanation.

"I have no answer for you, Calum."

After a long while, a lone rider entered the clearing in front of the cottage. He dismounted and glanced in their direction before entering. He was smaller built than the others. James guessed correct - someone else wanted him in this prison and he shuddered at the thought that it just might be a Cameron. Maybe Fergus was blackmailed into capturing him, his own family threatened. That would explain a lot.

James turned to Calum, his blood surging through his veins.

"I don't know how much time we have before they come back out. I'm having one of your bad feelings about what may happen when they do. These posts are secured underground, but the wall bases are not. Find a rock or anything to move the soil. Swift now lad, work like your life depends on it. Because it probably does."

Calum needed no more encouragement. A roar of laughter

from inside the cottage was incentive enough for James to fall to his knees and dig like there was no tomorrow.

Chapter Eight

Her opinion of James had been challenged much in the last few hours. Aileana was still irritated by him, but couldn't deny the raw attraction that coursed through her body every time he was near. The intimacy they shared did little to comfort her. She could not afford to let him possess her.

She opened the door to her chamber and found her gown positioned so she could step into it. She trailed her hand down over the length of the deep green velvet. Would James have liked it?

What an annoying thought.

It was no matter what he thought of her gown since she didn't need flattery or romantic designs from the likes of him. Still, she had developed an acute awareness of him. His nearness in the solar made the task of rationalizing their danger challenging. Part of her wanted to send Father Addison away and run her hands all over his muscled torso. The other part of her was surprised to discover his presence a comfort. She would not think about the kiss, no she would not.

She stretched to unfasten the clasps at the back of her dress, her fingers fidgeting. She had just begun to remove the garment when Gwen entered. "Oh, I'm sorry my lady, I didn't know you were in here or else I would have knocked. Getting ready without me, are you?"

Gwen's smile calmed her and almost made her feel like everything was normal.

Normal. Just a few days ago things were just that. How quickly life could be turned upside down testing the limits of inner strength and stretching it beyond all sensible boundaries.

"I was trying." Aileana tried to sound confident, but her declaration was met with raised eyebrows. "But to be honest, I probably would have ended up stuck halfway into my gown with the castle under attack and unable to do anything but crawl under my bed."

Her blunt attempt at humour resulted in a short burst of laughter from each of them.

Gwen sobered first. "Do you think we're in any real danger here?"

It was the same question she'd posed to James a short time ago.

"I believe we're safe for the time being. Come, let us ready ourselves and make the most of the evening, for our guest's sakes. I believe our demeanour is a guide for those around us."

Gwen smiled and nodded while she scurried to tuck, pin, and fuss over Aileana. When they returned to the hall, the room was transformed and capable of accommodating twice as many guests as present.

"My dear, an unexpected guest has just arrived." Aileana turned as Sheena approached; her expression solemn. Over her aunt's shoulder Gawain stood, wearing a broad smile, as though the world was in perfect order. He came to her, took her hands in his clammy, willowy ones and pressed cold hard lips onto each palm.

"My lady, how radiant you look this evening," he said. "I've thought of nothing but you since I was overtaken with grief when I visited you last. I apologize for my hurried exit and my harsh words. I was too much a coward to have you view my unmanly tears and so I fled. Being here, in this castle, knowing my cousin would never grace its great hall again was too much, and even now threatens to crack my resolve to comfort you."

Aileana tried to remain calm. His swift departure and his hate-filled words that day had mortified her. When she needed a friendly face and the comfort of someone she could trust, he fled. She was still guilt ridden over how he discovered the letter, yet she was certain of one thing - he was lying about the reason for his *hurried exit*. His current demeanour was baffling. This was the most attention he'd ever bestowed upon her. She could think of no reason to justify this about-face. A sick sensation passed through her. Would he try to woo her? Now?

She never minded Gawain's thin frame or pale skin, however, she found herself comparing him to another and the skin of her palm tingled in repulsion from the feel of his lips on her hand. Instead of a broad chest with fabric curving around the muscle beneath, Gawain's tunic lay flat and almost hollow against him.

"Fear not, dear cousin, you are as welcome to these stone walls as you've ever been. I accept your apology. It's been a trying time for us all. You're with us now and so I trust you intend to join our celebration?"

He smiled but it did not reach his eyes. Aileana moved to take her place at the head of the table; Gawain followed and positioned himself to do the same. An awkward moment passed while she watched his smile disappear.

Gawain opened his mouth and closed it again. A couple moments passed before he spoke. "Why Lady Aileana, is that not the setting for Lord MacIntosh?"

Sheena interjected and recounted the events leading to James's absence. She finished with, "'Tis Lady MacIntosh who is entitled to sit at the head of the table in his Lordship's absence."

"Ahhh, but she does not yet hold that title, does she?"

Aileana stiffened. "I do not yet hold that title, but this is still my home. The man who does hold that title, endangers himself for our benefit, and would not object to my taking his place."

Gawain bowed his head, conceding the point.

"The MacIntosh is brave and will protect us from these fiends," Sheena said, boasting.

Aileana tried hard to look anywhere but at Gawain. His clothes were impeccable and his entire air was too polished. His former brooding was predictable. This new Gawain was a mystery. Her unease grew and she wished for James's immediate return.

"We are fortunate indeed to have the MacIntosh as our protector," he said. "I for one will sleep better tonight knowing he tracks our would-be attackers. At least on that front, he is a committed man."

Aileana caught the sarcasm in his voice. "Dear cousin, do you think to insult a man who is absent and therefore unable to defend himself, but also willing to place himself at risk for our protection?" Though James's reputation was well known, hearing it from Gawain like this, on this day was too much.

"My lady, I apologize if my assessment of the MacIntosh has offended you. I assumed you had knowledge of his appetite since you are to marry him. He spends so much time at the king's court as the man's Highland spy, that I assumed you would possess some understanding of the man and his politics."

"Common knowledge or no," Sheena said, "discussion of such matters is highly inappropriate in the presence of a lady, especially the one to whom the gentleman in question is betrothed." Sheena raised her chin and scanned the dinner table for agreement from the other guests.

Had she blinked, Aileana would have missed the loathing apparent in the glare Gawain directed at her aunt. When Aunt Sheena turned back from surveying the guests, Gawain had smoothed his features with a tight smile. Aileana's flesh broke out in goosebumps.

"My sincerest apologies again, my lady, for my impudence," he said. "I humbly beg your apology."

"My betrothed's history is of no consequence to me, dear cousin. Only his future concerns me," Aileana said and turned toward Sheena who smiled and nodded.

Gawain unsettled her.

Or did the topic unsettle her?

Either way, she would not continue this discussion. Sheena engaged her in an exchange about the wonderful springing time thus far. She settled into a conversation designed to prove her extensive knowledge of the estate's tenants and its production. In the end, she feared Gawain's comments would remain forever branded on her guest's minds.

The rest of the dinner improved her spirits somewhat. The servants produced bowls of steaming roasted pheasant and vegetable stew served with heaping platters of warm bread for soaking. The main course consisted of succulent wild deer, roasted pig and duck complimented by baked puddings, roasted vegetables and large drawing bowls of dark gravy. Warm mead and wine flowed free and no goblet fell below half full. Trays of wild berry pies, layered custard cakes and cream-filled pastries completed a grand feast she was proud of.

Though the mood was somewhat sombre, everyone complimented the servant's hard work. After dinner, most of her guests paid their respects and retired to their rooms for the remainder of the evening. Fear of an attack had doused the merriment from earlier that afternoon. Those who remained joined Aileana and Sheena on large cushion-covered, wooden benches, which were arranged near the stone hearth. Thankfully, Gawain had chosen to retire with the majority of the other guests. When he kissed her hand goodnight, her hair prickled at the nape.

Once she retired, Aileana lie in her bed listening to the noiseless night and couldn't help but pull the covers right up to her chin. The longer she spent in Gawain's company, the more uncomfortable she became. He'd watched her, just as James had earlier, but his gaze did not excite her - it scared her. She stood the two men side by side in her mind and the effect was rather startling.

The cold look Gawain had given her a few days ago and his almost too smooth demeanour tonight were sides of him she'd never seen. Was this the true Gawain, dark and false? Was the loss of the estate and betrothal to her such a blow to him, his entire person had changed?

The two men were so different. Would she ever understand either? Aileana relaxed and drifted toward the edge of sleep all the while wishing James would resolve the issue with the raiders and return by daybreak.

She awoke as soon as the hidden door on the tower stairs creaked. Aileana held her breath, but the sound of a boot scuff on the stone floor near her bed brought her straight upright. Her heart pummelled. Before she could scream, she was bound and gagged where she sat. The darkness prevented her from seeing who would dare such an act. Her breaths were short and laboured and tremors shook her body as they wound rope around her arms and legs. Her stomach burned with fear. She struggled as they dragged her from her bed into the narrow passageway. Her arms were looped around her captor's neck while he crept through the channel leading outside. She knew this route, but hadn't used it since she was a girl.

They made almost no sound and she tried to sway her body

to break free, but the man whose back she rested on was large and held her still. Her face was forced into his hair and the scent was clean. Lavender? This must be a dream. No, it was her worst nightmare.

Once outside the castle boundaries the man broke into a run. She bounced up and down and was sure her arms would pull from their sockets. Just when she couldn't take any further punishment, she was lifted off his back, her arms re-bound, she was then placed into a cart and covered with layers of canvas.

Her nostrils filled with the stench of rotten cabbage. She was going to vomit if she didn't get the gag out of her mouth soon. Aileana managed to slip her bound arms from behind her back, down across her body and work her feet through the loop. Once in front of her, she used her hands and teeth to work at the gag and loosen the ropes around her wrists.

Free from her bondage, her body convulsed. She had feared little in her life. Her uncle had not often raised his voice to her, much less his hand.

Somewhere between shock and hysteria, conversations in her mind consumed her about what to do. Much of the grief and anxiety she had repressed over the last few days found a feeding ground. Her anxiety escalated causing icicles to settle in her stomach.

She longed for safety, but the hard jolting cart was a constant reminder of where she was. She even imagined her uncle calling to her. "Aileana! Fight back, love, with all that you have and all that you are. Fight back!" She longed for his strength to guide her, though could only weep for him, and for herself.

She swallowed salty tears and focused hard on the image of his face. If his strength couldn't help her nothing could. That wasn't true. She had strength. She'd proven it earlier that day in the solar with James. He'd been proud of her.

Think dammit!

Her thoughts cleared; her best option was to jump out of the moving cart. She'd risk injury on the fall, but that was better than any alternative with these brutes. A little clarity gave her all the courage she needed.

Aileana shifted to the edge of the canvas and peeped out from underneath. A surge of confidence evaporated when the cart stopped. Oh no!

They hadn't been travelling that long. She didn't know on which road, though, and tried to work out where that distance could have taken them, in all directions. There may be an opportunity to escape yet.

To her dismay, when she was hauled out, she viewed a small cottage she'd never seen before and so wouldn't know which way to run, even if she did break free.

The large man holding her arm asked, "What have you done with your ropes, m'lady?"

The mocking tone he placed on 'm'lady' heated her cheeks. He would offer a term of respect in this situation? He had all the control, yet he would mock her attempt to flee. She glared at him and he chuckled.

She was shoved inside the cottage and re-bound, this time tighter. The man placed her on a chair, tied her arms behind her and her feet to the chair's legs. She was relieved she'd not been tied to a bed. From her current position, she'd be difficult to ravage. Her body shook anew with the mere thought of the word.

Her captor, who she could see clearer now, said, "Maybe this'll keep you secure."

"Who are you? Why have you taken me? What is it you want?"

The man raised his eyebrows.

"All in good time, Lady Aileana, all in good time. You will

not be harmed, if you stay quiet."

Her other abductors were also inside the cottage and smirked at his comment, but said nothing. Their silence was unnerving, yet after the initial encounter, she was relieved when they left her alone. No one spoke to her or bothered her in any way whatsoever. Whatever they had in mind, they were taking their time about it. An act of ransom? Those were rare these days, yet so far, their behaviour suggested it.

Time crept by and her bindings dug into her hands and feet. Her back ached and her mind spun. With the men occupied by doing little and ignoring her, she could try to figure this mess out.

The silence was endless. Her captors were relaxed and she prayed that meant they didn't intend to harm her. In fact, from the way the biggest one peered through the window, it seemed like he waited for someone.

She memorized every last detail of their faces, their bodies, and their clothing. If she ever got out of this horrible situation, she would make sure these men were held accountable for their treachery.

She counted eight of them. The man who'd removed her from the cart was well over six feet tall and looked older than the others. He was rather well dressed, for a barbarian. His tunic was properly arranged and belted. He wore deep blue, black and green plaid with a large silver brooch attached at his shoulder.

She blinked when he strolled over to check her bindings and she saw the single arm raising a sword stamped into the brooch, which made bile rise in her throat.

Manu Forti—With a Strong Hand. MacKay. She shuddered.

Aileana glanced away before he caught her staring. The last thing she wanted was any attention, yet her breath came in shallow pants. She continued making mental notes about her captors; tall, brownish black or flaming red hair, well dressed, calm. She came to the troubling conclusion that if she were to sum any of them up in a word, barbaric would not be suitable. Focused? Certainly. Powerful, too. Even though they were responsible for dragging her from her bed in the middle of the night and binding her as she was, she could not bring herself to label them barbaric. There was an air of quiet patience about these men that made no sense. These were the men responsible for the horrific MacKenzie attack.

"Drink."

Aileana snapped her head up. The leader stood beside her, holding a cup of water. She cursed her nervousness. He helped her drink and she was thankful for the cool liquid hydrating her parched throat. How did he know she was thirsty when she hadn't known it herself? He took the cup away and she resumed her downward gaze.

His single act of pity piqued her curiosity and forced her to glance up at him again. He'd already turned away from her and was again looking out the window. She dared a glimpse at the other men. They had no interest in her either, instead played some kind of game with dice.

The ease with which they abducted her was startling. How did they know where to find her room? Who was the mastermind of this scheme and who would they negotiate with?

James.

It was not possible for an organized caper such as this to be planned without knowledge of the MacIntosh's relationship to her. Oh, but they were bold indeed if that were the case.

She wondered about James's reaction once he returned to Chattan Castle to find her taken. Would he be desperate to save her or annoyed at the inconvenience? She couldn't say. At times it appeared he had taken quite a fancy to her and at others he appeared irritated by her presence.

The man who hauled her out of the cart placed a woollen blanket around her shoulders, drawing her from her troubled thoughts. His expression softened before he turned and sauntered out of the cottage.

Aileana was at a loss and stared at the door in utter disbelief. A grunt on the other side distracted her just before James exploded through it.

Chapter Nine

Digging underneath the prison cell hadn't been difficult, considering the wet spring they'd had. They had managed to dig a passage and escape into the woods behind the cell. James's fingers throbbed from the exercise.

Once he was confident of their hiding place, he tried to rationalize which direction to move. That question was answered once the other men exited the cottage. He overheard enough to discover that Aileana was in another dwelling close by. He had no idea if she was there by choice or not, but he intended to find out.

Dawn had broken just enough so he could see some of the men. Fergus McKay was among them. His guts dropped like they were full of lead. The winter had no doubt been rough and he was responsible for some of Fergus's hardships, but this was nonsensical. Was this about money? If so why wouldn't they just come to him for help?

Before he could dwell on what he'd like to say to Fergus, Gawain stepped into view. He had a good look at the man the day he stormed out of Chattan Castle and later in the garden. James was sure of his identity. Visions of the rendezvous he'd interrupted in the garden crept into his mind. His throat dried and blood pounded in his ears. They'd made a fool of him.

Damn them all, he'd make them pay.

James was crouched and feral and ready to pounce. Calum placed his hand on his shoulder and shook his head. It was enough for James to ease up a little. His brother's clear head was full of reason. Though Aileana was close, they still didn't know where she was. By remaining undetected for a short while longer, they could glean her location.

Though appearances would suggest otherwise, his instinct still told him to trust Fergus. The man must know who his captive had been. James frowned. So a Cameron had not blackmailed Fergus after all. What then? Was this some bizarre form of protection? His head swam with the implications.

From well behind them, James saw the flash of crimson tunics. The message he'd sent to the King's Guard earlier had given them enough time to assemble. His scouts had been in the area when they were taken and created a trail. His men were good at carrying out their assignments and he was forever in their debt. Within minutes, twenty of King James's guards surrounded the McKay clan and Gawain, odds even Fergus wouldn't take. No one would escape now.

James erupted from his hiding place. "You! You're behind this?" He growled and lunged toward Gawain, caught just in time by Calum and two guards.

Gawain sneered. "It was all her idea! She wanted to run away with me. I've had her many times over the years and she wanted to feel me inside her again and again—"

James broke free from Calum's hold and smashed Gawain's jawbone with a sickening crunch. Pain shot up his arm and he suspected Gawain's jaw was not the only thing broken. Holding his throbbing hand close to him, he pounded the man with his other fist.

Gawain would pay for this hellish night; he'd pay in the king's dungeon or he'd pay with his life. Gawain dropped to the ground, writhing and moaning. Breathing hard, James turned away from the disgusting sight of him and wiped his bloodied hands off in his tunic.

Gawain claimed they ran away together, and James could do nothing to disprove it. Still, the lass was somewhere close by and he was still responsible for her. Damn Gawain and damn Aileana for involving everyone else in their scheme to run away. Fergus's capture, an event he'd been trying to avoid for months, had occurred on James's bidding and he didn't even care. After all their hard work to uncover the truth surrounding the MacKenzie attack, Fergus's own stupidity would land him in the dungeon or worse.

Aileana Chattan was responsible for this. A clear path led in the direction the MacKays had been headed and James took off toward it followed by several guards. In the moments it took him to get to the other cottage, all sorts of images of the Gawain and Aileana together exploded in his mind. His blood surged through his veins. He ran through the first MacKay he encountered and burst through the door, with no weapons, to confront the woman he despised. Oh how she would pay. The moment their gazes locked, she fainted.

* * *

Aileana floated along on a cloud, bobbing up and down with James's strong arms around her, holding her tight. Fluffy pillows spread out for miles around them and were so irresistible she reached down to touch one. She couldn't quite reach it and so leaned down a little further.

* * *

James caught her just before she fell off Arion's back. Once he had roused her from fainting and had her settled atop Arion, she fell into a slumber. He was grateful for the momentary respite from the night's chaos and focused on returning to Chattan Castle. What he would do with her once there, he did not know, but her limp body quelled some of his fire. She'd proven much more troublesome than he'd ever imagined and, unfortunately, he was responsible for dealing with her. And deal with her he would. At least now that he'd been captured by the King's Guard, the cousin was out of the picture. James's fist still throbbed, but in a satisfying way.

He peeked over her shoulder. Aileana still dozed. He would have thought she'd at least act upset that her plan had been thwarted, but she hadn't even pressed him for information about her lover. Instead, she lay limp and relaxed in his arms as if everything was in order. What game was she playing?

When they returned to the first cottage and his former prison cell, the Guard had already secured their prisoners and was on their way back to the larger encampment several miles west. From there they would proceed south to court to meet their fate. Good riddance to them all.

Aileana's soft and yielding body moved against him as Arion trotted forward. James shifted in his saddle to move away from her warm body. Damned if she didn't move closer to him in her sleep.

All the times he imagined them plotting and scheming were not just fleeting impressions. He'd been right all along. It took everything in him to not send her off to the dungeon as well. He was angry enough with her, but her punishment would not come from a cold, rotten hole in the ground. Hers would come from careful planning once he calmed down.

They rode in silence while the gray morning mist lifted around them. He searched for the right words to say to her while she slept, knowing she would lie to him the minute she awoke. He would trap her in those lies.

Calum trotted beside him. "Was any of that real?"

James's voice was flat when he answered. "Aye, Brother. I believe it was."

Calum shook his head. "Have you spoken with her yet?"

James looked down at her soft profile to see her eyes still closed.

"No, not yet. There's plenty of time to get into that. I just want to get her home first. I don't think she's going to like what I have to say or the new security measures I'm going to impose." He glanced down at her again and smiled.

"Security measures?"

"Oh aye, she'll not escape again."

"Escape? Is that what you think?"

"You heard Chattan, they ran away."

"You can't be serious? Did you not remove the bindings from her wrists and ankles yourself? She wasn't running away."

"Yes, I'm sure 'twas all a good show to appear as though she was not a willing partner. You've no need to worry, she'll not go to the dungeon like her lover. She will learn her place, however, and discover that she cannot play these games and expect no consequences."

"Oh my poor, poor brother." Calum shook his head. "You are in this far deeper that I ever imagined."

James glared at him. "I don't know what you mean, and considering the night we just shared, I'm in no mood for your games. I will say one thing though, my visit to Edinburgh must happen as soon as possible." He pushed Aileana's bottom forward a little to ease the tightness gathering in his loins. "While Fergus's involvement in this crime baffles my wits, I would not see him hang for the MacKenzie attack when I know he's not responsible."

Calum pulled back on his horse's reins and stopped.

"James, do you think 'twill make a difference if you attend the court and speak for Fergus? The Stewart is not tolerant of Highland conflicts. Your presence alone will not make the difference so the argument you present must be sound."

That was exactly why he was so determined to go. He dearly wished he could have spoken to Fergus, if for a moment. Any discussion with him would require the king's approval—not an easy acquisition.

He slowed his pace while Calum caught up with him again and took note of his surroundings. They were almost at Chattan Castle. He couldn't wait to see how she would face all who would be waiting. He glanced down at her relaxed countenance, avoiding the angry red marks on her wrists.

* * *

"You're almost home." His breath tickled the delicate skin beneath her ear. His deep voice roused her and she became aware of his firm thighs and the thick chest muscle cradling her head.

Her body flooded with warmth. She opened her eyes and discovered they were almost home. The familiar road had never looked so good. Conscious of her casual position in front of James, she straightened her back, trying not to lean on him.

"No need to move away, lass. I don't think anyone will be concerned about how much you've warmed up to me once they learn of our ordeal." His voice was a husky whisper.

Her face grew hot at his meaning and she was thankful for her long tresses hanging around her face. In her semi-awake state she forgot the peril she'd encountered mere hours before and had taken wanton comfort in the MacIntosh's arms. He had saved her after all. Still, some decorum was in order.

"I realize I haven't yet thanked you, my lord, for my rescue."

Aileana turned her head to the side to glance up at him and noted how much he towered over her even seated. Her heart skittered along in an insane drumbeat inside her chest.

"Your rescue indeed, my lady. 'Tis my hope you'll find a way to thank me for my services and my discretion." His tone

105

was no longer husky, it held a warning.

"Your discretion?" What did he suggest? "My lord, I'm certain I have nothing to hide." Her chin shot up and her back straightened to the point of cracking.

"Oh aye, I'm certain we'll come to an understanding." He smirked and looked ahead as if to dismiss her. "No one need know of your treachery just yet."

"Just what are you implying?" Her fists clenched. She had no intention of repaying him with any sort of 'services' as he put it, or his discretion. She had nothing to be discrete about! Her cheeks burned again, but with anger this time not desire. Before she could recover, her clansmen spewed from the castle. Aileana had been so absorbed in him, she didn't realize he'd brought her right to the front door.

James dismounted in one fluid movement and reached up to help her down before she could swat his hands away. His firm fingers tightened around her waist, and for a moment he stared hard into her eyes, as if searching into her soul. Infuriated and semi-aroused, she was powerless under that gaze. She shuddered to think where that could lead her and was grateful for the people who descended upon them.

Father Addison was the first to greet them. Behind him was Aunt Sheena who motioned for Gwen's assistance. Together, they ushered her inside the castle's protective stone walls. Once in her chamber, Sheena and Gwen couldn't do enough for her comfort. While they prepared her bath, servants arrived with a large platter of roasted chicken, bread, cheese and a pitcher of warm mead. When she had devoured most of it, she recounted her story to the two women.

"Aileana, love, you do realize who was behind it all."

"I do not. I assume there will be an investigation. I would not want to fear monger, however, one man wore a MacKay crested brooch." Her body shuddered with the realization she was lucky to be alive.

"Aye, there might be MacKay involvement, but I can tell you with certainty your cousin Gawain, the foul man, was also involved. I saw him leaving early this morning." Sheena crossed her arms over her chest.

"How is that possible? Gawain would do me no harm." Gawain? Did this have something to do with the MacIntosh's evasive accusation?

"My lady, please do not gag me any longer on that man and his intentions," Gwen said.

"Gwen, what is it you wish to say?"

"That he was behind the whole thing and meant to hurt you because of your uncle's plan to marry you to the MacIntosh."

"I know you have never liked him, but do you believe him capable of intending harm?" There was no doubt Gawain was different, but was he so bad?

"I believe it with my whole heart and have watched him over the months since his return." Gwen paced and fisted her hands at her sides. "He slithers in and out of the castle like a snake." She stopped. "I know of a kitchen maid who lives not far from here who had the unfortunate bad luck to encounter him one night at a tavern in Moy." Gwen swallowed hard. "She was beaten so bad she couldn't work for a fortnight."

Gwen's face had never been filled with so much worry. "Gwen, surely 'tis vicious rumour you speak of and not hard fact."

"No, my lady. 'Tis true. I know because I was asked to heal her. I've kept this from you because you asked me not to speak ill of him. I will never disobey you my lady, but you've given me the freedom to speak, and speak I shall." Gwen wrung her hands. "I admire your ability to see the best attributes in every soul. That speaks to your goodness, but there is none in him."

Aileana opened her mouth.

"And I saw him, Aileana. With my own eyes, I saw him right after you were taken." Sheena said.

"How?"

"I was on the far side of the courtyard. Gawain didn't notice me and must have thought no one was up at that hour. I was leaning against the stone wall waiting for day to break, a habit I picked up after William passed on. Our last moments together were spent just before dawn on the day he died.

"The sky had not yet brightened and his slight frame gave him away. Once he left the courtyard, I couldn't resist knowing what he was up to. I entered the same door he exited and lit a candle to find my way through the dark passageway. It didn't take long to find your room. I entered and discovered you missing. I then opened your chamber door to alert the guards.

"It wasn't long after that, most of the castle was roused and a plan of action put into place. Two of MacIntosh's men were sent to track Gawain and leave a trail for the King's Guard. The other two went in the opposite direction to alert them."

Aileana was speechless. This was incredible. All this time, he'd plotted against her. Did he despise her uncle too? What a fool she'd been to trust him, believe in him.

The day he'd seen the letter he seethed. That was the real Gawain. Not the one she saw last night with his cool demeanour to gain entry to the castle. Gwen had been trying to warn her forever.

"I've been such a trusting fool." She looked at Gwen who stopped wringing her hands and let out a long breath as though she'd held it forever.

Sheena stepped towards her. "No, Aileana. Never say that. Gawain is at fault here, not you." Her aunt wrapped her arms around her and squeezed tight. "You've endured enough. I want you to soak in that bath and forget about everything except that you are safe and sound. Nothing can hurt you now."

"Aye, Aunt, I thank you. I believe a bath is the only thing I can comprehend at the moment."

Aileana poured herself into the hot, rose-scented water. Each limb welcomed the heat as the stiffness and ache in her joints melted away. Gwen and Sheena lathered and massaged her back, legs and arms. Though tight, the bindings had left red marks on her wrists and ankles.

Sated by the heat, Aileana stepped clear of the tub to sit by the fire. Sheena answered a knock at the door and left with Father Addison.

With only Gwen in the room, it was impossible to hide any of her truest emotions.

"Oh Gwen, I was so confused and afraid. I didn't want to say so in front of Aunt Sheena but the moment James came through that door, I was so relieved I fainted."

Gwen blinked through tear-filled eyes.

"We were so worried about you. We couldn't understand why your aunt was causing such a commotion. She woke the whole house and it took Father Addison quite a while to calm her down. In the end I think it was the valerian I slipped into her mead that settled her enough to tell us what she saw."

Aileana smiled and sighed. "'Tis all too much to take in. I believe you, but I will need some time to adjust to Gawain being someone I must fear. And you knew all along. When I am rested, you must tell me everything you ever viewed in him to earn your distrust."

"Of course, my lady. You must be weary."

"I am, but my mind will not settle."

"I thought as much. I have a gift for your betrothal."

"Oh Gwen, you don't need to give me gifts. 'Tis I who should do so for you for your excellent care."

"Nonsense. Besides, this gift is somewhat selfish in nature, it is to protect you in the only way I know how." Gwen's brow knit. "I never knew fear like I did today."

Gwen produced an enchanting pewter cross on a chain which she placed around Aileana's neck. From a distance it looked like a Christian cross, though upon closer inspection, the Celtic circle of infinity was there as well.

"With this gift of the cross I lay, protection here both night and day; and the one who should not touch, let his fingers burn and twitch; I now invoke the law of three, this is my will so mote it be."

"'Tis lovely, thank you." Aileana's eyes filled with tears.

"You're welcome my lady. And since it is a cross, no one will suspect 'tis been blessed in a different way than usual." She smiled.

"I am proud to wear it."

"I am glad you like it. I considered a ring at first. You know, the ones in which you can carry substances?"

"Gwen," Aileana said. Her tone held a warning note.

"Like cowbane."

"Oh dear," Aileana smiled.

" Or belladonna."

Aileana couldn't hold back her laughter. "Stop."

"Perhaps wolfsbane would have been useful last evening. But I thought it might be better if I didn't make a murderess out of you."

"And I thank you for it, my friend. Now, before I fall asleep sitting up, I must lie down for a while."

"Of course."

She tried to get up, but stumbled a bit. Gwen helped her into a fresh shift and into bed. Aileana wanted to talk more of the incredible night's events, but instead fell into a deep weightless sleep.

Chapter Ten

James watched the priest wipe tears from his eyes as Aileana was ushered into Chattan Castle. He stood just outside the entrance and was at a loss for words. So she would stick to her story of being captured. He shook his head and entered the keep. If she wanted to play games, he'd give her one, but she'd lose.

The guests crowded him, wide-eyed. Who else was in on this little show?

"How did you rescue Lady Aileana?"

"Was it dangerous?"

Even the priest chimed in, "I was convinced she'd never come home. Surely m'lords, God was watching over you and guiding your hands to enact her safe return."

It was sickening. If they only knew.

He and Calum followed the crowd into the dining hall where pitchers of ale and trays of food were brought out; no doubt from last night's feast. His gut rumbled approval. James was desperate for a washtub and a bed, but that would have to wait. Father Addison insisted they fill their bellies and share their story but not before the priest recounted all he knew. Secret passageway? That piece of information was intriguing. He'd have it examined and ferret out her plot.

He didn't know whether he should concede she was captured or tell the truth that she was running away with her lover. He scanned the faces around him. These noblemen and ladies were good people. Even, if her inner circle of servants at the castle were aware of her scheme, he'd bet his life these people were innocent victims just like him. Did they need to know of her deceit?

"Last night, Lady Aileana was—" Calum sat up a little straighter beside him. He wanted to say running away, instead he said, "— abducted from this castle and, in fact, from her own bed."

Several gasps around the room were not loud enough to mask Calum's heavy sigh. He had worried over what his brother might reveal.

"'Tis true," Calum said. "Gawain plotted the whole thing with help from the outlawed MacKays."

"The Constable? I can't say I'm surprised." Father Addison shook his head and clucked his tongue. "My poor, poor lady. You are true heroes, m'lords."

James narrowed his eyes and scrutinized the priest's expression for some form of acting.

"Do you think there will be any further danger of raids now these MacKay beasts have been captured?" the priest asked.

"I believe the immediate danger we spoke of last evening has passed." He looked around and remembered why they'd come. "I will consult with Lady Aileana, however I'm certain she will agree there's no longer a reason to delay the festivities."

Visible relief swept across the room as James turned to Calum and smiled.

"James, what are you doing?" Calum whispered.

James leaned in close. "Showing the lady she can't play us for fools and expect to slink away without answering for it. She'll find out what her secrets have cost her when she wakes."

"You don't believe she was kidnapped?"

"I do not."

"She doesn't deserve this treatment from you."

"Nor do I deserve such treatment from her." James got up to leave. Enough already.

"M'lord, do not worry. Get some rest and we will see to all the particulars for tonight's feast." Father Addison clapped his hands and called for Andrews, the kitchen maid and someone named Colleen. The man all but bounced out of the dining hall.

James walked away shaking his head and hadn't noticed Calum walking beside him until he claimed he wanted extra food to nibble on, and doubled back. James carried on toward his chamber and the promise of respite.

As James passed Aileana's door, he had a sudden urge to walk in on her. In what state would he find her? Upset? Plotting?

Instead of interrupting whatever she was up to, he ordered one of his men to locate the secret passageway. Apparently it led outside and he wanted to know its every nook and cranny.

"Go in there and map every square inch of that passageway, especially to and from her room. When you are done, stand guard in her stairwell out of sight." Until he could be rid of her, he'd know every last detail of her comings and goings.

James smiled as he sauntered off to his chamber. A hot bath and a manservant waited inside to attend him. He peeled off his soiled clothing and sank into the hot water. Damn but he was tired. The servant helped him as required then pulled back the covers and left the room.

James couldn't wait to see the look on her face when she found out about tonight's feast. He had the urge to march down the hall to tell her, but the bed was too inviting. He got out of the water, dried himself and slipped into the bed wearing nothing. A traitorous image of her in the same state floated into his mind just before he drifted off.

* * *

Mid-afternoon. The castle was quieter than ever. Following the hellish night she'd survived, the silence while unusual, was welcomed. Still, a visit to the tower would help her sort through the unbelievable turn of events and how wrong she'd been about Gawain.

Aileana should have trusted Gwen's judgment. That much was clear. All the times he was distant, did he plot against her? Even before her uncle had died? Or were these actions retaliation for his loss of fortune? She had no answers. Everything she thought she knew was turned upside down. She'd been acquainted with him for years, yet she didn't know him at all. He must have had some underlying dislike for her all along. To take such drastic measures made no sense whatsoever. Aileana slipped on her dressing gown and padded up the stone stairway. About half way up she ran headlong into a man standing in her way. She dashed down the stairs again and bumped into Gwen upon tearing open her chamber door.

The maid grabbed Aileana by her arms to steady her, but she fought back.

"My lady, is there something amiss?"

"There's a man in my stairwell! A man! What's he doing there?" Her voice's pitch was far higher than normal, high enough to make the dogs howl.

At that moment, Sheena rounded the corner and hustled the women back inside. Aileana made for the door again when Sheena broke in. "Aileana, I'm sure the man is there for your protection. I assume the MacIntosh put him there to ensure no one got near you again. There, isn't that better?"

"Better?" She had no words for her outrage. How dare he

post security in her room without her permission.

"Well then, let's get you settled so we can discuss what you'll wear tonight—"

"Tonight?"

"Aye love, tonight. The MacIntosh spoke up earlier and said the festivities would continue. Aileana?"

The room tilted just enough to make her to stumble. She grabbed the bedpost and held on for dear life. Aileana drew in a deep breath. "Who does he think he is hiding a man in my room without my knowledge? And now he's planning events at the castle?"

"Aileana, he was trying to protect you, dear."

"Protect me? Or scare me half out of my wits?"

"There, there, I'm sure that's not what he intended at all. About tonight, according to Father Addison, he offered to extend your continued hospitality for your guests—"

"That's right. *My* guests." The MacIntosh clansman shuffled his feet near the bottom of the stairs and she turned her fury on him. "And you! Remove yourself from my room this instant!"

"But my lady—" The man's face turned red.

"Until her Ladyship recovers from her ordeal, sir, I believe you should take her advice," Sheena said. He nodded and left.

This was all too much. It appeared his earlier appreciation for her input was fleeting. This was just the kind of arrogant, insufferable man she feared he was from the beginning.

Sheena closed the door behind the frightened-looking man. "Aileana, please sit down and let's talk this through."

"I don't want to talk it through. Aunt Sheena, I know you mean well, but I have no intention of placating that man's arrogance with submission. Would you please locate his Lordship and ask him to meet me in the solar in half an hour."

"As you wish, love." It wasn't hard to tell Sheena didn't

agree with her, but she had no desire to debate her feelings.

Once Sheena was gone, she paced.

"My lady, you have to admit, it was easy for those men to kidnap you through the passageways."

Gwen was right, but she was unable to let go of her anger so easily.

"There's more to it than that. He's making all the decisions here. This is my home, not his yet, and I intend to remind him of that." Aileana had no real argument there. Once the betrothal agreement was in place, he could do as he pleased. She sounded a little like a spoiled child, but it didn't matter. Decisions affecting events occurring in this castle were hers and that was not about to change. He could do as he pleased in his own home.

She hadn't given the betrothal ceremonies a single thought once she'd gotten home. Sheena and Gwen had rushed her into the castle and up to her room so quickly, she did not notice the guests had made preparations to leave—direction she had given the previous evening.

Aileana had not informed him of her role in the past. That was a mistake. She was disappointed, but not surprised he wouldn't realize the importance of appearances in front of everyone. By making the announcement himself he'd established a commanding precedent. She could not allow that.

Gwen fussed around her and was just finishing her hair when Sheena re-entered. Aileana looked in the mirror and took note of the maid's work. Gwen had chosen a cream gown with gold embroidery on all the edges. The square neck was meant to accentuate her figure and the extended sleeves were graceful. Her hair cascaded down her back. Her outward appearance was in stark contrast to the turmoil bubbling inside her.

"Aileana, he has no idea you're so upset. Please give him a chance to explain himself."

Sheena's words fueled her confidence. She nodded to each woman in turn, squared her shoulders and left the room.

The distance to the solar gave her more time to compose herself. She was ready for battle when she entered the room and found him seated on a chair near the window reading an account scroll. His casual appearance added to her anger. Insufferable man. He could do what he chose. He had already made himself at home here, but this was her home too and she was not about to let him forget it.

"My lord, can you tear yourself away from your reading and allow me a few moments of your time?" Her tone was harsh and his surprised expression told her he had no idea what was coming next.

He placed the scroll on the desk and walked toward her. She watched him take in her appearance from the top of her head trailing down over her features to rest just above her neckline. A lazy, sensual smile rested on his lips.

"My time is all yours, my lady. Did you rest well?"

His hand reached towards her hair, but she pushed it away. She couldn't believe he'd missed the anger in her eyes. Did he think she'd come to enjoy his company? The arrogance.

"I am displeased, my lord, with your presumptions earlier today. I'm here to inform you we are not yet wed, and until such time, decisions concerning events at this castle and matters of security shall be conducted in consultation with me."

James blinked. His grin disappeared and his gaze narrowed, sending flutters across her belly.

"I would not wish to interrupt your pleasure, Lady Aileana. I intended to speak with you about the guests, but you see, I was tired from last night's adventure and as it was, I fell asleep before the opportunity presented itself."

She could not think of a retort before he continued.

"On the second issue concerning security, I placed a man in your stairwell and I will continue to do so until the time comes when your husband is in your bed to prevent you from leaving it."

She gasped. He was too bold. James stood mere inches from her, forcing her to look straight up into his face. Her heart pummeled.

"My lord, do not make any further presumptions on my part. 'Tis not my wish to have you in my bed at all. And given the choice I'll take the man on the stairs."

She seethed. She glared at him and he glared right back.

"But your lover can come and go into your room as he pleases, is that it? Tell me, is that how you met? By secret passageway?"

"I beg your pardon?"

"Do not play innocent with me Lady Aileana." James turned his head, but kept his eyes focused on her. "You need to understand though, while you are still betrothed to me, you will not conduct yourself in such a manner again. Once our troth is broken you may do as you please. It's no wonder your uncle was so anxious to be rid of you."

Her mouth fell open. She searched his narrowed eyes. Oh dear God he believed what he said. Gawain? Her lover? After a terrifying night spent pondering her fate, she would have never suspected this further abuse.

"My lord, you are mistaken." Aileana thrust her chin up. "I will defend myself on this matter once and you may take from it what you choose. I was removed from my home last night and detained against my will. I only later learned Gawain was involved. We are not, nor have we ever been lovers. It appears my judgment is lacking on many accounts."

Aileana trembled. She'd never been treated with such disrespect in her life.

"Your judgment does not concern me. Only your conduct, and as much as I would like to believe you, I cannot." James crossed his arms over his chest. "You claim you and Gawain were not lovers, yet you were crying the day I revealed your uncle's letter. You admitted you expected him to be your husband and I later saw him in the garden, no doubt waiting for your signal to steal away for a tryst."

"You saw Gawain in the garden? When?"

James shook his head. "Oh you play the game well, Lady. When I came to collect you. He watched you from the hedge. Do not try to tell me you did not know he was there."

"I did not." Was Gawain trying to capture her even then?

"And I don't believe you. It is of little matter, however, as I will leave here on the morrow and gain the king's blessing to break this contract. Without your uncle available to concede, it is the proper way to handle this situation. Once all the particulars are explained, I'm certain he will assist in wiping this blemish clean."

That's what she was, a blemish? She bowed her head. How much further abuse would he dish out this day? She didn't deserve it. James MacIntosh may have all the power in this situation, but she was not about to lie down and take it. If no one else would stand up for her, she'd damn well stand up for herself. Aileana raised her head to meet his gaze.

"Oh the king will assist will he? Of course he will. You may give him my regards from my dead father while you're at it. It appears that man will be forever responsible for my unhappiness."

"What did you say?" James cupped her face with his strong hand.

"Nothing that matters to you, my lord." She wrapped her small hands around his forearm to shove him off but he would not budge. She should be afraid; instead she wanted to drive a dagger in his gullet.

"You mentioned your father and I will hear your meaning. Now."

"Surely you know of my father's involvement with your precious king?"

"I confess I do not. Your father was a good friend to my family and I was told he died while travelling to London."

"Of course that's what you heard. Especially if the king had any part in the falsehood."

"You border on treason with those words."

"I care not for treason! I've lost a beloved parent to that man's cause and I will not be silenced for it!"

His grip on her face tightened. "I don't believe one word that falls from your lips. You have the gall to claim King James is responsible for your father's death. Lady, you go too far."

"I don't care what you believe!" Aileana twisted enough to break free from his grasp. Her hands fisted at her sides and her chest heaved.

James's eyes darted from her face to her bosom. "But you will care. Do not think for a second your crimes against me will go unpunished. I regret the feast tonight, but we will both suffer through it and I will leave here tomorrow for Linlithgow. It is unlikely you will see me again."

He could go with her blessing. Aileana tilted her chin up. "You may go with my good riddance, but know that I am no liar. My father was sent to England for surety of King James's ransom. How much was it again? 40,000 merks?" Now that she was out of his grasp, she couldn't resist making her point. "It seems to me the palace at Linlithgow becomes more lavish by the second. Perhaps the king never intended for my father and the others who were sent away from their families to ever come home."

"Enough! I'll hear no more of these villainous words from you."

It was good to see him rattled for a change. "And as for the crimes against you? I have been the victim here. Twice. Yet by your account I am faithless and a treasonous liar. However do I manage it?"

"Do not mock me," he warned.

He stepped toe to toe with her, so close their bodies almost touched. Her breath came in short gasps. Their faces were so close she could feel his breath as he fired his hateful words at her. Hers were no better, but at least they were the truth. He was so blinded by his devotion to his king, he couldn't see anything else.

She had never been so incensed by anyone in her life. She couldn't fathom what her future held with him bearing down on her. She needed to get away from him and clear her head. As she turned to leave, James caught her by the arm.

"Where do you think you're going?" he asked.

"To see to the dinner preparations."

James turned her to face him, holding her arms in his large, strong hands and stared into her eyes. "You'll go nowhere without me this day."

"I'll go where I want, my lord, and with whom I choose. You can rest assured, it will not be with you."

"Oh no? We'll see about that. You'll do what I want while I'm under this roof and responsible for you."

He held her arms too tight. The distance between them had disappeared again and she could scarce draw breath.

"Tell me my lord. What do you want?" She dared ask.

James didn't answer with words. His hand grasped the back of her head and drew her forward to capture her lips. This kiss was not like the first one. His mouth moved over hers with urgency, his tongue hungry for her response. She was frightened by the intensity of her own reaction when it came. A great surge moved through her body urging her towards him. Her hands moved up to curl around his neck as his hands moved to her waist to pull her in tight. She was lost in the liquid heat coursing through her veins as they pressed against one another.

As the kiss deepened, her head swam. James carried her to the bench and pulled her onto his lap. His hand gripped her thigh. He traced the outline of her hip and slid his hand further up to rest on her full, round breast. She stiffened at this touch, but he did not break the kiss or his hold on her. He reached up to slip her gown off one shoulder, his fingertips traced her neck, collarbone and further down to the top of her breast.

She should stop him. That was the right course of action. She despised this man who made her feel like she would burst into flames at any moment. His mouth and hands sent thrills of sensation through her. He burned kisses all along the path his fingers explored and her head fell back a little as he tasted her neck. Oh God his mouth must be a cardinal sin. He reached the rosy pink bud jutting out from her breast and moved his tongue over it, encouraging its fullness. He took her nipple into his mouth and sucked hard, the sensation jolting through her was almost too much. She grew desperate for something she didn't yet understand.

Her blood pounding, her breath in shallow pants, Aileana gripped his hair tighter as his hot mouth tortured her body. She could feel his hard muscles beneath her thighs and wanted him to touch and taste every inch of her.

"James." His given name was on her lips before she could correct herself.

He grasped her hips and turned her way from him. His fingers dug into her soft flesh as he pulled her backside toward his thighs. She pressed down against him, the hard length of his shaft pressing against her bottom. Only their clothing separated what she desired more than anything - he desired it too. The intense urgency raging through her was frightening and her whole body went rigid.

He stopped. "We must cease this madness." His voice was strained.

His tortured words sobered her just enough and she jumped off him. Her body pounded with desire as she fixed her gown over her quivering flesh.

He stood abruptly and walked toward the door. She wanted to say something to him, but no words seemed fitting. Before she could think on it any further, he opened the door to reveal Father Addison with his fist raised about to knock.

Chapter Eleven

Aileana dashed to the door to greet Father Addison. His raised eyebrows told her he had some sense of what had transpired between her and James. Her cheeks heated and she clasped her hands together in front of her, not making eye contact with either man. It was awkward, considering she stood between them.

"My dear, your aunt was worried you came in here to have heated words with his Lordship." Father Addison turned to James. "I assume, m'lord, because you were leaving, all has been resolved?"

Aileana peeked up to see James's expression. She caught a light pink flush cross his features.

"All is well Father." His voice was flat. Controlled. "Some heat passed between us, but we are discovering the limits of our discourse. I thank you for your concern."

She was sure she sensed increased tension in his body, as if an invisible tether joined them and she would forever detect any change in him. If the fates were kind, a large hole would open up beneath her and swallow her up. She would not be so lucky, and despite the lack of sudden and immaculate intervention, she forced a weak smile.

"Aye, we are quite well, Father. How are the preparations

coming for this evening?"

Father Addison looked heavenward and smiled. "My child, everything is in order. Your delightful presence is all that is required."

With that, she turned to James, but still could not meet his eyes. Instead, she fixed her gaze on the stubble on his chin. Her skin tingled at the memory of it scraping across her flesh moments ago.

"I won't take up any more of your time, my lord, I must see to my guests."

She bobbed a curtsy to him and left the solar. Once outside she tried to clear her muddled thoughts before anyone else could see her. She walked toward the great hall hoping no one noticed her shaking legs. Inside she trembled, sure she would come apart at the seams. Anger at the man's heartlessness and her desire for him warred inside her. She prayed the result wouldn't vanquish her in the process. As she turned the corner she encountered Andrews.

"M'lady, it is good to see you up and about." His smile was tight and his gaze darted from her eyes to the floor and back again.

"Is it John?" She was irritated enough and didn't have the patience for this.

"M'lady, considering last evening's horrible event, I believe it is time I disclosed your uncle's motives."

"And you don't think that's a little late, and just a bit obvious?"

"Maybe so, but my duty to you and your uncle have altered. You should know everything."

"Very well, please come into the dining hall. 'Tis unlikely we will be interrupted in there."

Once seated by the stone hearth, John wrung his hands. It was strange, she was about to learn the information she had coveted just a day ago, yet she didn't care anymore why Gawain had fallen out of favour with her uncle. It all seemed so irrelevant. Andrews would not reveal anything she couldn't already suppose. Still, the man appeared shaken and if unburdening himself would give him peace, she would not deny him.

Andrews drew a deep breath. "I was present when your cousin first came to visit us many years ago. One day I witnessed his bath and noticed marks on his back that I couldn't make sense of. I mentioned it to your uncle so he and Father Addison examined the boy closer and concluded someone had attempted purification on him."

"Purification? You mean beating?" The thought of it was horrifying and while she knew some parents believed their children to possess evil spirits, she had never seen one harmed. It was not something people discussed. Still, a bubble of pity swelled inside her for Gawain, and a little nausea.

"Aye," Andrews said. "We estimated by the number of scars on his back it had been occurring for quite some time."

"My God." She swallowed hard. She knew little of her uncle's first cousin and was glad the man had never accompanied Gawain on his visits.

"No. Not God. In the name of God in someone's twisted mind perhaps. Your uncle, generous soul that he was, tried to adopt Gawain and at least salvage something of a life for him. His father would hear none of it and insisted upon the laird's commitment to secure the boy's future at Chattan Castle. As you can imagine, we all worried about the state of the boy each time he visited. It took the first couple of days to even get him to talk."

"I never knew."

Andrews rubbed the back of his neck. The information was a burden to him. It also belonged to her now as well.

"Gawain was often here for two or three days before you were ever aware. The laird tried hard to protect you from the horror."

"Is that why he wouldn't commit me to him?"

"Not entirely. As the years passed, the boy grew into a man and where there was once a sliver of hope he could be salvaged, time revealed a growing seed of cruelty in him."

Andrews reached for her hands and squeezed.

"Cruel? In what way?"

"At first it was in how he mistreated livestock. Then he degraded and beat some of the peasants from the village. He preyed on the weakest souls he could find. The laird was beside himself with rage. He arranged for Gawain to take the knight's training to teach him to discipline his mind."

"Uncle did that?" So much had been kept from her. Aileana understood her uncle's need to protect her, but her ignorance had not served her well last evening.

"Aye, and once knighted, the man appeared transformed— so much that the laird hoped for Gawain's salvation once again. Your uncle offered him the constable position here and believed Gawain had come into his own." Sadness swept Andrews features. "Then we received more disturbing reports."

"What sort of reports?"

"I will not provide you with details except to say several young maidens in the area will never be the same."

"He raped them?" She was going to be sick.

"He brutalized them. Your uncle wanted to be rid of him, once and for all. While he lamented the man Gawain could have been, the laird was not about to put any more of his people at risk. He was about to fire him and banish him from the family."

Aileana placed her hands together and raised them to her lips. "Was Gawain there the day Uncle died?"

"Aye."

No. After all her uncle had done for Gawain. Her thoughts raced back over encounters she'd witnessed between the two men. Her pity vanished and blood pounded in her ears.

"Did he—" She couldn't say the words.

"I cannot say. Gawain followed us and neither he nor the Laird was in my sight when the tragedy occurred. I couldn't prove anything so couldn't move to have him arrested. Thankfully, he's in the king's dungeon of his own doing and you're safe and sound."

Safe and sound indeed. How wrong she was to trust in anything she saw on the surface of Gawain Chattan. She'd mistaken his cool demeanour for shyness, instead it held his cruelty.

"John why didn't you warn me after Uncle died?"

"Because there was no reason for me to think he meant *you* any harm. One would expect with the laird gone, he'd woo you to earn your favour."

"I do not wish to point out how wrong you were."

"You may, m'lady, but I don't think you can punish me any more than the hell I went through last night." Andrews lowered his head, his shoulders slumped.

"I am fortunate for your counsel and your service, John." She meant it. Of all the people who could harm her, John Andrews was not one of them. Truth be told, she was pleased to have this quarrel over with. She needed all the support she could get.

When he looked up, his eyes were misted. He cleared his throat and smiled. There was the kind man who would throw himself in front of a battering ram to protect her.

"Aye, well enough of that, lass. You are away from danger and with an honourable man who will never mistreat you. As your uncle wanted."

Therein was the problem. Aye, James was considered honourable, but on the score of mistreatment, she could not concur.

"Not so honourable I fear."

Andrews puffed up his chest. "Oh I am certain you will make a fine couple. He might turn a few heads lass, but he's a well-respected man, well admired by his tenants and at court."

"That he may be, however, he believes Gawain and I were lovers, and is bent to break our betrothal once he leaves here tomorrow."

Andrews deflated. "No."

"Aye, 'tis true. He even called me a liar when I told him about the king's involvement in father's fate."

"Your father. How did that topic arise?"

"It is no matter." Aileana shook her head. "There is no convincing the man of my innocence either, although I do not understand why he will force us to go through with this dinner tonight, only to ruin me tomorrow."

"Aileana, you must be mistaken."

She would relish the error if it were so. "Father Addison said the MacIntosh required much convincing before he would sign the contract in the first place. Now, he has a falsified reason to get out of it. And if that is his desire, he can go - with my blessing." With her uncle dead and Gawain a marked criminal, she had no one. Her betrothed would become her ward to do with as he saw fit, and considering his pigheadedness thus far, she wasn't hopeful of any sort of peace in her future.

"I don't know what to say. Would you allow me to speak with him on your behalf?"

"No, 'tis no point. He would counter you by saying I put you up to it. I don't know of any way to prove my credibility."

"What can I do?"

"God bless you for asking, but there is nothing except to help me get through this night and tell no one what we spoke of here."

"I will do as you wish m'lady."

"Thank you John," she said and kissed him on the cheek. Aileana left him before her overcrowded emotions could betray her.

She struggled to rationalize her thoughts. What had passed between her and James in the solar, and what she'd learned about Gawain, were heavy burdens. She pulled every ounce of strength from within to give her the courage she needed to face her guests. No doubt they would bombard her with questions and insist on every last detail of the previous night. The topic of Gawain Chattan would consume most conversations for many hours to come. She must endure all this speculation whilst under *his* scrutiny. The fates were cruel.

Once she arrived at the great hall, she was greeted by her aunt and several of the guests, all rested and ready to celebrate the betrothal and the rescue. She turned her attention to the conversation and focused on it, trying hard to keep her thoughts clear. She was awash with such a span of emotions from nervousness to residual fear and fought hard to remain calm. The anti-climax of the previous night and the unexpected desire for James left her shaky and unsure how to behave. An uncommon feeling for her, and she didn't like it one bit.

One night. That's all she had to suffer through to put an end to these hellish events. Her body and mind couldn't take much more and it would be a relief when she had her home back.

The question was what then? With the contract broken, James would be responsible for arranging another for her. If only the king weren't involved. She might plea with a sheriff to let the contract lie dead and find a way for her to keep her home without the shackles of a husband, but she wouldn't even know where to begin to make this happen. Either way, between James and his precious king, she would have no say in what was to come.

Aileana entertained her guests throughout the afternoon with grace, but there was no way for her to hide the fact that James was absent. He'd already broken their arrangement. Why was he torturing her by forcing her to endure this pretense? Alone.

Aileana straightened her back and forced a smile while she envisioned sticking a dagger in him. Each moment he remained absent, she seethed. He dared think her capable of every lecherous act and then attempted to seduce her. Vile man. He was a raving lunatic. She'd show him. If he thought for a moment he could humiliate her and get away with it, he was mistaken. She'd find a way to retaliate, somehow.

* * *

The priest stopped him before he could leave the solar.

"Lord MacIntosh, you're an honourable man to be sure. You're well respected amongst your clansmen. That much I know. I also know you are a man of the world and have never been married. What I'm trying to say, if you will permit me, is that young woman is near and dear to us. I would not want to see her, or you for that matter, in a situation where you're both miserable." He paused. "These last days have been filled with a great deal of activity and emotion. I trust there are no decisions being made in haste?"

It took him a minute to digest the priest's meaning. "Father, I'm aware of Lady Aileana's attributes." *More than you know.* "You're correct. Much has transpired in the past days by way of excitement. You may be assured, all will turn out as 'tis meant and with the proper balance of justice."

Father Addison seemed satisfied with that and unaware of the real reason for the tension between he and the lass. What the devil was he thinking anyway? What was he doing with this woman? Rather, what was she doing to him? He wanted to make her squirm for her deceit, but he might just be the one to squirm. In truth, he'd rather hoist her over his shoulder, bring her back to the bench and finish what they started.

He needed to cool off. He couldn't continue these lustful thoughts of her, or else he was going to damned well explode with need. Of course bedding her and falling under her spell would land him under her thumb—exactly where he never intended to be.

The two men left the solar together, but instead of following Father Addison to the great hall, James exited the castle from the back and walked to the stable. The best prescription for a foul mood was a brisk ride and a cold swim. He rode hard toward a secluded pond he knew was close-by.

James struggled to keep his thoughts away from the obvious thrill that coursed through him at the memory of Aileana's response. No doubt it was what she intended. Aye, but she was good at her game. When she entered the solar, he was taken with her. It was not until she spoke he realized her intensity amplified her beauty.

She didn't respond like an innocent, oh no. On the contrary, she knew just when to yield to him. The woman was skilled in lovemaking. Hell, she could teach him a thing or two. His traitorous loins hardened just considering it.

He arrived at the pond and shed his clothing before diving in. The brisk water cooled his raging body. He remembered the taste of her skin, how she arched her body toward his. A wanton act. His name on her lips was just about his undoing. God how he wanted to bury himself inside her.

He dove into the water again and again until his body cooled enough to risk re-joining the party. He had one night to exact his revenge and at dawn tomorrow he would ride from

Chattan Castle and her forever. He would not let his lust for her rule him again.

At dinner, he was ever aware of her. She wouldn't look at him when he came into the hall and was quiet through the meal. Her expression was too masked to tell if forcing her through this event was having the desired effect. The crowd gathered honoured him, yet he couldn't help conclude the event was a mistake. The triumph he longed for didn't come.

"I never thought I'd see the day," Calum said so that only James could hear.

"Meaning?"

"Meaning, Brother, you're smitten and you are doing everything possible to convince everyone around you, especially yourself, you don't care about her."

"How much ale have you consumed?" James asked. It was a failed attempt at a jest. Calum did not even crack a smile.

"Oh you're serious?" James whispered. "I'm not smitten with anyone. The wench will soon discover what it is to be humiliated. When we leave here tomorrow, we will journey straight to Linlithgow to break this contract."

"You're serious? James, I've never seen you act so daft in your life. The girl was abducted for Christ's sake. What will it take for you to believe that?"

"I am less a fool than those gathered here. Look how she has them clamouring for her attention."

"And who among them would you see bed her?"

"What?"

"Who would you see bed her, marry her, be the father of her children?"

"I don't care who else she takes to her bed," he said. James shifted on his seat. He didn't like envisioning her with another man, no matter how necessary it was.

"Oh Lord 'tis true!" Calum said. Two people near him

turned their head. He hushed his tone to just above a whisper. "I suspected, but I know it for certain. You're head over heels for the lass aren't you? I can't blame you. She's stunning, intelligent, and that body."

"Don't you ever!"

Calum burst into hearty laughter. He leaned close to his brother's ear. "Jealous, too? Oh this is the greatest revelation ever."

"I'm not speaking to you anymore. Go back to your ale." James was irritated and turned away. The younger man got the hint and left the table though not before he drew the attention of several guests including Aileana. He didn't want her privy to that line of conversation.

Calum plopped down beside Aileana and flung his arm across her shoulders. "My lady, I understand you Chattans claim to be the best storytellers of all the Eastern Highlands. We MacIntosh can weave a bit of a yarn ourselves with the right motivation."

His voice was loud enough for those within earshot to chime in.

First, the Chattans yelled, "Aye!"

Followed by a MacIntosh who was even louder.

"Aye bring us out a barrel or two 'o ale an' we'll show ye!"

"Aye my lord, we are the best storytellers of all the Highlands, not just the Eastern region." Aileana's broad smile for Calum twisted James's guts.

Again, the Chattans chimed in.

"Aye m'lady, you tell that MacIntosh what we're made of!"

His heart was in his throat. The look of happiness on her face was intoxicating. He wanted her to smile at him like that. Her power over him was mesmerizing. He had to steady himself to recover. Somewhere in the back of his mind, Calum chuckled and it sobered him.

During the evening, both of their clansmen recounted tales of bravery and heroics, a welcome distraction. There were songs of war and peace, of love and death.

Aileana told Calum she had never felt so proud of her clansmen. "They've paid true homage to their countrymen through tales of the brave Scots who protected their homes and families from ancient and brutal Norse attacks." Aileana confessed she had always loved the stories of her people. He listened to her every word. Young though she may be, she was passionate and proud. Chattan's daughter indeed.

Aileana and James spoke little to each other during this time. So engrossed was she in the stories, and he in ignoring her, the majority of the evening passed without much exchange and he didn't like it. But there was still the dance. This was the part he looked forward to all night. When the ale was gone and the night grew late, the priest suggested the musicians strike the tune, so the exhausted couple could retire. A jolt of fire shot through him as he took her hand and led her to the dance area.

"Father, I believe that's the best suggestion I've heard all night," he said. Now he would see the extent of her shame and misery. She couldn't hide it from him at close proximity.

The pipers began an old melody while they positioned themselves. James took her hands in his and bowed, she curtsied. He placed his right hand at her waist as his left came up to meet hers which she placed flat against his. Her left hand rested on his arm.

From the beginning of the dance, Aileana would not meet his gaze. It was common enough during this dance at marriage ceremonies for the husband to scoop up his bride and carry her off to the marriage bed. He could see why. Their bodies moved in perfect harmony together and while she stared at his chin, he tried to remember all the reasons why he didn't just bed her anyway.

Enough of this cowering. He squeezed her waist prompting her to meet his eyes and once she did she didn't turn away again. This pleased him. The melody's slow tempo made him aware of the movement in her hips as they swayed together. Blood rushed to his loins as he envisioned them performing another kind of dance. The intensity building in him was difficult to douse. If the dance didn't end soon he would be in real danger of taking that to which he was entitled, but vowed to refuse.

The final note droned on.

A loud MacIntosh bellowed out, "Take 'er upstairs!"

Aileana blushed. Damn, she played the innocent so well. The aunt and the maid removed her from the festivities, not soon enough. Chattan kept some good ale in his buttery and James would need a good deal of it in order to keep him from her this night.

Chapter Twelve

Aileana dismissed both Sheena and Gwen after an hour of enduring their endless chatter. Sheena didn't know James was about to break the agreement and the last thing Aileana wanted was a discussion on that topic or, in truth, conversation of any sort. She needed sleep—good old sound, dreamless sleep.

She removed her dress, donned a thin linen night shift and moved to open the window shutters. The cool night air would calm her frayed nerves and enflamed senses. A light cough startled her. The damned guard. She'd forgotten all about him in the stairwell, by order of the overbearing and infuriating tyrant she would soon call ex-husband-to-be. She slammed the shutters in protest and was somewhat satisfied when the man scurried further up.

Just as she was about to crawl into bed, a knock echoed through her door. Aileana shook her head and stomped across the chamber. Which one of the ladies was this with some excuse to come in and pass more comment about the night, and on and on and on. She was in no mood for it and thought she had made herself clear. She flicked the latch up and tore the door open.

"I told you I am not in need of anything—" She stopped mid sentence. James's gaze fell to the flimsy garment she wore.

His lips parted and he didn't even try to avert his eyes.

"I beg your pardon, my lady." His voice cracked. "I heard your window slam and I feared you were in danger." His last words were barely a whisper.

I am in danger. She moved to position her body behind the door, but he pushed it further back so she had no way to conceal her body from the heat burning in his eyes or how they travelled over her. She could not let this happen again.

"Lord MacIntosh, as you can see, I am well and not appropriately dressed to receive anyone but my maid. I bid you good night my lord."

She turned to reach for something, anything to cover her body but he caught her by the arm and pulled her back against his chest. He smelled of ale. James reached down and grasped her bottom, pulling her tight to his hips. His erection throbbed against her, sending terrifying thrills to her core. She had no defence against him. Her traitorous hips arched against his and his resulting growl drew moisture between her legs. The sensation was intoxicating. He trailed moist kisses down her throat to the crook of her neck where he grazed his teeth across her flesh. She shuddered and clung to him.

Why did he have to be such a tyrannical oaf? He thought everything bad in this world about her, yet here he was, seducing her again. He wanted her misery and her passion and she would fight him to the bitter end. He shifted his hold on her, grasped her breast and encircled her nipple with his thumb, the garment she wore offering no barrier from his onslaught. Her body pressed hard into his. Her control slipped. If she didn't stop him now, she soon wouldn't be able to.

"Please let me go," she said.

"I don't want to. I want to bed you Aileana, and I know you want me too." Even his ragged breath increased the heat down below.

"You're drunk, my lord and I'm not decent."

"That I know. I would like to share in your indecency - over and over, in truth."

He leaned down capture her lips. She didn't have the strength to fight him off and in his current state there was no way to reason with him. Perhaps the man on the stairs could serve purpose after all.

"You there! On my stairs, come man, help me with his Lordship. He's drunk and about to fall."

She was happy and sad when James's head snapped up to glare at her.

"Anyone but me, is that it?"

"You don't know what you're saying."

The guard approached him and attempted to lend aid.

"Get off me man, I don't need your help." James glared at Aileana. "And she has just proved she doesn't need protection either. You are relieved."

The guard sighed and left the room. She had nothing left to save her from James's advances. Though, the look on his face suggested he'd not make any more this night. His hands clenched at his sides and his frown grew.

"I leave at daybreak, Lady Aileana. I will send word of the king's decision as soon as the deed is done."

He didn't wait for her response and left her chamber. With that, she closed the door and latched it. Thank God her uncle had insisted on inside latches years ago.

Aileana listened at the door and heard no further movement. She crossed the room to reopen the shutters to discover she had broken them and could not make them give without causing a further racket. This meant she couldn't enjoy a cool breeze to still her thoughts.

Throughout the night, she tossed and turned, having wicked dreams of James's body on hers, his mouth tasting hers, her hands exploring him. She woke in the middle of the night bathed in sweat.

Come the morn, James MacIntosh would no longer torment her. She longed for life to return to normal, at least for a little while, or long enough for her to figure out how to regain some control over her future. Exhaustion from the events of the past two days set in and she drifted into the deep dreamless sleep she wished for.

Aileana awoke the next morning when Gwen arrived with a pitcher of mead and a tray of food. She had no appetite for anything besides solitude.

Gwen fussed over her with extra care and she was more than willing to allow it. She longed to speak of her encounters with James but wasn't sure how to begin. Her mood was quiet and Gwen was quieter than usual too as she fixed Aileana's hair.

Aileana tried not to think of James and focused instead on what Gwen was doing. The ribbons and beads the maid put in her hair matched the long crimson gown she had chosen. James might have already left, but her neighbours would remain for part of the morning and she was responsible to see to their comfort and extend her hospitality as long as they were here.

Today she was still Lady Aileana Chattan.

"Gwen, is something bothering you?" Aileana asked, unable to bear the woman's unusual silence any longer.

"My lady, 'tis I who should ask you that question. You need not concern yourself with my feelings."

"Since when should I not be concerned with your feelings? Gwen, you are my dearest friend. If there's something bothering you I want to know about it. Is it a man? Have you begun another affair? You don't look happy though so that can't be it."

Gwen's face broke into an exasperated smile. Half laughing, she said, "Please, teasing is my job not yours." Gwen sobered. "I'm worried about you. I see a connection between you and the MacIntosh, but you don't seem happy about it. Please tell me if you don't wish to discuss it, but that is the only man on my mind, I swear."

Aileana didn't believe her, but she would get to the truth. She wanted to talk to Gwen about her feelings and while she was reluctant to bring up her awful situation she would surely burst if she didn't speak of it to someone.

"I have been hoping for some opportunity to discuss certain encounters between myself and my former intended," Aileana said.

Aileana was unused to voicing her true feelings. She had always been able to rely on her uncle for counsel, however, on the topic of James MacIntosh, she could use some *experienced* advice.

"Former intended?" Gwen's eyebrows shot up.

"Interesting how you don't sound surprised."

"Well, I—"

"Come on, out with it. Did Andrews talk to you?"

"Andrews? No of course not. My lady, I have much to share with you but I'm not sure you're ready to hear any of it."

"If you have news to share please do so. I've been lied to and omitted in far too many important discussions of late to tolerate any more."

"Very well. My source for information is Calum MacIntosh. Almost from the moment he entered the house, we took notice of one another." She smiled. "We've become...friends. I beg your pardon, but he has been interested in your reaction to his brother's foolish behaviour. He believes—"

"He believes what?"

"—that the MacIntosh has developed feelings for you, but

won't admit it to himself."

"Oh I can assure you, Gwen, his brother has developed feelings for me, but they are not anywhere near romantic or kind. He believes me capable of the worst sort of venom."

"I know. Calum told me what the MacIntosh thinks. He also said that there's a lot more to his brother than appearances would allow. You see he was rejected."

"I don't mean to be rude Gwen, but I have to be honest with you. The man is on his way to Edinburgh to acquire the king's consent to break our betrothal. He doesn't need that consent, but for some reason, the man can't form a thought without his precious king's approval."

"Calum spoke of that too. My lady, there's a lot more going on here than we realize."

"Like what?"

"Calum wouldn't go into full detail, but I trust him. He asked me to tell you his brother is wrong and he will do everything in his power to sway him back to the right path."

"And which path is that? The one where he slanders me, marries me off to someone else, or the one where he seduces me?"

"Seduces you? My lady, considering his current course of action, are you sure he was seducing you?"

Aileana recounted all conversations and encounters with James from the last three days, beginning with the embarrassing meeting on the road and ending with the knock at her door the previous night. She swallowed her pride and left out no detail in her account. Gwen stayed quiet for once. Only her frown showed her concern which made it easier for Aileana to disclose such private information. As uncomfortable as the subject was, Aileana needed clarity.

"Have I lost my sanity? Why does the man have such an effect on me? I can't keep my thoughts sane enough to have a conversation with him much less negotiate with him. If I want any control over my future I need to keep my wits about me and I can't seem to do so."

"Aileana, he is meant for you alone."

This marked the first time in their relationship Gwen had ever spoken her first name. The impact of it and the simple truth of her statement pinched Aileana's heart.

"That may be true, but am I meant for him? Is it possible God made a mistake and put several women here for him? Or made him incapable of opening his eyes long enough to see either one of us?"

Sheena knocked once on the door and entered. Her aunt had found the perfect time to interrupt. Aileana didn't think there was anymore she could say anyway. The MacIntosh and his brother had left at dawn and most of the guests waited to have the morning meal with her and, they too, would take their leave. The excitement of the last three days had taken its toll and she longed for the afternoon and the opportunity for solitude.

The table in the dining hall was adorned with fresh wild flowers and bowls of glazed fruit. Once she and Sheena were settled, the rest of the room followed and the servants presented platters of meats, breads, cheese, and cured fish.

At a time like this, Uncle Iain would have boasted about his cook and explain that foods could never be too fresh and the care necessary for correct presentation. He loved to entertain. She thought of him often during the morning meal, but with pride this time instead of sadness. Whatever became of her, she would make him proud. That was all that mattered.

Once the meal concluded another receiving line formed and she thanked all the guests again as a departing gesture. Of course, no one was ready to leave at that precise moment, but it marked the point where all formality ended.

Aileana strolled to the back gardens, straight to her little haven. Some time alone surrounded by buds of the flowers she liked to list and just contemplating bloom was the right prescription.

For the next several days, she came to this exact spot to reason out her choices. Life had not returned to normal as she hoped. Instead, she became more anxious by the moment when no word came from James about his meeting with the king.

What now? Had he returned home? Had the king agreed? She needed information soon or she would explode.

James cleared his throat to reveal his presence. Aileana's eyes found him and his far too direct stare put her on edge.

"I hope I've not disturbed your respite, my lady. I'm on my way to Moy Hall, but assumed you would wish to hear of my trip."

As she looked at him, her apprehension and confusion grew. She was relieved to see him, but her belly was ready to let all its tremors loose at once.

"You do not disturb me, my lord. I trust your visit to Edinburgh was pleasant."

James sat next to her on the bench and she turned her full attention to him.

"Pleasant?"

It was a poor choice of words as he did not look happy.

"Productive then."

"My visit to Edinburgh was—"

He scrubbed at his stubble and stared at her as though she could provide the words he sought.

"My lord, did you acquire the consent you desired?"

His eyes darkened upon her last word and her insides clenched. Dammit. She would not let him do this to her again. The past sennight's contemplation had not quelled her body's need for him.

"What I desire is another matter," he said, his voice deep and husky.

Her breath caught in her throat as she watched his gaze drop to her lips. Despite the growing moistness at the junction of her thighs, she was angry. She'd gone more than a sennight with no word from him and now that he was here, he was going to play the seduction game again? Not this time.

"My lord, if the decision was so confusing why did you not ask a scribe to write it down?"

"What?" His gaze shot up to lock with hers.

"You have me at an advantage, you see. I do not like waiting to hear news which will decide my future. Would you mind getting on with the king's decision? My life hangs in the silence."

His jaw slacked. The look of shock on his face was almost humorous. Almost.

"You are angry with me?"

"Of course I'm angry with you. You've falsely accused me of wrongdoing when I am innocent, take measures to ruin me, and stammer when you should share information."

James swallowed hard and his expression turned cold. "Very well Lady Aileana. I had a conversation with the king about the unique nature of our circumstances."

He paused.

"And?"

"And he was about to grant consent to break the contract."

"But?"

"Calum interfered."

"Interfered how?"

"It is of no matter. The result is, King James and Queen Joan wish to meet you."

"They what?"

"They wish to meet you. I will make all the arrangements."

"My lord," Her voice rose to a pitch wolf hounds would appreciate. "Am I to understand you were not capable of breaking the contract?"

"I am not to blame, it was Calum's fault."

This was worse than breaking it off.

"And what is expected of me when I meet them? Box your ears in front of them so they are exposed to the extent of my loathing?"

He stood, towering over her with his eyes shining like emeralds and filled with anger. "I will not debate the reason your presence is requested, but I intend to see it through. I will retrieve you on Monday next. Be ready."

"You are to escort me? I cannot go on my own?"

He leaned down so that his face was as close as possible to hers without touching. He smelled like leather and her heart drummed. The scent caused her thoughts to scatter every time.

"I intend to escort you. Your conduct will be impeccable and this business will be concluded. Am I clear?"

She nodded.

"Be ready."

As he stalked off she had the irresistible urge to throw a rock at the back of his head.

Chapter Thirteen

"You know, Brother, a wise man once said 'Patience is virtue high'. Who was that again?" Calum asked with a lazy smile.

"Chaucer, as you well know." He'd informed Aileana he would collect her after the morning meal and now wished he'd said crack of dawn. Waiting shred his patience. James paced.

"Indeed. You may wish to heed his advice."

"What the hell does he know? He's English. Quit your riddles and speak your mind!"

"You are troubled about the lady you're anxious to collect, whom you wish to discard. I wonder why you appear agitated. Have you changed your mind about keeping her?"

"Changed my…what? Of course not. This business would have been concluded by now had you not interfered."

Calum had insisted James was in total denial over the lass and anyone who saw them in a room together would come to the same conclusion. The king and queen were quite in love themselves and so played into Calum's game. It was well and good for the king and his lady to enjoy their romance, but Calum had no business implying there was anything between him and Aileana Chattan. A love match indeed. How absurd.

"Ahhh, but then you would have no excuse to see her again," Calum said.

"Don't you mean you would have no excuse to see the witch?"

"Do not call her that."

"Oh. Hit a nerve have I? Serves you right for shoving your gigantic nose into places it doesn't belong." James grinned when Calum's hands flew to his nose.

"Well that aside, one day you will thank me for my interference and for pointing out what a prodigious ass you've been."

James stopped pacing and glared.

"I see you like to dabble with your life, Brother. That line you enjoy dancing around becomes thinner by the second."

"Very well. Let me speak plain if you will hear it."

James folded his arms across his chest. "This should be good."

"I am not jesting when I say Aileana Chattan is an incredible woman. I don't understand why you insist on making her out to be something she is not. For God's sake, James. Open your eyes and see what you have before you. When was the last time a woman preoccupied you the way she does? Ever? Do not try to tell me she does not stir you because I have watched you when she is near. You can scarce look elsewhere. And yes, I have discussed this with Gwen."

James huffed.

"Scoff all you like, but I can tell you with certainty the lass is just as affected by you."

"The maid told you this?" It shouldn't matter, but somehow it did.

"Yes, but the lady has just as much doubt about you. Perhaps even more."

"What doubt?" James had a vague sense of being caught in a sticky web.

"She thinks you're arrogant."

"Pffffff."

"Self-centreed."

"Ridiculous."

"Irrational."

"That's enough."

"Insensitive."

"I said that's enough."

"Pigheaded."

"Calum!"

"Dim-witted."

"Enough!"

Calum stopped speaking. That he wasn't smiling added no comfort. Damn but the words made James feel like a heel. All he needed to do was present the lass, show how incompatible they were and he'd be done with it. Except, he had never once considered her on a level where she might have feelings. Even deeper than that, she might have formed false opinions about him. Thinking her a vile deceiver was easy. Considering her to be something much less was unnerving. If he allowed himself to go down that path, he would lose more than his self-respect.

When he arrived at Chattan Castle, the steward Andrews informed him Aileana was almost ready. As a distraction, James reviewed the itinerary with the man again to ensure he could contact her should the need arise. From here they would travel together in his carriage. The roads were dry this time of year and passable. One overnight stop was necessary at Perth and they would arrive at Linlithgow Palace late afternoon on the fifteenth. The length of their stay depended on King James and whatever it took to satisfy the man to break the contract.

The irony of the situation was not lost on him. A short time ago he was prepared for a decision like this; one where his king would determine his fate. Hell, he was willing to accept it without question for what he considered the greater good.

Somehow that had all changed. There would be a decision. This one he may not be prepared to accept.

Then there was the issue of Fergus. Damned daft MacKay. What a fool he'd been to lend safe harbor to the man to have his hospitality thrown back in his face. He hoped this trip would bear some fruit, and the MacKay would be released. Although it appeared the odds were stacked against both of them now.

When Aileana opened the door to the front courtyard, his thoughts scattered. She looked wary yes, but there was an undercurrent of reproach in her demeanour, or was that his mind playing tricks with ideas Calum put there. Did she think him so foul?

"You're early my lord. I trust there is nothing amiss to foil our travel plans? Or are you anxious to see the deed done?"

Anxious indeed. He'd misjudged what he saw. She wasn't wary or reproachful. She was angry. He noted her raised chin and how her breasts thrust up as she marched past him. Her fury fueled his lust. The realization was intriguing. He wanted her. Right there and then he wanted to lift her skirts and bury himself deep within her.

This would be a long journey.

Desire's familiar pull swept him as he guided her to the back of carriage. As she stepped up, he noticed how her girdle hugged her waist. His fingers itched to slip inside the belt and tug her backward toward him just to see how she would react.

"Nothing at all amiss," he said. "I only wish to arrive at Perth before dusk."

Aileana sat on one of the long benches just inside the carriage, but he'd yet to let go of her hand. He pulled her back towards him, bringing her inches from face. She blushed right down to the swell of her breasts, his view enhanced by her angle. Damn, but it made her perfect skin even more inviting to touch. Her eyes flashed fury, amusing him and setting his blood afire.

He released her and helped Gwen inside as the servants loaded their luggage.

He and Calum entered and took the opposite seats from the two women.

James watched Aileana smooth her hand over the cushioned, velvet seats. Reserved for special travel, the carriage was wide and covered with leather. The interior was roomy and comfortable with deep, thick seat cushions. A small woman could easily slumber on one. Watching her drink in each detail was intoxicating. James longed for her to worship his body in the same manner.

"My lords, are we collecting the king on our way?" Aileana asked.

Calum chuckled. "'Twas a gift from my father to my mother a few years back. She preferred the comfort of a carriage to a saddle and my father enjoyed lavishing extravagance, but only when it came to her. He commissioned the most comfortable one he could."

"He sounds like a loving husband." Aileana looked down at her hands in her lap.

How could one small comment tug at him?

"Aye, he was a loving husband. I know he would not object to another fine lady possessing it," Calum said.

James turned toward his brother. What was he playing at?

"I do not ken your meaning, my lord. Are you offering to sell it to me?" Aileana asked.

Calum laughed. "Sell it? Of course not. James and I wish to give it to you. Don't we, Brother?"

James had no use for the carriage. It had sat idle for years, but his brother's manipulation was enough to make the walls close in. Aileana looked wary and there was no doubt she expected him to rant and roar and say it wasn't so. Perhaps that's what Calum expected as well.

Self-centreed, she had called him. Irrational even. The cost of the carriage would be worth the shock on their faces when he agreed.

"Of course it's for you, Lady Aileana. Consider it a gift for your fine hospitality under more than difficult circumstances. Please accept it and our gratitude."

He watched her brow furrow while the maid gasped beside her. Without turning his head, he reached toward his brother's face and pushed his bottom jaw back up to where it belonged.

"You have my thanks, my lords. While I will say, such lavishness isn't necessary, I'm certain my back will thank you on the morrow when 'tis not aching from a stiff saddle," Aileana said, smiling at Calum. James waited for her to bestow the affectionate gaze to him, but it did not come.

Her rose scent soon floated across the carriage, fuelling his already heightened senses and sending his thoughts further down improper paths. He envisioned her straddled atop him with her bare breasts at perfect sampling level while he thrust himself into her. He squirmed to hide the growing evidence of his desire. The movement drew her attention and the moment their gazes locked he could see the misery there. Cold water on his loins could not have doused his lust better. This was what he wanted wasn't it? Her misery. So why didn't it make him feel any better?

* * *

They arrived at the first stop in good time. The carriage was equal heaven and hell and Aileana couldn't wait to escape it. Even the light drizzle offered her more comfort than what she'd suffered for the past few hours. At least it held no hidden meaning. It was clear and possessed a plain purpose. The MacIntosh, when not scowling, confounded her with his elaborate gift. She'd been convinced Calum had made it up to tease him, but his reply was a complete surprise—just as he was turning out to be.

She entered the cosy tavern with Gwen in tow. The establishment was small and dark, but comfortable and warm. Her stomach grumbled and a large pot by the hearth sizzled and spit its reply, indicating its contents were ready for consumption. They were guided to a well worn oiled table and told today's stew was rabbit. Her favourite. The steaming bowl she received was a comfort she needed.

While friendly enough, the wenches serving them paid much more attention to the two men at the table. Time and again, the ample bosomed servers lingered, offering more bread, pepper, salt, tankards of ale; Gwen and she received not a second glance.

"We've had good travelling thus far, I expect the next leg of our journey will be much the same, don't you think so, Lady Aileana?" James asked.

"Aye."

"At this rate we'll arrive at Linlithgow by tomorrow noon as planned."

"Very well." It didn't matter to her whether he flirted with the serving wenches or not so why did he try to engage her in conversation? He could fill his boots with them if he so chose. Yet, without looking up, the heat of his potent gaze burned her. It was bad enough he humiliated her with the ordeal, why did he want her attention too? She preferred he let her suffer in peace.

Aileana grinned when the servers gave up their fruitless pursuit and left them alone. More than once, she noticed Calum stealing glances at Gwen. Was he the reason Gwen had been so quiet the morning she'd confessed all about James? Thus far Gwen had still not revealed anything of significance.

Had there been a tryst between them, Aileana would know by now.

Once back inside the carriage, the men informed them they would ride for a while. Though pulled by four horses, the carriage required only two. The others were brought so James and Calum could get some exercise. She didn't mind. At least she'd have some breathing space.

"Such an interesting gift for you, my lady."

"Oh don't start with me, Gwen. I'm in no mood to discuss James MacIntosh, or his gifts."

"Oh he has gifts aplenty."

"As does his brother, I suspect." Perhaps if she turned the table on Gwen, the woman would brood and leave her alone. It was cruel and she didn't want to hurt her, Aileana just wanted to clear her mind for a while.

"His brother is of no concern of mine."

"I suspect we are better off without either of them," Aileana smiled across the carriage. When Gwen's gaze met hers Aileana saw resolve. Perhaps in time Gwen would share her feelings. For now, it appeared she'd get the peace and quiet she craved.

Aileana stretched out on the cushioned seat and drifted off to sleep. Before long, the carriage pulled to a halt again outside the inn at Perth.

James had prearranged four separate rooms and the group checked in just before the evening meal. Aileana and Gwen were at the end of the upper floor, far removed from the potential ruckus of the entertaining rooms downstairs. James and Calum were assigned rooms on the first level. Thank goodness, and all that was holy, their rooms were not near one another.

Aileana knew this place well as she and her uncle had often stayed here when they travelled. It was relatively large and happened to be situated half the distance between Edinburgh and Inverness-shire. As such, it welcomed many travellers, including members of Parliament.

While Gwen unpacked all the necessities for their overnight stay, Aileana changed into fresh clothes. Gwen had chosen a gown meant to convey her position as a lady. Even if the serving wenches at this establishment were as bold as the last, there would be no repeat of inappropriate conduct. Frivolous as it may have seemed, establishing rank among the classes was necessary and could be communicated without speaking a single word. And so, Aileana wore a sapphire satin dress with square neckline and gold stitching. Her hair, still pinned from earlier, was an elegant plaited design. No one would doubt she was a lady.

They made their way down the stairs toward the dining hall. The room was decorated with rich-coloured tapestries hanging on the walls and tall-cushioned chairs surrounding oak tables. The room drew a body in. Despite the warm spring evening, a fire glowed in the hearth and several people were already there, sipping mead or ale and waiting for their meal to arrive.

James and Calum stood when Aileana and Gwen entered the room and escorted them to their seats. Aileana was careful not to meet James's gaze. The table sat eight and she was surprised when four other men joined them. James made introductions around the entire table. She struggled to hide her shock when he included three MacKay clansmen. What was he thinking? She was ready to jump out of her seat, grab the nearest horse and flee back to Chattan Castle.

James leaned back into his chair and rested his chin in his palm. He listened to the MacKay sitting next to him with a smile on his face. Aileana had clearly missed something critical.

The Mackay clansmen dressed well, without even a hair out of place, which struck her as it had when she'd been in the cottage with others of their clan. Aileana's body tensed as she compared her assessment of those men to the ones in front of her. The same impression came to mind, powerful but not barbaric. Gwen's hand found hers underneath the table and the comfort it brought her was immeasurable. Aye, there was at least someone else in the room who understood how confused, terrified and furious she was at the moment. The more Gwen squeezed her hand, the better she felt.

Aileana focused on her breathing which came in short bursts. They accepted James's introduction of her without any prior hint of her existence. Was it possible they were not aware of her involvement with their clansmen? She doubted it. How could James sit with them at the same table appearing unconcerned? Perhaps he'd decided her torture was not vast enough. Aye, that was it. He didn't just want to ruin her, he wanted to make her as raving mad as he was.

She listened closer to James, engaged as he was in a general discussion with a MacKay about Fergus's trial. He was aware with whom he spoke, so she looked to Calum who wore the same casual expression as his brother.

"Of course this leg of the journey was the shortest part for you three. And was there any indication why the trial was delayed by a sennight? It seems odd considering our king's handling of Highland conflicts to date. We all assumed he'd deal with it straight away, but when word came back of the delay we were all surprised."

James gave no indication of hidden intent at all in his question or comment; in fact, he could have been speaking with Calum about any number of topics.

"We don't know either, MacIntosh. We were just as surprised as you. We received word through the king's advisor about it. Can you imagine, a prisoner allowed to send word to his clansmen about when the trial would be? You'd think 'twas an invite to a celebration."

The elder of the three, Allain, went on to explain how they'd stayed away from the main roads as there were still many who would not wait for the trial to determine guilt. This far south, there didn't appear to be as much of a threat so they'd enjoy a soft bed for the night and perhaps some soft company. He spoke to James as if they were friends. Their behaviour was confounding.

The discussion continued while the meal was served. Roasted vegetables and glazed boar were complemented by steaming mounds of warm bread. The combination of cinnamon and cloves from the dark fruit puddings warmed her on any other given day, but the disturbing conversation taking place in front of her chilled her to the core.

Aileana stopped herself time and again from relaying her opinion of what King James should do with Fergus MacKay and the rest of his clan - and with himself for that matter. She stole several glances at James, but none were returned. His manner and expression were relaxed and comfortable. He must know how this affected her.

After about an hour and a half, James turned to her.

"Ladies, we still have a good ride ahead of us tomorrow. We start early and so I shall escort you to your rooms now."

She stood so fast her chair almost toppled. Aileana nodded to those present, careful not to meet the eyes of the three MacKay. While James led the way to their rooms, she waited for him offer something, anything, about what had just transpired.

Gwen went into the chamber while Aileana waited in the hallway for James to offer an explanation. A sudden thrill ran down her spine. Privacy with him was dangerous at the best of times. She was too agitated from the mix of emotions at the evening meal to ward him off if he tried anything. As it happened, she needn't have worried at all. All he offered was a curt bow and a quiet, 'Goodnight' before turning to disappear down the hall.

She stood frozen in place.

Unbelievable!

It was bad enough his behaviour all evening was confusing, but to add insult to injury, he wasn't going to explain anything to her. She stormed into her room and slammed the door securing it with a loud click.

"So he's just going to leave us here? He didn't even tell me to lock the door! At least he could've given me a dagger or sword to defend myself. At Chattan Castle he posted a guard in my stairwell and here with kin of the barbarians who abducted me and massacred those poor MacKenzies under the same roof, he simply says good-night?"

Her voice grew louder and her pitch higher. She was careful not to shout because she didn't wish to draw any attention, but she wanted to scream the house down!

Gwen's brow furrowed. "I have no idea what's going on here either. But I can tell you one thing, the MacIntosh has shown concern for your safety time and again. I believe we must trust that he knows what he's doing."

"Oh he knows what he's doing all right. Whether he's willing to share his master plan or consult with anyone else is quite another story. If he is the man God put here for me, 'tis a torment He sent and nothing more."

"Shall I help you with your evening ritual?"

The nightly hair brushing ritual was unnecessary, but there had been times when it served to relax her, maybe tonight would be one of those times. She'd try anything to quell the burn in her belly.

"Aye, now is as good a time as any, but on one condition." She waited for Gwen's nod. "That you sleep in here with me tonight. The bed is big enough and I would feel much better if there were two of us to fight off those brutes, if necessary."

"Of course, if that's what you wish."

That settled, she went over the conversation between James and Allain MacKay again. Both men seemed sincere. James didn't appear afraid or concerned. That meant one thing. James MacIntosh was not only familiar with the MacKay clan, but he was also sympathetic. But how could that be? Everyone knew they were guilty, their battle flag was found; there could be no doubt. Trying to figure it all out was exhausting. Aileana was weary from travel, worried about who she was about to meet, and irritated with the cause of it all. Fed up, she crawled under the heavy quilts, pinched her eyes closed and prayed for sleep. The last thing she heard was Gwen's light snoring.

She tried to hold on to her slumber but her rocking body would not let her drift away from her tormented thoughts. Eventually, she lost her struggle and opened her eyes to see Gwen sleeping across from her in the carriage. They sped along at an even pace and she had to blink a few times before she remembered how she'd gotten there.

James had come knocking early. "Please dress yourselves and meet me downstairs."

His abrupt command was a no surprise. Brute. So, he would begin the day off in the same manner.

When they met him at the carriage, his expression had been unreadable. He ushered them inside, passed in a basket of food and secured their luggage. As the first streaks of pinkish gray crossed the sky, they left the inn and headed toward Linlithgow.

Chapter Fourteen

James looked down just as she peeked out from between the folded leather flaps on the side of the carriage. He watched her sleepy expression turn hard as she spied his horse and lifted her gaze to meet his.

"Lady Aileana. Good morning to you. Is there something you require?"

She looked as though she would bare her teeth any moment. A sudden thrill passed straight to his loins. *Careful, you know how arousing her temper is.*

"Aye, my lord, there is something I require. Answers to some questions would be a fine start. First, why did we sit through a meal last evening while you entertained known murderers? Second, why did we stay at that inn with those same murderers in close quarters? Third, why I was roused from my bed at an ungodly hour to be bounced along in a carriage travelling faster than 'tis meant? It won't be much of a gift if you insist on pounding it to the ground."

Aileana's pitch continued to elevate with each new point she made and it made him grin. By the time she was finished, he was chuckling. He couldn't help himself. She was a little wildcat and it stirred him beyond measure. By God, he'd given up trying to be cross with her. The more time he spent with her the more he wanted her beneath him. To hell with what would never be, he had no reason not to quench his thirst before he was rid of her. She wasn't an innocent so why deny himself? Just to see how she'd react, he leaned back to reveal Allain MacKay riding next to him.

Allain was a clever man with a good heart. He didn't take offence to her insult. "It appears now is a good time to share our situation with your young lass."

James nodded and ordered the carriage to halt. He dismounted and stepped inside, but rather than speaking to Aileana, he turned to Gwen instead.

"Do you ride lass?"

Gwen grinned and nodded.

"I happen to own one of the best horses in all of Inverness-shire. Would you like to try him and stretch your legs awhile?"

"I thank you, my lord, for your kindness". She was eager and could be considered a pleasant sort upon further review—for a witch. He'd keep his guard around her, but a conversation was in order regarding the golden haired viper he was about to set straight.

James stepped back to let Gwen out. She mounted Arion in a swift and graceful motion and Calum looked pleased. James re-entered the carriage to find Aileana's eyes ablaze and fists clenched in her lap. Oh she was ready for war. This was going to be fun.

"Those are good questions," he said. "But before I answer any of them, I have one for you." He sat so close to her that their thighs brushed and he flung his arm around the back of the seat behind her. She did not cower and he admired that, but her eyes told him she'd like to stick something sharp into his flesh. There was that thrill again.

"Despite our differences, do you trust me?"

He liked how her chin came up and her lips pursed.

"I assume you're referring to my safety, my lord. As it is, I'm not accustomed to others deciding all aspects of my life for me without my counsel. Obviously you know what's going on here and have not seen fit to inform me."

Her arrogance was the like he'd never seen. God it set him on fire. How much farther could he push her?

"Not accustomed? I take it your uncle disclosed the particulars of our betrothal to you then? If that were the case, dear lady you would've had a part in it. However, I was under the impression you only learned of our contract when I presented your uncle's letter."

She blinked several times. He'd found her breaking point, yet when she spoke there was no tremor in her voice.

"I'm sure my uncle had good reasons for holding back details of the arrangement he made with you, sir. And I am certain one of those reasons was that he died before he got the chance!" Her voice took on a husky tone. She swallowed hard and burst into tears and he couldn't have been more shocked. Breaking point indeed. He wrapped his arms around her and held her close.

"Shhhhhh. I'm sorry if I've upset you. 'Twas not my intention to bring you pain." What the hell was his intention? As if prompted, Calum's laughter boomed from outside. Bugger off. Not that anyone could know what was happening between them at the moment, but the silent curse toward his brother helped. Anything would do to interrupt the gnawing in his gut.

Aileana sobbed into his shirt and held onto him like her life depended on it. He knew women who could spring tears on command, yet the weeping lass he held seemed genuine. Everything else aside, he had no reason disbelieve she truly cared for her uncle. His comment was a low blow. But what if he was wrong about the rest of it? Not possible. He had too much evidence to prove otherwise. Still, he never intended to make her cry.

Once her tears subsided, he lifted her chin and brushed off each tear stained cheek. Christ. Now he wanted to comfort her. He was in serious trouble here.

"I meant what I said. I won't intentionally cause you pain. Your words bring out the beast in me as your mouth and body bring out the man in me."

He bent his head low, but she stopped him by placing her finger on his mouth.

"My lord, weren't you about to give me an explanation?"

He replied by taking her finger into his mouth and slowly encircling it with his tongue. He watched her tear stained cheeks grow pink. She appeared transfixed by his action just as he was by watching her. At that moment, the carriage jolted bringing him back to his purpose, whatever that was.

"Why is it I can't think straight around you?" He cut her off before she could speak and put a prudent distance between them by moving to sit across from her.

James sighed and rested his elbows on his knees. "Let me start at the beginning. The MacKay clan is not responsible for the attack on the MacKenzies last year." He put his hand up when Aileana made motion to speak. "Please, let me finish, there's much to tell."

She settled further into her seat.

"Last fall, Calum and I travelled north to speak with the MacKenzie chief about a farming proposition. It was a rough, time consuming trip so we intended to find a bed for the night. It was then we smelled smoke and saw flames. It didn't take long to hear screaming down through the glen. We rode hard and fast, but we were too late. The sight that met us was almost too much to take. We scanned the devastation and helped those we could. Aileana, as I'm sure you've heard, the MacKay battle flag flapped in the wind.

"We knew the work was fresh and raced to follow the trail. We didn't know what we'd do when we found them but we couldn't turn back."

The memories were painful, even after so much time had passed.

"We followed their trail north for two days and eventually caught up with them. The closer they came to their own lands, the more careless they became and therefore, easily identified. They were MacKay's bitterest enemy—Sutherland. We realized soon after, we weren't the only ones tracking them. I met Fergus MacKay himself that day. He and a band of his closest clansmen also tracked the barbarians.

"Fergus wasn't surprised Sutherland would frame him but had no idea why they chose to attack MacKenzie. Knowing the king's distaste for clan feuding, we agreed that the longer Fergus and his men were out of the king's reach, the better chance we had to determine what was going on and clear his name.

"I encouraged Fergus and his men to stay on my land. I fed them and I hid them. I don't know what possessed Fergus to get caught up in Gawain's and your business, but I will get to the bottom of it when I next speak with him."

He ignored her gasp and again put his hand up when she was about to speak. And right on cue the intoxicating little glare was back in her eyes.

"I meant to visit Fergus when Calum and I were taken. My hope now is to speak directly with the king. We've gathered some weak proof to present to his Majesty, but in the end, he will have to take our word for it. Considering how much he dislikes our way of settling disputes, I don't know if 'twill be enough."

James sat back further in his seat.

"We've been careful with whom we've shared this information. I believe someone else is involved with the Sutherlands in this terrible ordeal. This means we have another faceless enemy still at large. Last night before I slept, I made sure your door was well secured Aileana, but not from the three MacKay clansmen. While I didn't foresee any danger with the other patrons present, I'm sure you noticed that I knew each and every one. I wouldn't take a chance with your safety, not while you are still under my care."

She stared at him for several minutes before speaking. Many expressions crossed her lovely face during that time, some he'd seen recently, some were new like the one now which was...gratitude?

She crossed the carriage and sat next to him never tearing her gaze from his.

"Aye," she whispered.

James's brow furrowed.

"I trust you."

It was his undoing. He slid his hands into her hair and tilted her head back. Her mouth was open and waiting. He inched closer and marvelled as her breath quickened. If he kissed her, there would be no turning back. He wanted her more than he'd ever wanted any other woman. For all that she was, he cared only that she was in his arms and anxious for his touch. He was under her spell and there wasn't a thing he could do about it.

He brought his mouth down to hers and it was she who darted her little tongue out to meet his first. Christ, but she tasted sweet. He grabbed her hips to straddle her legs across his lap so he could touch her everywhere at once. Her hands tugged at his hair as the kiss deepened and her tiny whimpers did all sorts of mad things to his insides. Already erect, every time she moved her delicious curves against him he was brought to a higher plane of torment.

She could not be coaxed away from his mouth so he ran his

hands over her breasts, stopping to slip his finger inside the edge of her gown. It nipped him when she inhaled and she groaned and tilted her head back. This was the access he craved. He pulled her dress down past her breasts, trapping her arms, and drew her toward his mouth. As he tasted her creamy skin, one of his hands held her firmly in place while the other slid down her body and across her hip to the hem of her dress.

His fingertips brushed across her ankle then glided toward the outside of her calf before turning to caress behind her knee. He pulled her gown up as he caressed her silky skin. He meant to excite her by inching up her leg, making some advancement before backing off a little and inching up again.

She arched toward him and moaned as he flicked his tongue across her taut nipple. God she was wild with need and he'd scarce touched her yet. A man could lose his senses with a woman who was so in tune with her body.

He moved from one breast to the other, taunting and teasing each nipple to full extension by flicking his tongue one minute followed by gentle rushing air the next. He released her and made use of his free hand to gather the rest of her skirt on the other side. He pulled it up to her waist ever so slowly and slid his thumbs inward. Her hot wet flesh welcomed him as he stroked the folds of her womanhood. She was as ready for him and he was for her. He slid his fingers along her slick heat in a gentle rhythm while his thumb found and played with her small hardened bud.

He shoved his hose down and grasped his erection scooting her forward at the same time so she could slide against him. As soon as their excited flesh made contact, she went rigid.

"Oh no," she whispered.

"Oh aye."

He grabbed her hips and positioned her to receive him, dying a little at her dishevelled state atop him. He could wait no longer to sheath himself within her.

"My lord!" She gasped as he pressed into her and discovered her maiden's barrier.

"What the bloody hell!" He looked at the woman he was about to impale and noticed the mortification in her eyes. "Why did you not say something." He could barely get the words out as his raging body screamed for release. He lifted her up and plopped her onto the seat.

"I—I told you I was a maiden," she said. She tried to cover her body, her flesh the colour of hot embers.

James turned away. Dammit it all to hell he could barely control himself because his erection still throbbed as if to say, 'Hey! Where did she go?'

He stomped his foot on the floor of the carriage and fixed his clothing with trembling fingers. As soon as it slowed enough, and without another look back, he jumped out of the still moving vehicle. He needed a great deal of distance between him and the never ending frustration that was Aileana Chattan.

* * *

Her head was in her hands when she heard the flap lift and slap back down again. She didn't need to look up to know it was Gwen.

"I won't ask if you are unwell."

Aileana sat up and tried to act nonchalant, but instead burst into tears.

"I wish to rearrange myself, would you help me please?"

Gwen sat close and worked on her hair.

"Will you tell me what happened? Did the great beast hurt you, Aileana? And believe me when I say, it's not just me who wants to know. Calum is ready to throttle him."

There were no words for what had just happened. She didn't understand it herself and her body still raged for release.

"Please, talk to me. Did you and he, you know, was there—penetration?"

"What?" How could she know? Aileana was going to be sick.

"I'm sorry. I just assumed. It's just—your clothes are all askew, and the way he stormed out of the carriage. He practically yanked me off his horse. You'd have to be blind to miss his passionate state. His tunic lay open at the waist and did not cover his hose. I could tell—by the bulge."

"It was visible?" Dear God would her mortification and shame never cease? She'd acted like a wanton tramp no better than the common wenches in her kitchen who'd ogled him before the betrothal.

"Oh hush, I'm sure I'm the only one who knew how aroused he was. And he tore off so fast I'm sure no one else will."

"He's gone?" Incredible! The slow burn of shame in the pit of her stomach disappeared and her entire body stiffened.

"He rode off like his life depended on it."

Her fury knew no bounds. "Is he a man or a child? Stop the carriage!" Those were the only words she could manage. She would not let him confide in her, seduce her, and leave her too confused and upset to meet Scotland's monarchy alone.

Gwen tapped the floor and they came to an abrupt halt. Aileana jumped out and began walking back toward Perth.

"My lady, where are you going?"

"Home. I will not be subject to any further abuse. If that man wishes me in anyone's company, he can bring them to me!" Her stride was fierce. She was a strong and could make good time back to the inn at this pace. It would be dark, but she'd get there eventually. Too bad she never thought to carry a dagger, or one of those small knives honourable men displayed upon entering a friend's home, and dishonourable men kept hidden.

Walking was good. It helped calm her frayed nerves. Irritated with her hair, she pulled pins out one by one as she strode along. If anyone had happened upon her, she was sure they'd run the other way, she must look a fright. Let them come. Let the whole damned country come and see what the high and mighty James MacIntosh to could do to a woman.

Bastard.

The sound of hooves behind her did not break her stride or her determination to get the hell away from him. She'd been walking for an hour and her legs were still mid stride when he scooped her up and placed her face down across the horse. He would not dare!

"Put me down this instant or I swear I will——"

"You will do nothing!" He didn't leave her any room to argue and in her current predicament, she had no rebuttal.

The horse slowed and turned around. Would he slow enough to toss her inside the carriage or did he expect her to jump? He allowed for neither, but keep right on going past the carriage and on toward the palace. The palace! He couldn't mean to present her like this.

"My lord! You cannot mean to arrive at Linlithgow in this style!"

She was fuming and struggled to reposition her body so that at least she would be in a more dignified position before they met anyone. His hand pressed down hard on her bottom.

"Be still and I will consider it."

There was fury in his voice, but she wasn't afraid to push it further. He was the reason for all of this, not her and it was high time he learned to admit when he was wrong.

"You cannot think to blame me for your brutish, narrow-minded, pig-headed ways!" The words felt good as they spewed from her, and speaking them to the horse's sweat-sheened forequarter shielded her from the glare James no doubt wore by now.

"Be quiet and be still."

"I shall not be quite whilst you hold me in such an undignified manner, sir! If my uncle were here he would flog you to within an inch of your life. You uncivilized, dim-witted, philandering oaf!"

The horse stopped. Her stomach clenched. She could feel movement from him. Shaking? Was he reaching for something to hit her with? She turned to see his head bowed low, eyes closed and—laughing?

This time when she tried to reposition herself, he did not prevent her. In fact, he dismounted and assisted her with her footing. He was still smiling and laughing at her. It was true. He was a lunatic.

"Have you lost your wits?"

This sent him into a further fit of laughter. Calum caught up to them and she could only shake her head in reply to his questioning expression. Gwen and Calum slipped off his horse and approached. Their eyebrows raised.

"James, are you well?" Calum asked.

After a few moments to compose himself he produced the most spellbinding smile she'd ever seen - for her.

He turned to Gwen, "Please take your lady inside the carriage and see to her presentation. We will have to abandon it near the peel and ride the horses across the drawbridge. The palace is only a short distance away and we can leave the carriage in a secure area just up ahead."

He smiled at her. Perhaps the king's surgeon would be available at the palace to help him.

"Lady Aileana, there are four horses, but I would be honoured if you would ride into the palace atop Arion with me."

He waited for an answer to a question he'd never asked. Arion appeared agreeable and he nudged her back and snorted. The man and his horse were too tiresome for their own good. She only had energy enough left to nod at him and walk back to the carriage.

"My lord, where are we staying tonight?" She thought to ask.

"At the palace," he said.

Of course they were. Because his torment knew no bounds.

Chapter Fifteen

Linlithgow, Scotland

Arion really was the largest horse she'd ever seen, yet considering how tight James pressed against her, she'd swear they were atop a much smaller young mare. His proximity added to her battle between confusion and mortification. His complete change in demeanour was impossible to explain and neither she nor Gwen had come to any conclusion except that he had truly lost his wits.

She'd lost more than that. She was tainted now. A fresh set of tingles meandered their way down her spine at the thought of what they'd almost done. His broad chest and rock hard thighs rammed up behind her didn't help either. As much as she regretted her unfortunate behaviour, she couldn't deny the man's effect on her. It was no wonder he'd been rumoured to have had so many women, for who could refuse him when he was so determined? Well, she would. With every ounce of convincing she could muster, the king would agree they were mismatched. After that she would have no choice but throw herself on the man's mercy and hope for the best.

Each step Arion took was like an extra weight pressing down on her. The torment seated behind her was one thing, but she was about to face the man responsible for her father's death. Did she have the strength to resist accusing him? She'd have to. Even after everything she had been through she would need to keep her thoughts to herself.

They rounded the bend and the palace came into view. Her jaw dropped. It was hard to believe only six years ago a tragic fire had laid the area to waste. The structure standing so proud overlooking Linlithgow Loch was likely the most beautifully situated dwelling in all of Scotland. Aye dwelling, if one could call it that. The east entrance was the like she'd never seen. A large drawbridge was flanked on both sides with canopied niches housing statues of a bishop and a noble. The central niche above the drawbridge housed the Stewart crest and an angel with outstretched wings. She'd heard the palace was like none other and if the inside was anything like this grand entrance, she could believe it.

"You're trembling," James said.

"'Tis beautiful."

"Are you nervous?"

Why did he have to give voice to her inner turmoil? To hell with keeping her thoughts to herself, he needed to know just how affected she was by these events! "Of course I'm nervous. My fate is about to be set by the man responsible for my father's—"

"Do not speak those words inside these walls," he said, his voice low and dangerous.

"And why not?"

"Because you will end up in the dungeon with Fergus and his men and there won't be a thing I can do about it."

"Why do you care? You're only here to dump me at the man's feet aren't you?"

When he didn't speak she turned to see if his expression might offer some clue to his bizarre behaviour. She was not prepared for the hurt in his eyes.

"You will come to no harm while under my care. Do you understand me?"

"Aye, I understand you are the only one permitted to abuse me. I understand that all too well."

Just before ascending the bridge, he stopped Arion and turned her to face him.

"How have I abused you?"

"You ask me that after accusing me of being faithless and impure? Even after you discover that I—when we—"

"That you didn't share your body with Gawain?"

Put like that, his words were much less cutting than when he first accused her.

"Aileana, I am sorry I accused you of lying with him."

"And?"

"And what?"

"And the rest of it! I didn't run away with him either, yet you still treat me like I did."

"What's past cannot be undone. I am willing to forgive you."

"Forgive me? For what?"

He sighed. "For deceiving myself and countless others. Aileana, I don't know why you continue this pretence. I said I am willing to forgive the past. Doesn't that please you?"

She couldn't speak. Perhaps he thought because she was still a maiden he was in a better position to barter with her life. No wonder he was almost giddy. After all, it wasn't damaged goods he peddled any longer.

She turned to face the yawning drawbridge. "What will please me is to be brought directly to the king and be done with this business."

"As you wish, my lady." There was a definite hint of laughter in his voice. What the hell did he find so funny?

The sound of Arion's hooves clip clopping over the planked bridge grew louder and she mused this was like being sentenced, but without a trial. Well she'd let him tell all the lies about her he wanted. The sooner she was done with him the better.

They passed under the portcullis, through a wide archway and on to the inner courtyard. After they dismounted, a young stable boy took Arion's reins and scurried off to tend to the beast. She took note of the bustling activity around her. Dozens of soldiers trained horses and each other; there was no doubt of the palace's security.

James led her to a doorway on the left. She looked back once to see Gwen and Calum following a distance behind. They were deep in conversation and looked almost...oh! She recognized the look on Gwen's face. So she was seeing someone new. Before the day was done, she intended to find out just how deep her friend's feelings ran. Gwen's throaty laugh was the kind only meant for her lover's ears. Aileana sighed. Would she ever know such a feeling?

They ascended a winding staircase which led through a narrow hallway and into the great hall. Were the circumstances different, seeing it for the first time may have evoked a feeling other than resentment. The grandeur was almost sickening. She stopped, forcing James to as well.

"My lady, we must address our host."

He was right, they must, but she couldn't budge one inch from where she was rooted to the stone floor. For all the courage she had a few moments ago, the well was empty.

James turned her to face him again. "Aileana, I promise you, this will all turn out for the best. You told me in the carriage you trusted me. I'm asking you to keep that trust for just a while longer."

He seemed so sincere she didn't know how to reply. She

wished he trusted her. She nodded and the smile she received as a reward took her breath away. Would he ensure she was taken care of? He hadn't seemed as cold since the carriage and so, had his opinion of her changed so much because she was a maiden still? Her nerves were far too frayed to speculate on what he might have planned and so she would have to act as sheep to the shepherd for this meeting. She'd have her answers though.

Just as she was about to agree, she realized everyone in the room had become aware of their presence. Far too many eyes scrutinized them, or was that just her imagination?

"MacIntosh! How good to see you, my lord."

A plump and pleasant looking fellow practically bounced over to them and grasped James's hand. His brocade tunic worked hard to cover his ample gut; his hose just beneath the skirt leaving little to the imagination.

It was then she noticed James was much more formally dressed than his usual attire. The belted tunic he wore today had a full skirt and his hose were barely visible between it and his high leather boots. He towered over the man and she was struck by how regal James appeared. Regal and breathtaking. How could any woman refuse him?

"Norrington," James said. "How fares your work for his Majesty?"

"Good, but never mind that." Norrington turned his gaze to Aileana. "Where did you find such a delicious creature?"

James curled his arm around her waist and pulled her close. It seemed odd behaviour considering why they were here. Norrington didn't appear threatening in any way.

"Norrington, may I introduce Lady Aileana Chattan of Inverness-shire? Lady Aileana, this is Joseph Norrington, the most infamous and shrewd solicitor in Lothian."

"In Lothian? Why you insult me my lord. I'd rather you

boasted in all of Britain." He turned his attention to her and said, "My lady, it is my deepest pleasure to meet you at last."

"At last, sir?"

"Aye. Didn't his lordship tell you?"

She turned to James. "Tell me what, my lord?"

James opened his mouth to speak, but Norrington cut him off and claimed her waist in the process.

"Tell you that it was my council he sought in order to test the validity of your uncle's contract right after he signed it. A clever man, your uncle. Only the king can break this arrangement, you see, and James wouldn't believe me at the time. I told him I've never seen this kind of written, signed and sealed document broken in any other manner. If our Laird MacIntosh here were not a baron and vassal to the king, well—"

She knew James wanted to break it now, but didn't realize he'd wanted to do so right from the beginning. Oh what a fool she'd been! He must have thought her too young and naïve to match his worth. And he would have been right, at first. Somehow since, she'd grown her mettle and this little game Norrington played didn't intimidate her.

"Oh aye, well those details are insignificant, Mr. Norrington, for we will have the king's blessing momentarily. Won't we, my lord?"

James studied her face. He looked displeased, but that was not her problem. "Not exactly," he said.

"What do you mean not exactly?" Her temper flared and the slow burn returned to her belly. Norrington squeezed her waist and led her forward toward the people gathered around the dais at the far end of the hall.

"My lady, his royal highness is rarely present at Linlithgow during the day. Most of the people you see here are bent on impressing her ladyship, the Queen. All serious royal business is conducted at Edinburgh Castle."

Aileana shuddered at the thought of Edinburgh Castle and its dungeons below. The last time she and her uncle had visited she swore she could hear faint screaming coming from somewhere in its depths. She was more interested than ever in Fergus's fate after what she'd learned. He was in those dungeons at that moment. As was Gawain. The first didn't deserve it, but the latter did and wasn't worth another moment of her time.

Norrington boasted about the palace while they moved forward as though he had input in its appearance. She'd heard much of this great hall and nothing was exaggerated. The long walls leading to the hearth behind the head table were decorated with statues, tapestries and other ornate hangings. Every sculpture, table, and vase expressed grandeur. This was in stark contrast to the intimidating structure on the other side of Edinburgh and most other noble residences in the country. This king was bent on promoting a new image of Scotland's monarchy with little consideration to the vast resources required to create his palatial dwelling. The residence was no fortress, rather it represented extravagance. She tried to mask her disgust, but it was difficult.

As they moved further toward the end of the hall, she looked closer at those gathered. The majority were women fitted with the latest fashions. She was pleased enough with her own appearance and wasn't concerned with how well she would compare. She wore a beaded circlet trimmed with a wispy veil hanging past her shoulders, and braided mesh covering buns at her temples. Her hunter green gown was trimmed with wide knotted embroidery on the square neckline and floor length sleeves and accented by a long girdle made up of many gold squares.

Most of the ladies wore a similar style gown, but some wore

a different and new fashion headdress. One lady in particular wore a truncated cone and had shaped the veil covering it into two peaks forming a butterfly henin. It seemed an awful fuss. Aileana preferred her hair loose and uncovered and wore it like that often when at home. The men wore tunics with varying skirt lengths, some revealing more than she would prefer to see, similar to the man who had led her forward earlier.

After receiving many dissecting glances, Aileana passed through the crowd and stood before the most beautiful woman she'd ever seen. The queen was pregnant and perhaps that was why she glowed, or perhaps it was the rumoured love the woman shared with her husband. They had been married while he was still in England awaiting settlement of his ransom and she heard he even wrote her poetry. Aileana was wrong to stare, but she couldn't help it. The English Queen of Scotland was stunning.

James recaptured her waist just as the queen and all those gathered at the table focused in on Aileana.

"I believe, Lady Aileana, the description of your beauty has been grossly understated."

"I apologize, your majesty," James said. "The understatement was mine and directed to any man who would look upon her. If I thought I could get away with it, I would keep her locked in my room so that only I could enjoy her delights." James replied in a far too flirtatious manner.

Aileana's shocked expression prompted a chuckle from the Queen Joan.

"I can see why you'd feel that way. I'm glad my own husband is unable to see past me or else I fear the sovereignty of this country could be at stake."

Aileana re-directed her shocked expression towards the dais.

"It appears there has been a change of heart since we last met, Lord MacIntosh."

"Indeed, your majesty. Much has changed. I'm certain my brother will revel in his accurate assessment on that day. I doubt I shall live it down."

"Is that so? And you Lady Aileana, have you had a change of heart as well and accept this man as your future husband?"

"I do—"

"Accept," James said. "Lady Aileana has had an exhausting journey, Your Majesty, and if it is your wish, I would like to see her rested."

"Oh course Lord MacIntosh. Cameron will see you to your chambers. Lady Aileana, I urge you to rest well for we shall celebrate in your honour tonight."

Aileana couldn't wiggle one word in between them and after James offered a curt thank you, he tugged her in the opposite direction and toward the guest chambers.

She was somewhat disturbed to learn her room was adjacent to James's with a small hallway and side doors connecting the two. Gwen was placed in a nearby room and Calum's was on the other side. Before she could turn around and catch her breath, she was alone in her room with James.

"My lord, I urge you to speak your purpose. Why have you brought me all the way here only to lie to the queen about our arrangement?"

"I have not lied to her majesty for I believe that would be punishable by hanging. I value my neck," he said.

"Then I suggest you tell me exactly what is going on here? You've dragged me half way across the country to inform me we will remain betrothed?"

"I have and we will."

"I see and will you please explain why that is?"

"I can tell you I didn't plan it so."

She was a fly caught in his web once again. He stepped toward her and she stepped back.

"Did you intend to break this arrangement when we left Inverness-shire?"

"Yes."

"What changed?"

He stepped toward her again and this time snaked his arm around her waist so she couldn't step back.

"This."

He leaned in close and she stopped thinking. All the anger and confusion rushed out of her and was replaced with immediate and intense desire. His lips grazed hers and her head swam. His free hand dove into her hair as the kiss deepened as he and claimed her mouth. Her body arched toward his and she had a niggling feeling somewhere far away that she should stop, but she couldn't get past the power he had over her.

He raised his head and looked deep into her eyes. His sparkled with purpose and she couldn't have protested anything when he held her captive like this.

"Calum and I will ride to Edinburgh Castle with haste to speak with the king. According to the queen, he will give us an audience to speak in favour of Fergus before the trial. I hope as well he will allow me to speak with Fergus, even if for a moment. I am uncertain how long I'll be gone, but I want you and your maid to stay here unless the queen herself bids you to her. Do you understand?"

Aileana tried to hide her disappointment. She wanted to know more about what had changed his mind and just realized she'd been coerced into submission. Her temper flared once again and she broke from his embrace.

"My lord, I will stay on these grounds if you feel 'tis necessary. I hope your meetings will not keep you too long as we have much unfinished business here."

"Aye, lass that we do." He leaned toward her again and his proximity muddled her thoughts.

"My lord, I'm speaking of your abrupt change of heart. I will have satisfaction from you, sir."

"As will I from you," he said, his voice husky making her moisten in anticipation.

"I shall return as quickly as I can, I promise."

James brushed his lips over hers one more time and crossed the room, glancing back with a look that told her she would need all the strength in the world to get the answers she sought.

Chapter Sixteen

"If it is your wish to gloat, be done with it and let us focus on how to aid Fergus."

"Oh I intend to gloat and will drag it out for a long time," Calum said. "May I ask what prompted this about face?"

"You may, but I won't answer except to say I've begun to understand the complexity of her attributes."

"And what the hell is that supposed to mean?"

"Nothing you would understand. Speaking of bewitching women—"

"Don't start."

"Seriously, Calum. I've noticed you around her. What are your intentions?"

"I don't have any to speak of at the moment. Do you know who she is? Or was?"

"I do not."

"Her father was William MacGregor."

"Aye, we acquired his farms several years back."

"That we did. He was a drunk and a gambler and squandered away the family's fortune. Our lady's maid is Gwendolyn MacGregor, a former gentlewoman herself who was forced to go into service in order to provide for her mother."

"Did she offer this information to you freely?"

"No, I suspected there was more to her story when at times I heard her slip 'my lady' instead of 'm'lady' used by someone of lower birth."

"I see. One word from her and you determined she had a hidden past?"

"Aye."

"The fact that you are attracted to her played no role in your hanging on her every utterance?"

"Of course not," Calum said, smiling.

James was grateful when they both fell silent. He didn't yet understand what had changed between him and Aileana only that the thought of any other man ever touching her made him want to smash things. He wasn't ready to admit what was in his heart and so turned his thoughts to the task before him. Suffice it to say, her virginity made a big difference in how he felt about her.

Looking around them as they entered Edinburgh, the king's vision was apparent by the new construction in parts of the city. Around him, commerce erupted and it was clear Scotland was on its way to greater prosperity. More and more people arrived in Edinburgh every day, eager to find work. Markets bustled with everything from construction material to fresh produce.

It was an exciting time, yet the castle still loomed foreboding, an eerie reminder of its dark past. The two men climbed the cobbled road leading to the majestic structure overlooking the entire city. Built on ancient volcanic rock centuries earlier, Edinburgh Castle offered impressive protection from attack because of its extreme height over the land surrounding it. The altitude and the stench grew as they climbed higher. With prosperity came all new sorts of challenges. Was the city ready for the influx of people?

James and Calum approached with cautious determination. This king, with all his good intentions for the country, lost his patience when trying to understand the complexity of Highland life. It was the king's vision for a united Scotland that first impressed James. Despite his severe methods, the king was on the right path to securing his beloved country's future. His Majesty may have preconceived ideas about how Highlanders should live, but he also appeared ready to listen

. Hopefully this would keep them out of the dungeon, at least until Fergus's fate was determined.

James and Calum crossed the esplanade and passed through the gatehouse. They left their horses with a stable-hand and climbed the stairs leading to the courtyard. The king took no chances with visitors, no matter whom they were, and that was apparent when the brothers' weapons were removed and they were escorted by two armoured guards. They were led into a large hall occupied by several Scottish nobles enjoying a test of strength between the king and another nobleman.

The king won the match and motioned to James and Calum.

"Ah, there you are. I wondered if I'd see you this day. I trust your journey was uneventful?"

One event from his journey sprung to mind, but James was not about to share it with the king. "Thank you Your Majesty, our journey was safe indeed. I hope now is an acceptable time for our visit."

The king nodded to James and motioned for him to follow. They were accompanied by his Royal Advisor, Lord Beaufort, a cousin of the queen, who was also English. James calculated this could weigh in his favour. It was clear to anyone who paid attention that this king wished to model aspects of Scottish Parliament and court after the English which he studied during his imprisonment.

James hoped Lord Beaufort's presence would prevent the

king from making any rash decisions affecting Fergus's fate. The men entered a side room and each took a seat around a thick, polished wooden table. On cue, servants arrived with refreshments and pitchers of wine.

"Well MacIntosh, what is so urgent regarding the savages I hold in my dungeon that it cannot wait until the day after tomorrow? You have no misplaced faith in our justice system do you?"

James recognized the king's baited question.

"Savages tho' they may be, Your Majesty, they're not guilty of the crime of which they are accused. I have proof of their innocence, information I expect you will find of dire importance to the safety of all the northern clans, as well as yourself."

"Those are big claims, MacIntosh. Your source for this information is solid?"

The king was intrigued and would listen. There was hope.

"As solid as the rock this castle is built on, sire."

When the king said nothing further, James recounted the tale he'd told Aileana earlier, leaving out no detail of the attack. He described how he and Calum had tracked the Sutherlands northeast to their lands and how they met up with Fergus and his clansmen while tracking, proving they were not involved.

He was cautious as he described how he hid Fergus and his men these past months. If Fergus was found guilty of murder, he was guilty of harbouring fugitives. James also described his and Aileana's abduction, hoping that if he included every detail, King James would be more willing to believe him.

At the end of his account, James pulled something from inside his tunic. Lord Beaufort started to rise, but the king raised his hand and the man resumed his seat. James tossed the object across the table and watched as it captured the interest of both men.

"Where did you get this?" The king demanded.

"It dropped from one of them as they retreated north. We found it in a clearing after they'd stopped to eat. There's no doubt, sire. That's a Sutherland plaid pin."

James watched as the king rubbed his fingers over the silver object. *Sans Peur*—Without Fear. Sutherlands at least witnessed the carnage.

The king took his time considering the evidence before him. When he spoke his tone held a warning note. "Is this all the proof you have? Do you expect me to put myself in the middle of a feud which has kept Mackay and Sutherland at each other's throats for decades?"

James chose his next words carefully.

"I have no further proof except what I have witnessed." He paused. "Sire, I believe they were not the sole party involved. Someone else is responsible for this. I suggest, Your Majesty, there will be a great deal of outrage if the MacKays are put to death by the justice they find here. I believe the real question that should be asked is: who has the most to gain by your decision to put innocent Scotsmen to death?"

He had gone too far with that comment, but he needed to use the king's mistrust of all Highlanders to further his point. The Stewart needed to realize that not all Highlanders were his enemies and not all Lowlanders were his friends.

Lord Beaufort rose to his feet. "Lord MacIntosh, is that a threat? I would be careful, if I were you, so you do not end up in the dungeon with your friend."

"Easy Beaufort," the king said. He moved to the window and rested his arm above the frame. When he turned back to face the men he smiled.

"James MacIntosh, you have either doomed us all by your suggestion or saved me from a dire fate. If I am to trust your tale as fact, condemning the men I hold below would be a severe mistake indeed. However, if I set them free without knowing for certain who's responsible, I run the risk of allowing another savage attack. I'm willing to accept your information as plausible, enough to grant you the meeting you requested with the MacKay. I'm certain you'll agree, if you are correct, and I do mean *if*, appearances will be important to uphold until the scheduled trial. Do you think it likely the so called partners in this crime will attend?"

"Yes, Your Majesty, I believe that's exactly what will happen. I believe, whoever these partners are, their entire agenda rests on your decision to wrongly condemn Fergus MacKay and his clansmen. Care must be taken to ensure escape is not permitted should their identity be discovered. I suggest you consider anyone who would have the means and inclination to carry out such a plot."

The king indicated he didn't need to consult anyone as the clan chief who topped that list was Alexander MacDonald. He admitted, releasing the man after having him secured as prisoner was a mistake, even if it was to prevent further carnage from the man's supporters. The Lord of the Isles wanted revenge.

"The MacKay and his men will remain in the dungeon until then. Although, I believe I can see fit to make them a little more comfortable."

The king came around the table and grasped James by the shoulders.

"I have many enemies MacIntosh, however, I believe today I have forged a permanent alliance with you. I understand you've an interest in Moray. Help me unravel this mess and it's yours." With that, the king and his advisor left the room.

James couldn't believe his ears. He and Calum turned to one another in shock, but before they could discuss the king's offer, a guard entered indicating he would escort them to the dungeon. He had one fleeting thought before being led away: with the Earl's title bestowed upon him in this way, he could marry whomever he chose.

The air grew increasingly foul as they descended the narrow steps leading to the castle's depths. Along winding stairs and through low ceilinged stone corridors, they arrived at the series of cells holding the twelve MacKay. The stench of rotting men and excrement was unbearable.

"Fergus MacKay!" The guard bellowed and hit the cell door with his blade.

Fergus didn't look up. "Who wants to know?"

The guard snickered through his black stained teeth. "Looks like you've go' a visi'or, although I don't know why anyone would want to see the likes o' ye. On your feet, you rotten cur."

James watched Fergus glance up. His face was stone as he obeyed the guard's command. He looked to James with raised eyebrows. When James shook his head indicating this was not an escape attempt, Fergus shrugged and followed the guard to a small room with four chairs and a table.

The guard left and locked the three men in the room together. "You go' ten minutes," he said, "If ye live that long." The guard whistled a light tune as he walked away.

"How do you fare?" James asked.

A grunt from Fergus was followed by his low, deadly voice. "I'd fare better if I weren't left in a dungeon to rot by someone I thought I could trust."

James's anger surfaced. "You idiot, I didn't force you to take on side jobs and get yourself caught. I wouldn't have sent for the guards if I knew what you were up to! And what the hell do you think you're doing abducting me anyway?"

James fists clenched and his jaw twitched. He was ready to make Fergus answer for his actions before doing anything further to assist him. He could have had the conversation with the king a sennight ago, but instead chose to let Fergus stew a little.

"We were idle. All we had to do was get rid of an unworthy gentleman and hold a lady for a while. My men needed a little action after months of only catching deer and rabbits. They were so idle they were ready to turn themselves in. How were we supposed to know it would turn out to be you and your little flower?"

"You were on my land! It didn't occur to you it could be one of my clansmen or me?"

James's furious reply was met with a scowl from Fergus and Calum took that opportunity to intervene.

"Look, as entertaining as it is to watch you two growl at one another, we have limited time. We came here for a more important reason than to point out who should have made better use of their common sense."

James was not going to let it go until he was satisfied that he did not need to worry about Fergus again. "Fergus, I need to know I can trust you. I've put my own arse up as collateral and I need your assurance you will never do anything so stupid ever again."

Fergus eyed him for a long time and sat back. "You have my word, MacIntosh. I expect that outside of your brother here, you can trust me more than any other living soul."

James hadn't expected anything eloquent, but Fergus's declaration was more than a simple 'Aye' and it served him well enough. James relaxed as did Fergus. James took the moment to change the topic altogether and launched into their larger problem.

"I've spoken with the king and gave him the pin. It seems to have piqued his interest and I believe he's at least intrigued by my version of events. I don't know how much I swayed him, but you will have a good meal tonight, I expect."

James waited for Fergus to react. Nothing.

"The trial is the day after tomorrow. I'll speak to what we witnessed in detail if asked to, but you must promise me something, Fergus." James waited for Fergus to acknowledge him. Fergus nodded his understanding and James continued. "You must promise me to hold your tongue. If you shout the place down, the king will look past the story I told him today and you'll be drawn and quartered by sunset."

Fergus contemplated this for a minute and let out a deep chuckle.

"I don't know what it is about you, MacIntosh, but there are few men who could get away with saying that to me. I understand loud and clear. Are all of my men here?"

James knew who he meant. "No, Fergus, your brother is not here. I corresponded with him all these months as you asked, but I've had no news from him since your capture. There's one more thing. When this is all over and you are forever in my debt for saving your life," James said with a grin. "I want to know every detail of your encounter with Gawain Chattan. I intend to see that he's not granted the freedom you and yours will enjoy."

"What do you mean not freed? Gawain is not here. He must have slipped past the guards when you went to rescue your woman. He wasn't brought here with us and I have no idea where he is."

James stopped breathing. When he spoke again it was with a dangerous, almost deadly tone. "You mean to tell me that bastard is still out there? That I left Aileana unprotected and he could've come back? And you said rescue. She was not part of the plot?"

"Of course not." Fergus cocked his head to the side.

Calum interjected. "Wait a minute, one of your men must have seen him leave and someone must know where he would go."

Fergus shook his head. "I thought you knew. If I had been able to speak with you sooner you would have known."

James was furious at himself for not ensuring Gawain was behind bars like the innocent MacKays. *Aileana.* She wasn't running away. He was overjoyed to learn of it.

"Well friend," James said. "Looks like you will be able to help me when you get out of this hell hole. Think you could endure a continued partnership with me a while longer to go on a rat hunt?"

Fergus responded with a deadly smile James knew was not meant for him.

"I'd be happy to, my friend. Happy indeed."

The guard returned and motioned for Fergus to follow. When they returned to his cell, a large platter of food and a pitcher of ale awaited. For one brief moment, James had the benefit of seeing true gratitude spread across the warrior's face.

As James and Calum left the area they noticed each of the other MacKays receiving the same courtesy. The king had been good to his word and James was grateful.

The guard led the two men back to the stable and they mounted their horses to return to Linlithgow Palace. Just before leaving the grounds a young page ran up to them with a note from the king himself.

MacIntosh:

I was pleased with our meeting today. Your 'real question' as you put it earlier has given me much pause for thought and I wish to discuss it with you further. The queen and I would be honoured if you and your party would dine with us this evening at Linlithgow Palace. Our servants will provide you with anything you desire.

J.S.

James passed the note to Calum before turning to the page with his reply.

"You may inform his Majesty we accept his invitation."

James thought about Aileana and hoped she wouldn't mind delaying their discussion until after dinner and he further hoped dining with Scotland's monarchs wouldn't fuel her anger. Then again...

James kicked his heels into Arion's sides a little harder than usual as the thought of Aileana unprotected caused his heart to beat a little faster.

Where was that little rat Gawain hiding? He was certain he'd not seen the last of that wretch. He was also determined Gawain would never get near Aileana again and groaned inwardly at the coming battle he would have with the lady over the new security measures he intended to impose without delay.

Chapter Seventeen

James returned to the palace in plenty of time for dinner, but it wasn't until he was dressed that he attempted to speak with Aileana. In truth, he was nervous. No barrier remained between them. Thinking the worst of her made it easier to ignore how much she meant to him. He had put her through much and she had every right to be angry with him. She'd have to resolve her feelings, in any case. He would not accept a refusal from her.

He rapped on her door. She tore it open and drew him into the room.

"I've been anxious to hear of your meeting since your return. Did you speak with the king? Did he let you see Fergus? Is he going to release the MacKay?"

James smiled. He would be pleased if her anxious state was also out of concern for his welfare.

"Easy love; one question at a time. I met with the king and he listened to my story with interest. Fergus and his men must still stand trial, but I believe the king is on our side. I saw Fergus. He and his men are well."

He was unsure how she'd react to the rest of his news.

"My lord, what is it?" He enjoyed watching her search his face. "There's something else isn't there?"

She was perceptive.

"Aye, there is something else you need to know." He took a deep breath. There was no way to say it gently. "Aileana, Gawain was not imprisoned with the MacKay. He must have slipped away from the guards when I came to rescue you. None of Fergus's men have any idea where he went."

Her face lost all colour. "Did I hear you right?"

"You needn't worry since I don't intend to let you out of my sight until he's found. And we will find him." He placed his hands on her shoulders. "Do you understand? You have nothing to worry about. He will never get near you again." James searched her face for a sign that she understood him before he continued. "There's more. I hope you'll agree what I propose is to ensure the protection I promise."

Aileana frowned. "Go on."

"I plan to ask the king for permission to use the palace chapel."

Her eyes grew wide.

"It will be difficult for Gawain to stake a claim if you're already married to me. Furthermore, we are not going against your uncle's wishes if we expedite the marriage since we've already had our committal ceremony. Only the king's permission is necessary to do this tomorrow."

"Tomorrow?" He couldn't tell if she was about to accept or lash out at him.

"Yes, tomorrow. Is that acceptable?"

He watched her draw a steadying breath. "You used the term rescue. I have spent a lifetime trying to convince you I was innocent in Gawain's scheme and one word from Fergus MacKay convinces you?"

"Aye."

"And you expect to march in here and tell me all is well and we can marry straight away? You are right in that I don't have a better choice for protection, but hear me MacIntosh, I have not forgiven you for what you've put me through."

"I am sorry." He didn't know what else to say. He deserved her anger, and if she refused he didn't know what he would do. She'd endured more than he thought her capable.

"I don't know if that is enough."

He didn't know how to make her see that he would lay down his life for her. He'd made a mistake and he needed her forgiveness. He reached for her, but she put her hands up.

"Do you not see I am trying to make amends?" James asked. "I give you my hand and my protection." *And what about your heart? Shut-up, Calum.*

She stood a little taller lifted her chin. He didn't take one ounce of air into his lungs until he heard her response. He watched her scrutinize him for sincerity. She weighed her options and he prayed her decision would tip in his favour.

"Aye, James MacIntosh," she said after an eternity. "I will marry you tomorrow."

His heart swelled. He reached for her and was delighted when she didn't resist. He kissed her cheeks, her forehead and then her mouth. His desire for her burned in that kiss. He gave her no time to recover and made a promise to come back in half an hour to collect her for dinner.

* * *

Aileana stood in the middle of her room with a torrent of emotions flowing through her when Gwen re-entered.

"My lady? Are you unwell? I must admit, your betrothed appears in good spirits. He practically picked me off the ground when I met him in the hallway. He said something about taking extra care of you."

Aileana swallowed hard. "We're getting married."

Gwen's brow knit. "Well I'm pleased to hear he's changed his mind with his daft idea to break the betrothal."

Aileana moved toward Gwen and grasped her shoulders with her small hands. The woman didn't understand. "Gawain was never apprehended. He's not in the castle dungeon with the rest. He's out there somewhere likely plotting against us again and I didn't know. How could we not know?"

Aileana released Gwen and paced.

A chill swept through her. The man had been bent on destroying them and she was not convinced he was finished with them. Marrying James was the right thing to do, she believed it, but would any event in her life ever come without some extenuating circumstance? What a turn of events. James MacIntosh was to become her savior—from Gawain. Uncle Iain must have always known it. He had tried to secure her future and keep her safe all along. As much as she was still angry with James for mistrusting her, she never doubted her safety when he was near.

"We marry tomorrow."

Gwen clasped her hands together and laughed. "The MacIntosh isn't going to let anything happen to you and nothing is going to happen to him. Marrying him is the single best thing you can do to ensure your safety."

Gwen's confidence eased Aileana's anxiety, enough to let her words sink in.

"By this time tomorrow, we'll be married."

"And this is bad?"

"He doesn't love me."

"Neither did Gawain, but that never bothered you."

She stopped and stared at her maid. Gwen was right. She'd spent so much time worrying over what James MacIntosh thought of her and never stopped for a moment to wonder why. Clarity tumbled over her like a cart of cabbages. She was in love with him! Dear God in Heaven, how could that have happened while she was cursing his every breath?

"I'm marrying him."

Gwen laughed. "Yes, my friend, I believe you are."

The thought brought a nervous smile to her face. Thoughts of Gawain could be pushed to the back of her mind when she pictured James.

Gwen's face lit with a sudden thought. "You must promise me something. You must promise not to think of Gawain any more until after your wedding night. If you let your fear of him overshadow what you and Lord MacIntosh share, he will win. Don't let it happen, my lady. Don't let him take away your wedding night. Promise me you won't."

Aileana was amazed at how well Gwen put the situation into perspective. Here at the king's palace, there was no way for Gawain to reach her. Gwen was right again. She did no justice to herself or James by focusing on her fear.

"Of course you are right. I shall think only of wedding James."

"And bedding him," Gwen said. Aileana grinned. Gwen always had a way to lighten the mood.

A knock on the door prompted a quizzical glance between them before Gwen rose to answer it.

"I beg your pardon ladies, but I wonder if I could have a moment of your time?"

Aileana stood at the queen's first word. "Of course, Your Majesty, please do come in. This is, after all, your home."

The queen entered and gathered Aileana's hands in hers.

"I've just heard the news. I came to offer anything I have to you. I understand you've just reached this decision?"

Aileana nodded.

"I imagine you did not bring wedding clothes with you?"

Oh no! She hadn't thought of that.

"Well, it's a good thing I came. Ladies come with me. My seamstress is the best in all of Scotland and we'll prepare a gown fit for, well, a queen."

They followed the queen through the palace, along several corridors until they arrived at a warm room with heavy tapestries covering all the walls. It was welcoming. A slight, young woman busied herself inside with several reams of unrolled fabric.

"This is where my personal dressmaker works. Ladies, this is Abigayle. She's a miracle worker, trust me." The queen turned to Abigayle who had just lifted the corner of an exquisite piece of vermillion brocade. She dropped the fabric and bowed deep.

"Abigayle, would you please create a masterpiece for this lady? If there's anything you need, I will have the pages scour Edinburgh for it. Now, I must go and pass along our regrets for dinner and arrange it for here instead. I'm sure our men will understand we have more important matters to attend."

The queen left and Abigayle set to work, employing Gwen as well, asking the size of this and the length of that. By the time Queen Joan returned with a gaggle of servants carrying platters of food and pitchers of drink, Abigayle had already marked out the panels for the skirt.

Aileana said little as the commotion erupted around her. It didn't take long for her to see the true extent of Abigayle's talent. Aileana's dress would become a pale blue brocade *houppelande* with broad gold lace trimming and floor length sleeves. It would be cut square around her breasts and rest on the edge of each shoulder. The bodice would be gathered high on her waist by a black velvet belt matching the under-sleeves.

As soon as the initial fittings were complete, Aileana and the queen sat apart from the others to enjoy their meal. Aileana couldn't help notice the lady's beauty.

"You're very kind, Your Majesty, to offer your servants and your hospitality to me."

The queen smiled.

"The MacIntosh and you are good people ensnared in unfortunate circumstances. I'm certain you would do the same for another." She frowned. "I fear the world lacks kindness these days. I have known what it is to fear for my husband's safety, and that of my children and myself." She seemed far away for a moment, but composed herself. "Besides, you'll only have one wedding night, you know. I have seen the way the MacIntosh looks at you and see no harm in showing off some of your assets on this occasion. I am certain you will both enjoy the results," she said.

Aileana's cheeks burned at the queen's comments. If she only knew.

"I take it, by your blush, you don't require any wedding night advice?"

Certainly not. It was one thing to have this conversation with Gwen, but quite another to have it with the queen.

"I thought not. Enjoy your fittings tonight, Lady Aileana. I'll send along my maids to assist you in the morning." Queen Joan stood. "I must retire. The days are more exhausting for me. I swear there are ten babies in my belly this time. The king is convinced it's a boy and insists upon my rest. I bid you goodnight. If you require anything at all please, just ask."

The queen bent towards Aileana and kissed her cheek before leaving the room. Abigayle gathered Aileana and continued her creation. Within an hour the better part of the dress was cut and pinned. Abigayle indicated she would not need Aileana further and insisted she worked better in solitude. The poor girl had been given an enormous task.

"I cannot begin to thank you for your work. If you are ever in need of my assistance, I shall do everything in my power to grant your wish."

Aileana kissed Abigayle's cheek and left.

Gwen and Aileana returned to the guest chambers. They

entered hers first to find a large vase of fresh bluebells and a note addressed to Aileana. She took it out and read.

Lady Aileana,
I wish to inform you his Majesty the King has approved our request to use the chapel. I trust this meets with your satisfaction. Please join me at the hour of one. Sweet dreams. Mine will be filled with thoughts of you.
Yours,
James

Aileana smiled and re-read the note.

"Would you mind if I went straight to bed?" Aileana asked.

Gwen embraced her. "I would not mind at all my lady. I wish you sound, dreamless sleep. And in the absence of that, I wish you a full alphabet of flowers to ponder."

Aileana smiled at her lady-in-waiting, her best friend. When Gwen left, Aileana removed her gown and stockings and was standing only in her shift when a deep voice startled her from behind. She had not heard James enter.

"Would you please not remove that just yet? I wish to keep my wits about me to address an issue with you."

He leaned against the side door. The last time she stood in front of him in her shift she had some resistance. Tonight she had none.

"Well sir, if you knocked on a lady's door instead of barging in, you wouldn't be met with such an unpleasing sight."

His lips curled at her jest.

"Unpleasing? Oh, that's an opinion that would be better formed after much exploration." James closed the distance between them and drew her into his arms. She delighted in his touch. "And exploration like that could take hours…or days…or a fortnight…" As he said each word he placed a kiss on each exposed shoulder and on her forehead. He smelled good enough to devour. Masculine. Virile.

"Aileana, I want you. Now. I don't want to wait another night." His voice was a soft whisper against her skin. "Please ask me to leave."

Between his scent and his voice, she could resist nothing he offered. "I cannot. I want to finish what we started in the carriage."

She had no idea where her courage had come from. She only cared about his strong arms surrounding her and his skilful mouth on her trembling flesh.

"Ask me to leave," he said. "I won't stop unless you ask."

She replied by pulling his face close to hers and brushing her lips against his, but pulling back just as he was about to seal the kiss. This man had driven her crazy, yet she couldn't imagine loving any other. She arched towards him and was aware of his thick erection pressing against her belly. Oh aye, the time was now. Wedding night be damned.

She moved her body back and forth and was thrilled when he scooped her up by her bottom and strode to the bed. She began tugging at his clothes and noticed the look in his eyes as he watched her. She'd seen it before but now recognized it for what it was. He might not admit it, but she suspected he felt as much for her as she did for him.

"Aileana, if you do not ask me to stop—"

"I will not my lord. You've wronged me and I intend to let you make up for your mistakes."

"Oh Christ woman, what you do to me."

In one fluid movement, he shoved her shift up to her waist and hauled his hose down. A wild shiver passed through her as he spread her legs wide and grabbed her hips. He slid his erection across her slick opening. Her flesh quivered in response, her body quaking beneath his gloriously hard body.

The loud knock at the door startled them both. He cursed

but did not move an inch away from her. She could see the anger welling in him.

"If we don't speak, perhaps they will go away," she whispered.

"Lady Aileana, I must speak with you immediately." The king's tone was demanding and he knocked louder.

James hopped off her like she was a hot ember and straightened his clothes in record time.

"A moment, please Your Majesty, as I am not properly dressed," she said.

James stepped back from her. "I should go."

Oh he was not leaving her like this and with that man on the other side of the door. "No, you will not. I feel no shame in anyone finding you in my chambers and you promised to finish what we started."

"Then for pity's sake cover yourself. His Majesty will not stand on the other side of the door for long and your delicious curves are far too exposed in that garment for my liking."

"Indeed."

James looked positively stricken. At that moment, Aileana held more power over him than she ever had. The question was: would she use it? She donned her dressing gown and opened the door.

The king strode into her chamber, barely glancing at James. The man was agitated and the tryst he'd interrupted did not appear to be the cause. He paced before them.

"Your Majesty, how may I be of assistance?"

"Lady Aileana," he said. "Lady Aileana Chattan. Niece of Iain Chattan and daughter of Angus Chattan."

Oh God. Shame burned her cheeks as she recalled her reason for despising this man.

"Aye, Your Majesty." She couldn't help the sarcasm in her tone, or the tension which forced her chin to rise. James moved to her side and slipped his arm around her shoulder.

She didn't quite know what to make of the man who stood before them. His was a strong and determined face. She'd heard many stories of his ruthlessness and preferred in this moment to recall the ones of this undying passionate love for his wife.

"My King, were you not aware of Lady Aileana's lineage when I appealed to you before?" James asked.

"I was not," he said. "Lady Aileana, surely you are aware of the sacrifice your father offered for the sovereignty of my crown and this great nation."

"Sacrifice?"

"Aye, my lady, sacrifice. Were it not for brave men like your father, I may have never returned to claim my crown."

It was not how she had heard the story. Could she believe him and let go of bitter feelings for a past she had not witnessed?

"My father died whilst acting as surety for your ransom, Your Majesty. How many others who left their homes have since returned?"

James's arm tightened and she imagined his eyes had just widened some. She didn't care. She had an opportunity to learn the truth and by God he deserved the challenge she threw at him in her father's name.

"Aye he did and I owe him a debt for it. That debt falls to you as his heir and I offer it to you humbly. As for the others, I will repay the debt to their families soon enough."

King James, never breaking eye contact, sunk to one knee before her.

Chapter Eighteen

Aileana woke early to cheery birds singing in the distance. She rose and donned her robe. Her body tingled, her blood humming in her veins. She dragged her brush through her hair and debated sneaking to Gwen's room, needing the woman's council more than ever.

How was she to reconcile King James's show of appreciation for her father's sacrifice? Were today not her wedding day, she would question James on the matter. There was no way a discussion with him was possible until later, and she supposed, they'd have other things on their mind.

A knock sounded at the door and Gwen entered followed by a flock of the queen's ladies-in-waiting. This flurry of activity would no doubt keep Aileana focused. The first of them came with the large tub followed by several pitchers of heated water scented with rosehip and lavender. Her tension ebbed. She was scrubbed from head to toe, leaving her skin a healthy pink.

Aye, this helped. She had never been one to pamper herself, but this treatment stilled her scattered thoughts. She was directed out of the tub by maids holding cloth sheets to brush the water from her skin. They led her toward the small hearth where her limbs were relieved of their coverings and smothered in rich rose scented cream. Gwen brought over a tray consisting of fruit, cheese and meats all of which were placed out for a luncheon at her home.

She enjoyed nibbling on the delicious spread while Gwen directed the maids on how to brush dry her hair. After some attempts, Gwen became impatient and took the brush into her own hand. She wrapped sections of Aileana's hair around thick pieces of cloth and secured them close to her scalp. Her hair would take a few hours to set like this, which was why the ritual began so early.

Aileana's thoughts drifted to James. Their interlude last evening made her quiver. Tonight nothing would stop her from giving in to her most carnal desires for him.

Could she last that long?

This would be far from a private affair so she had no choice but wait. Oh how she longed to be alone with him, though. She had always thought she would have some trepidation about lying with her husband for the first time, but never imagined it would be with someone she loved. If only he could love her in return.

He had feelings for her, anyone could see that. Could a man like him even fall in love? He'd been with so many women. Knowing he would be a skilled lover was good and bad. He knew ways to achieve pleasure she couldn't even imagine. Even Gwen had hinted at things which shocked, yet she could envision doing them with him.

His experience also meant she may encounter some of his conquests. The idea of anyone else touching him was uncomfortable enough, witnessing women gawking like he was the evening meal was almost as bad.

By the time Gwen had almost finished her hair, the tub had been removed and most of the servants with it. Now, only she and four of the queen's private maids remained.

Aileana wanted to share her surprising visit from the king with Gwen, but was unable to do so without privacy. Hopefully, her friend would understand her cryptic comments.

"I'm grateful to you for my privacy last evening."

Gwen's brow furrowed. "Of course. I understood you were tired."

"Aye, I was tired, but my dreams were filled with tormenting images." Would Gwen understand? Aileana didn't dream and Gwen knew this.

"I see my lady. What sort of images?" Gwen leaned in closer.

"The first was that of a stag. He was strong and brave and pure of heart. I was a doe and he wanted me to trust him and become his mate."

"Aye, my lady, I understand that dream." Gwen's lips curled. "And the stag, did he rut with the doe?"

Aileana gasped. Leave it to Gwen to say something scandalous. Still, a thrill raced through her at the implication.

"The stag would have, but was interrupted."

"By whom? A second stag?" Gwen's grin widened and her eyes filled with a mischievous glint.

"Of course not!" Aileana laughed. "The stag and the doe were devoted to one another."

"Were they now?"

"Aye, but they were interrupted by a red lion."

Gwen cocked her head to the side. "Indeed."

"The lion wished to pledge his loyalty and service to the doe, for the sacrifices of her herd."

Gwen's jaw dropped. She looked astonished.

Aileana knew the feeling. She'd come to Linlithgow Palace expecting far less than appreciation of her family. Could she trust the king? She hadn't had opportunity to speak of it to James, but would. He knew how she felt about the man. Was it an act? Was this how he garnered allies and if so what did he expect to gain from her? She was more curious than ever about him.

"My lady, I have difficulty finding the right words. Your dream was astonishing."

"It was. I confess I am unsure what to make of it myself."

Gwen probed no further, but her brow knit until Aileana's head was full of curlers.

Throughout the morning, a few servants popped in and out, but it wasn't until Abigayle arrived to dress Aileana, nervousness set in. She smiled as Abigayle secured the back of her silk under-bodice. Fifty satin buttons, Abigayle boasted. The effect tightened the material around her chest and enhanced her bosom. This undergarment had been sewn for the queen before her pregnancy and would not fit her for several months. It fit Aileana like a glove. James would not smile, but she would enjoy the time it took for him to undo them.

Her gown was designed in two separate parts, the bodice and sleeves separate from the houppelande. A black velvet belt covered the seam just underneath her breasts and was secured at the back and extended to the floor.

When she was dressed, the maids and Gwen began the task of removing the cloth hair curlers. Dozens of golden curls cascaded down across her back. The movement was luxurious in contrast to the tight bindings. Her hair was crowned with a gold circlet which dipped at the middle of her forehead.

When she turned to admire herself in the looking glass, she gasped at the sight that met her eyes. She had never imagined herself looking so regal.

She turned to Abigayle with gratitude caught in her throat. Abigayle's eyes grew wide and she looked uncomfortable. "You truly are a magician, Abigayle. I thank you from the bottom of my heart for all your hard work."

Abigayle appeared almost embarrassed by the heartfelt thanks bestowed upon her.

She bowed her head. "You are most welcome, m'lady."

With that, the seamstress gathered her belongings and left the room.

Earlier, Calum had delivered a flat box Aileana was to open when she was almost ready. The delivery also contained a note concerning Gwen, but she was instructed to wait on that as well.

Gwen moved forward, her eyes filled with tears and placed the box in Aileana's hand. Gwen then removed the cross she'd given to Aileana for protection.

"You won't need this today," she said.

She looked at her friend and at herself in the mirror and pulled out the note Calum had passed her earlier.

"Gwen, I want you to go and get yourself ready please. You need not attend me any further this day as I wish you to be a guest at my wedding. Please be sure to take your time before returning for me. I believe I may need a few moments. Oh and by the way, there's a box in the side chamber for you. It was dropped it off earlier." Aileana tried to act casual, but her heart thudded.

The note from Calum told Aileana of the box and asked if she could relieve Gwen of her duties for the day so that she could be his guest. It had been difficult to give nothing away.

Gwen took the box and placed it on the bed. She pulled the scarlet ribbon, lifted the lid and peered inside. Her face dropped as she stared. Aileana moved toward Gwen wrapping one arm around her shoulders. She offered the note, to which Gwen shook her head.

"What does it say?" Gwen's voice lowered to a whisper. The tears in her eyes made Aileana's heart constrict.

"Looks like you may need some help getting ready too. Calum wishes you on his arm today."

Aileana turned to the four maids.

"I trust you can assist this lady?"

They giggled and nodded and ushered a slack jawed Gwen out of the room. She'd been right about Gwen and Calum. Something budded between them. Gwen deserved every happiness. She'd taken her family's plight in stride and never complained about her sunken status.

Aileana's thoughts paused on James as she admired herself once again in the mirror. The box Gwen had handed her still rested in her hand. She opened it to find a beautiful three stringed pearl choker with a gold pendant secured in the centre stamped with the MacIntosh coat of arms. Matching pearl earrings completed the set.

She read the note and smiled at the foresight of her brother-to-be. Calum had stated these belonged to his mother and had been sent to Edinburgh for cleaning and repair after the betrothal. Her lips curled. He had played a significant role in seeing her marriage to James come to fruition. She'd thank him later.

Gwen returned and the time had come to leave for the chapel. Aileana choked back tears when Gwen entered the room. The maids had been up to the task. Fine intricate braiding rested on Gwen's thick dark hair which was brushed to a shine. The braids were offset by a delicate gold wreath attached to a whisper thin gold edged veil. Her dress was the colour of fine wine and fit to perfection with its empire waist, flowing skirt and floor length sleeves similar to her own.

"You deserve to dress like this every day," Aileana said.

Gwen smiled and with trembling lips mouthed, "Azalea, amaryllis, aster—"

They smiled as they left the room together and continued to

whisper many more flower names and made it up to 'k' by the time they reach the chapel.

The queen intercepted them just outside and gushed at the 'stunning result of Abigayle's work' as she put it. She congratulated herself on her quick thinking the previous evening in assigning the dressmaker to the task.

The king arrived and gave Aileana an appreciative once over, offering his arm. "Lady Aileana, it would be my honour to escort you to your groom."

Was he jesting? Accepting his allegiance was one thing, but replacing her father on this day, was a leap she was not about to take.

"Your Majesty is too kind. I cannot impose upon you in such a way."

He smiled. "Of course you can, my lady. I will not have you unescorted."

His insistence was no surprise. She imagined he was more than used to getting his way and had no choice but smile and accept his arm with as much grace as she could muster.

From nowhere, Calum appeared and stopped dead in his tracks once he viewed Gwen. He smiled and offered her his arm.

"You look stunning sister." Calum spoke to Aileana, tearing his eyes away from Gwen for the briefest moment. "I see you are as delicate as my mother was. The choker fits you perfectly. I'm glad for my brother. I know you will make him happy."

Calum turned back to Gwen, his gaze devouring her. Aileana had to look away.

"Shall I escort you inside, my lady?"

She couldn't imagine how Gwen must have felt in that moment because her own heart was about to burst out of her chest with happiness at Calum's genuine appreciation.

The king urged them forward.

211

Aileana's thoughts turned to her uncle. He was the reason she walked up the aisle toward James MacIntosh instead of Gawain. His assessment of both men had been accurate. She sent thanks heavenward to her uncle for his good sense.

She walked forever to get to James. The chapel's ornate beauty was nothing compared to the man waiting for her at the end of it. His tunic was the same shade of blue as her gown. Intentional no doubt. She smiled, remembering the ridge of buttons on the back of her bodice.

Aileana stood before James, focusing on the lines she was to repeat. She gazed into his eyes and found more promise and sincerity there than she had ever seen. He repeated his words with emphasis on love, honour and forever and a shiver of anticipation ran through her. Before long, the ceremony was over and his mouth claimed hers. Just as she responded, he pulled away and winked at her. He was quite skilled at making her forget where she was.

They were led out by the king and queen and Aileana wished they could turn right toward her chamber instead. Within minutes they were in the great hall to where tables were prepared with more food than they could eat in a sennight. The hall was filled with guests, including several lords and ladies of the lowland region unknown to her but conversing at ease with James.

The feasting continued well into the afternoon. At times, James leaned close to her and whispered comments like, 'mine', or 'Lady MacIntosh', or what had become her favourite, 'wife'.

She tried to be polite to those who congratulated them, but her thoughts drifted to the man beside her and on more than one occasion, he said her name twice to collect her attention. His voice set her belly fluttering and the look in his eyes set her pulse racing. In a few short hours, she would be his in every way possible.

One guest in particular continued to catch her eye. The woman was stunning with flowing auburn hair and the deepest chocolate brown eyes she'd ever seen. The woman stared at Aileana so decidedly, making her wonder if they'd ever met.

As they mingled with the other guests, she could feel the woman's eyes on her. The stranger circled them at a wide berth. Aileana's hair prickled at her nape. Before she could ask James if he knew the woman, they were intercepted.

"James darling, I've missed you so much. Fare thee well my love? When I heard you were in the city and about to be married, I had to attend to see it with my own eyes. Tell me James, how many mistresses do you currently keep? Five? Or six?"

James stiffened the moment the woman came into his view. This kind of talk was not meant for any sensible person's ears, yet the woman smiled at the gasps of those nearby. Aileana's insides churned.

"Lady MacIntosh is it? Well my dear, I suggest you use him as much as you can before the night is out. No doubt he'll be back in another's bed by tomorrow."

James didn't speak, nor did he move. Instead he glared at the woman, his jaw clenching. She stared right back and smiled with her head held high. Aileana looked around; those within earshot had ceased their own conversations and watched the scene playing out before them.

Calum moved to his brother's side with Gwen on his arm.

"Jocelyn, nice to see you again. And where may I ask is your husband? Oh wait, I remember, you never married. You were too good for anyone who dared ask."

"Ah, the younger brother. I remember you. And who is this creature you have with you? I've never seen you before, my dear. Is she from out of the country or have you descended to the lower classes for companionship?"

"That's enough, Jocelyn." James's command was controlled, yet Aileana didn't doubt the fury just beneath the surface.

He gathered Aileana's arm and urged them in the opposite direction. How dare the woman show her face at her wedding and worse, cast doubt on James's fidelity toward his new wife. The woman needed to be put in her place.

"That's right, walk away. You never could live up to your commitments."

James turned to Aileana.

"My lady, with your permission, I would like to set the record straight so that neither of us has to endure her lies."

Aileana was grateful James consulted her, but out of respect for him she didn't want his past dissected in front of everyone. They could and would sort out the woman's accusations in private, but this woman was not about to consume one more minute of her wedding day.

"That would be an appropriate action to take, my lord," Aileana raised her voice so that all could hear. "However, I feel every moment that passes detracts from the time I have to spend with you this evening. As the Lady pointed out, I must make the best use of our time today."

She turned to Jocelyn who, as Aileana hoped, was just realizing she had underestimated James's new wife. The woman's smile disappeared and her mouth set in an ugly straight line.

"I thank you for your advice, Lady Jocelyn, I trust that concludes your purpose for attending my wedding?"

"I, well, I—"

"I thought it might. Good day to you Lady." Aileana turned her back on the woman and drew James closer to the dais where the king and queen sat.

The king, who Aileana was not aware had overheard, laughed. She turned to see Jocelyn escorted out of the room by the king's guards.

"Well put, Lady MacIntosh. Remind me to never call you out in public," he said.

A grin rested on his lips as he motioned for the music to start and turned to his beaming wife who nodded to them.

James's body still oozed tension. Aileana squeezed his hand to gain his attention. When he looked at her, she smiled to let him know everything was all right. His response was to reach down and kiss her cheek. The gesture was the best thank you she could have received.

The pipers began a familiar tune as James took Aileana's hand and led her to a large area away from the vast table. He put one hand around her waist and his other out flat. She placed one hand on his shoulder and laid the other flat against his. They moved easily together. Aileana didn't try to look away from him this time as she searched his expression for answers to her unspoken questions. He responded by mouthing three words that sent her head in a spin. She was ready to leave. Now.

When the dance ended, the king arose. "My Lords and Ladies, we have before us that of which poets dream and the lonely would lay down their lives to possess. I believe we shall burden our newly wedded couple with propriety no longer and bid them good night."

James nodded and to the king's approving laugh, guided her out of the hall with haste, through the palace and straight to their room. She hoped their pace wouldn't send her tripping over her skirts.

He paused outside, gathering both her hands in his and kissed them. "Thank you."

"For what, my lord?"

He cupped her face and peered deep into her eyes.

"For giving me so much. Everything beautiful in this world

is here because of you. You know that don't you? It's true I've been with other women, but the truth is that since you've come into my life, I haven't seen another. All I see is you."

God, but he was beautiful. She curled her arms around his neck and pressed herself against him.

He scooped her up and carried her into the bedchamber. James set her down by the bed moving away to lock the door with an audible click. She turned to face him and noticed flowers had been added to the room along with a tray of food and many candles. The bed covers were pulled back as well.

He sauntered toward her, releasing the belt holding his doublet as he inched closer. She didn't know where to begin with her dress, and so gave him a playful smile and shrugged her shoulders. He removed both his tunic and shirt and stood before her bare-chested. Her hands explored the hardened muscle contrasted by smooth skin. She pressed her lips to his flesh and he quivered.

James reached around her and with a couple of tugs, her houppelande loosened and fell to the floor.

"You do that rather well," she said, her voice but a breathy whisper.

He held her shoulders and kissed her neck. "One can do anything well when one puts one's mind to it." His reply came with a rush of air just beneath her ear, a place she hadn't known was sensitive until that moment.

James began a torturous trail of kisses searing her flesh in their wake. She tasted his skin and fought the urge to nip him with her teeth. He reached around her again, discovering the ridge of tiny buttons.

He spun her around. "What evil is this?"

He didn't wait for an answer and began pulling them off one by one.

She gasped. "My lord the queen's seamstress, Abigayle,

worked hard on those. I believe you do her work a disservice by destroying them."

He growled. "I extend no sympathy to any creature who would design a garment to torture a man on his wedding night. I promise you, no one will ever know, I'll stitch them back on myself if that pleases you."

He reached around to her belly and pulled her hard against him. A jolt shot straight to her loins and her nipples hardened.

"Only you please me," she said.

She heard the unmistakable sound of tearing fabric. The cool air at her back made her blood race and she shuddered. Satin covered buttons flew to and fro across the bedchamber. He turned her around and lifted her onto the bed. His gaze dropped to her mouth while his fingers caressed her shoulders.

"I will never willingly hurt you. You know that, don't you?"

She nodded. She didn't care about pain, only the pressure deep in her core, taking her breath away.

"This, what we are about to do, may," he said.

Aileana was touched by his tenderness and responded by pulling off her bodice and skirt and tossing them to the floor. She eagerly moved her hands to his crotch. His breath was ragged as she caressed his impressive offering. He was heavy and aroused and she reached inside his hose to grasp his thick erection, needing to feel him throb in her hands. She stared at it openly and stroked his hard length. She craved his body inside her. He panted hard.

He shuffled out of his remaining clothes and stopped her hands from their movement. James eased her onto her back raising her arms over her head and lowered his body onto hers, his hard, heavy body pressing her onto the soft coverlet. He found her mouth and plunged his tongue deep within. She opened her legs and shifted her hips, arching, urging him to take her.

His hands touched and teased every inch of her, stopping to play with her firm nipple before moving down across her trembling belly. She buried her fingers in his hair as she had so longed to do. He slid down her body and wedged between her thighs. His tongue was velvet heat lapping at her too sensitive skin. She moaned his name.

James's magical fingers slowly probed her wetness as he inched his mouth closer and closer to the source of her heat. When his tongue made contact with her moistened flesh, she became wild with need and bucked her hips. She had no idea what he was about to do next as he closed his mouth over her hardened bud, driving his fingers into her at the same time. Her body thrust off the bed in response. Liquid fire raced through her veins.

The heat swelling within her was almost painful.

"Please, James."

He groaned. His breath was ragged as he kissed and flicked his tongue upward again. He took her hardened nipple into his mouth and tugged hard. She almost came apart underneath him, every inch of her body screaming for release only he could give.

James spread her wide and entered her, stopping when he was just inside. His thick, hard member stretched her and the intoxicating pressure turned sharp and piercing. He hadn't exaggerated when he said it might hurt. He pushed harder. She was already full of him, impaled and he'd barely begun. Aileana opened her eyes to look at him. He strained, waiting for encouragement from her to continue. She pushed her body upward taking him into her, pushing further past the barrier of her maidenhood. *Oh God it hurts.* He didn't move for long moments and eased back slightly, thankfully taking some of the pain with him.

"You are so tight around me." His voice cracked. "Christ,

I've died and gone to heaven."

He eased into her again. It didn't hurt as much this time. He was right, it felt better. Pleasure built again as he slid in and out of her in a tempered rhythm. The movement was too slow and not what her body craved.

"James, more."

He obeyed and drove into her with increasing force, edging her across the bed. She hooked her legs around his waist and raised her hips to meet his every delicious thrust. She was close to something—like reaching for an unknown object she must have.

She pulsed around him, her orgasm finally washing over her. He slammed all the way inside her and tensed. Fluid ecstasy coursed through her veins while he throbbed inside her, her body milking his. She stared up at him. The wonderment in his eyes made her heart swell. He slid his arms under her shoulders and continued to pump into her as he claimed her mouth in a delicate dance of tongues. Each slight movement released another ripple of pleasure. They moved together like that for a time until the last sensation ebbed and a satisfied heaviness over took her limbs.

* * *

Before long, James realized she had fallen asleep. He watched her face. Her flickering eyelids told him she was dreaming and the tender curl of her lips had him hoping the dream was about him.

This eighteen-year-old virgin had shown him more about being a man and sharing his body than every single woman before her. He thought back to the dance and the three words he'd mouthed to her.

For the first time in his twenty-four years, he was in love. He continued to watch her expressions as he kissed her face, her breasts and at last her mouth. He didn't wonder anymore if she returned his feelings. He could see it in her eyes. He wanted to shout his newfound realization to the top of his lungs, but instead acknowledged the last wishes of an old friend.

"Chattan, you sly fox. You knew all along, didn't you?"

He made her a silent promise that he would move heaven and earth to find Gawain. That rat would never, ever get close to her again. James pulled the quilts over them and within minutes drifted into pure contentment.

Chapter Nineteen

James and Calum left early to attend the MacKay trial at Edinburgh castle. He could still smell Aileana's scent on him and couldn't wait to return to her. It would take precious little for his arousal to peak again, despite the passion they shared last night and again this morning. The trial would provide necessary distraction. He doubted he'd make it to the end of the lane otherwise.

"You're unusually silent this morning, Brother," James said to Calum. "Worried about the proceedings or are your thoughts more pleasantly engaged?" Calum and the maid had appeared devoted to one another during the wedding feast, so his frown seemed misplaced.

Calum grunted.

"Oh, I see. Let me guess, you wanted the lass, but she'd have none of you and you don't have enough experience to convince her otherwise."

"Wrong again. I'd appreciate it if you wouldn't pry me for details of my disastrous night. If you seek distraction please think on your own and leave mine out of it."

If the circumstance were reversed, Calum would never let up until he got to the root of the problem. Besides, James was too curious to let it go.

"Ah, I could do that and be pleasantly preoccupied all the way to Edinburgh. The truth is, I've never seen you so solemn and cannot quell my curiosity. What's put you in this foul mood?"

"I don't wish to discuss it, though 'tis unlikely you'll let it drop." Calum sighed. "Courting the wench was a mistake. I see that. My image of her was flawed and clouded by the attraction I felt. Believe me when I say, you're married to the only woman of the two with any virtue to speak of."

"She's not a virgin?" James stifled a chuckle. "Is that all?"

Calum didn't reply.

"I know your sensibilities prevent you from seeing past this aspect of her life but be reasonable man. Do you really like her? If you do, you'll look beyond her choices as I'm certain she'd look past yours. I know we've never discussed your future marriage plans, but I've seen you look at her and have never seen you look at any other woman the same way. Don't throw away something just because your views differ from hers."

Calum still didn't reply and James didn't see the point to push further. His own night was far better than he could have ever imagined. The woman he called wife was more than a match for him in bed. And oh God, the things she could do with her tongue.

She had come to him a virgin, there was no doubt there, but it was a little hard to believe no man had ever touched her before. She was so free with her passion. He shifted in his saddle as images of her desire flushed body flashed through his mind. Dammit, he needed to focus on something else.

Calum brooded. The lad had a lot to learn about women. Hell James had learned his lesson well enough. The thought of Aileana belonging to anyone else was not one he'd wanted to entertain. Now he didn't have to.

They crossed into Edinburgh and before long stood at the

gates of the castle again. It was intimidating to newcomers, especially those brought there by force and not invitation. James thought about the men in the dungeon - most never came out. He'd risked much by approaching the king with his proof and his theory. That risk had paid off thus far, yet caution prevailed. Without knowing who had betrayed the monarch, the trust earned could be lost as easily as 'twas gained.

They were escorted to the hall where the trial would take place. He thought back to the discussion he'd had with the king on the matter. Executing the trial here could work for or against their cause. By having MacKay and his men brought to court, the king would make the decision to release them or hang them without involvement from any other parliamentary or judicial body. Therefore, the man had absolute control. However, he also assumed sole responsibility in the event of an unpopular decision.

This plan could work if all the pieces fell together in the right way. It would be a bold act for someone to speak out against the monarch when he set the MacKay free, but he was banking on that sort of reaction to give something away, some signal to indicate involvement.

When they entered the hall, James and Calum took a seat on opposite sides. Their plan was to scan the crowd to detect anything unusual. The room was unencumbered with decoration; meant for the purpose of business rather than entertaining. A tall, ornate chair sat on a riser, empty and waiting for its regal owner.

The room filled. James remembered the note he'd received early that morning from Fergus. It stated, "The king believes us. Thank you. Say nothing unless he asks. All will be revealed in good time."

James assumed the king would craft his questions with care,

yet his gut knotted. So much could still go wrong at any point. Chains rattled and the prisoners shuffled toward the throne. Moments later, its owner entered from a side door and took his seat.

Before speaking one word, James Stewart eyed the prisoners one by one then scanned those in attendance. As his gaze dissected those gathered, the room fell silent. When he spoke, his voice was clear and determined.

"My countrymen, we are in the presence of traitors."

James's gut lurched as the crowd mumbled. The noise peaked and died away and the king said nothing more until they settled down.

"We have before us today, men accused of such horrific crimes one can scarce believe anything better than savage animals capable of committing them. The sentence befitting these crimes is death."

Again, the crowd broke into a rumble. Noblemen faced each other and nodded their approval at his words. James watched for those most animated.

"As it is, Fergus MacKay, your clan has been accused of murder, rape, destruction of property and many lesser charges too numerous to mention. I hereby release you of all charges laid against you, as per undeniable evidence presented to me."

That statement was followed by dead silence then erupted into jeers and shouts.

"What's this? Will you have me condemn innocent countrymen?" The king demanded an answer from the crowd.

Kenneth MacKenzie yelled back. "But their banner was found," he said. "They did the deed!"

The man looked years older than he was. The attack had taken its toll. James held his breath. Any moment, they would know. They had better. The king was not likely to hold his patience for much longer and this deadly game was far from over.

The Stewart's penetrating gaze roamed the crowd until it rested on James. He nodded. The trap was set. "I have information convincing me neither Fergus MacKay nor his clansmen are responsible for the crimes against clan MacKenzie."

Various clan representatives declared their belief in Fergus's innocence. It was more interesting to watch those insisting on the man's guilt. After a few moments, Alexander MacDonald rose. He looked enraged with his red cheeks and wild hair.

"Good King, if you choose to let these traitors go free, you condemn all the other Highland clans to the same possible fate. You cannot expect us to abide by your English laws if you do not protect us with them as well."

MacDonald. He turned to see the king's reaction. The man's entire demeanour had changed from calm to dangerous in a split second. He knew what it was to be pinned by that man's glare and he didn't envy MacDonald.

"Laird MacDonald, you believe letting the MacKays go free will condemn you to the same fate? Surely a large clan like yours is not afraid of a dozen men?"

MacDonald spat on the floor. "There were more than a dozen men!"

The king grasped the arms of his throne. He looked ready to spring.

"More than a dozen you say? How on earth would you possibly know that?"

The king glanced sideways and nodded to the captain of his guard. That signal prompted about twenty of his men to position themselves around the MacDonald clan. A great number more of them were present than any other.

"'Tis what everyone has said." MacDonald's gaze shifted between the king and Fergus Mackay. "The attack was too brutal to be carried out by only a dozen Scots."

225

"You're correct in your assessment, MacDonald. It wasn't carried out by just a dozen Scots. They had help in planning the whole affair. Do you happen to know of anyone who might want to attack MacKenzie and blame Mackay?"

Colour drained from MacDonald's face. Gasps were heard around the room. The few Sutherlands in the room were also surrounded.

"Oh, I see that you do." The king's tone was silky. "The question remaining is why would the MacDonalds and Sutherlands enter into such a plot?"

Shock at the implication was audible. James was impressed with the king's direction. Whispers of 'Sutherlands?' swept the room.

"It is interesting to note that, your men do not appear as surprised at my suggestion as most others here today. I believe you may know all about this plot, MacDonald, although I don't believe you'll tell me today. However, let's see how some time in my dungeon loosens your tongue. Take them out of my sight!"

The clan members did not struggle or fight back as they were herded out of the room. The king turned his attention to Fergus and regarded him evenly.

"Laird MacKay, you and your men are free to go."

At that moment, a young man burst into the room. He was travel-worn and distraught. He went straight to Fergus, but spoke to the king with his head bent in submission. "Your Majesty, I have terrible news to report to Fergus."

"Of course, lad. You look like you've seen the devil himself."

The lad turned to Fergus and blinked several times. His mouth opened and closed again like a fish gasping for its last drop of life. "Your brother did as you bade, Fergus. He tracked as far north as he could to watch their activity. We were near their lands, they must have detected us and set a trap." He paused and shuffled. "They took us by surprise, Fergus. We didn't expect them to be waiting. But, wait they did. At the first sign of us, they attacked. William was in front." The young man's voice fell to almost a whisper. "It all happened so fast. They took off and we couldn't catch up. We heard screams that night—I'm sorry Fergus."

Fergus made a small movement toward the lad and within seconds four of his clansmen were on him. Did the boy recognize how close he had just come to death? His wide eyes and pale skin indicated he probably did.

James stepped in between Fergus and the boy. "MacKay, you'll not touch the lad." James was in no mood to take on this giant, but take him on he would. He'd risked too much to save this man's neck to see him throw it away again. Fergus could do as he pleased away from the king's clutches, but here with so many witnesses, there'd be no way to save him from the noose.

James's words managed to reach the warrior. Fergus stopped struggling and shook off the other men before stalking out of the hall with the boy and his men laying chase.

Godspeed, Fergus MacKay.

James turned back to the king. "How did you know it was MacDonald?"

"Let's just say something you said two days ago set me thinking. Who would have the most to gain if I falsely accused a Highland clan of such a deed? Two years ago, I imprisoned MacDonald for legitimate crimes against the Crown. I let him go out of good will eventually. I've had him watched for some time, but obviously not close enough.

"The MacDonalds plotted my overthrow. If he could've convinced enough of the Highland clans to rise up against me, well, MacIntosh, I don't have to tell you what the end result of that would be, do I? You unravelled the plot. You just didn't know who was responsible. The two questions I still have though are, why MacKay, and why MacKenzie? My God, the atrocities inflicted on those poor people can never be reasoned. It's that precise kind of act performed in the name of feuding that I cannot abide. I don't believe even you, whom I regard as a noble gentleman, could justify it."

James considered the man's words. Although correct in theory, actual Highland life was much more complex. He couldn't deny who he was and he was not about to engage in debate with the king about it.

"And you're certain MacDonald is responsible? Outside of his peculiar behaviour here today, what other indication do you have?"

"I've received enough intelligence from trusted sources to verify Alexander MacDonald's hatred of me has not diminished in two years. A few months back, prior to the Mackenzie attack, I received an anonymous letter indicating he was meeting with Artair Sutherland. Unable to conger any logical reason for such a relationship, I disregarded it until you arrived with the plaid pin. Considering where you found it, your story fit with the timing of the letter and the events that subsequently transpired. MacDonald's behaviour here today merely secured my suspicions. Of course, he will have to be questioned."

James noticed the glint in the king's eyes. It was time to shake hands and thank him for his fairness and put the troubling business behind him.

The king smiled, shook James's hand and walked away. "One more thing," the king stopped and turned his head, "Moray correct?" James did not get a chance to reply. "It's yours. I will divert to your schedule for proper ceremony after your honeymoon." He invited James and his party to dine with him back at Linlithgow Palace later that evening to discuss the details.

As they walked out of the castle toward the courtyard, a frightened stable hand approached them with information that the MacKay had just rode off on Arion.

Calum burst out laughing. James had no choice but to share a horse with his brother.

"Shut up, Calum."

* * *

After James left to attend the trial, Aileana thought of a hundred things she wished she'd said to him. How could she help but feel anxious? If the king found Fergus guilty, James would likely be imprisoned as well. Had she thought of anything other than bedding James, she would have spoken with the king and begged for Fergus's freedom and James's security.

"Aileana, you must believe your husband and his brother will return safely. I'm certain all will be well." Gwen had joined her just after the men had left and bless her she tried, but only James's safe return would comfort her.

"How do you know that? Really, how do you know they weren't all thrown into the dungeon the moment they arrived?"

"If I thought reciting flower names would ease you, I'd surely have reached viola by now. You really should calm yourself, Aileana, it's not good for you." Gwen's voice lowered and she frowned. "I'm worried too." Her fingers endlessly linked and unlinked.

"I know you are, and I'm sorry we're having this discussion instead of the one I know you want to have, but I'm so frightened this will go so horribly wrong."

She wanted to know every detail about Gwen's evening with Calum, but she just couldn't seem to focus on anything other than the danger they were in.

Gwen swiped her cheek. "Will it help if I tell you how disastrous my night ended?"

The comment was unexpected as was her solemn demeanour. She noted the dark, puffy circles under Gwen's eyes and imagined her friend had endured a sleepless night.

"We sat together through the wedding feast, as you know," Gwen said.

She did know. Calum looked nowhere other than at Gwen the entire evening.

"He introduced me to other noblemen and ladies as if I were any other lady there instead of a servant. We danced, it was beautiful. He was furious when Jocelyn spoke against me. He made me feel important, and he was so taken up with me I thought, surely this can work."

Gwen paused and moved to the open window. A long lonely cry from a far away bird echoed through the room.

"We were the last to leave the hall. We walked back to my room arm in arm where he kissed me so passionately." Gwen's voice cracked and she placed her hand over her heart. "We moved into my room and I honestly thought he was going to make love to me right then and there. I was ready. I would have done anything he asked, but instead he wanted to talk. He explained how he'd never been with a woman before and how pleased he was to share such an important experience for the first time with me.

Gwen's laugh held no mirth. "You know my history. You can imagine how torn I was, having to tell him he wasn't my first. Worse, he wasn't even my second or third."

Just how many lovers had she been with?

"Three, if you must know." She looked apologetic. "I see the question in your eyes. I've been with three other men, obviously some more than once. I told Calum in the gentlest way I could that my opinion on the subject was different from his. I explained that my experience would help me choose my future husband.

"As you can imagine, he doesn't understand. I've lost him. How stupid was I to hope someone like him could ever love someone like me? He called me names I've never been called before. Maybe he's right, maybe I don't deserve the sanctity of marriage after all my affairs."

It wasn't fair. Gwen had made decisions Aileana didn't understand, but they were hers to make and it wasn't right for Calum to judge her without hearing them.

"Don't deserve the sanctity of marriage? My dear Gwen, how many women do you suppose my husband has been with before me? I would suspect the number is much larger than three. Why should the standard be so different for women? You must give him some time to absorb your confession as I'm sure it wasn't what he expected. I can speak with James if you wish. Surely we can confront Calum and make him see sense?"

Gwen said nothing only gazed through the window.

Aileana's thoughts drifted back to daybreak. She had awakened to find James sitting up in bed with his legs swung over the side, holding her gown in one hand and several satin buttons in the other. The sight of her naked husband intending to fulfill his promise, though she was sure he didn't know how, stirred her desires.

Aileana moved behind him and wrapped her arms around his chest while trailing kisses down his neck.

"I wouldn't start that, wife, if you want your dress fixed before I go."

"You don't know how." Aileana's teasing drew a cocky smile to his lips. What was once despised, she now craved.

She took the dress and buttons out of his hands, placed them on the floor and scooted in front of him to straddle his hips.

Warm ripples spread through her at the memory of the passionate lovemaking that followed. James MacIntosh had come to mean everything to her in such a short time and he felt the same way about her. Her heart was near bursting. Two people who enjoyed the kind of physical passion they shared, must possess deep feelings for one another.

What about Calum and Gwen? Didn't they also appear to have feelings for each other? Couldn't those feelings overcome any obstacle? How important was James's past to their relationship? She remembered the jealousy, thinking of James with another woman - Calum must feel the same way. Therefore, Gwen must mean a great deal to him. If he was ready to become intimate with her, did that mean he intended to marry her? Why should her past matter if he loved her?

A loud noise outside the room gained her attention. It sounded like a struggle. She motioned for Gwen to use the side door hoping she could find out what was going on. A guard was posted out there and by the muffled sounds coming through her door, she assumed he was being attacked - but by who?

Seconds after Gwen closed the side door, Gawain burst through the other. Her heart leapt up into her throat and for a few moments she couldn't even utter his name.

"Well, my love we meet again," he said, his voice low and menacing.

Aileana was horrified at the sight of him. Deep crimson splatters stained his shirt, his eyes were excited and wild. His face twisted into an attempted smile, but his deformed jaw prevented it from holding. Only his voice held any note of the former man.

Why did he carry a quiver of arrows slung across his back? "You—you're an archer?"

"Arrowsmith. It was the easiest way to gain access to the palace."

"But what are you doing here?"

"Why, I've come for my bride." Gawain stepped forward. "We'll be married by sundown and after our glorious wedding night, will return to *my* castle. Aileana, I must tell you, I'm disappointed in you. You've made it difficult for me to claim my inheritance. You understand, I'll have to punish you. Oh don't worry; like mine, the scars will heal in time."

She tried to force air into her lungs to scream, but her breath caught and her blood pounded in her ears. Gawain took a few menacing steps toward her and as he did she stepped backward keeping perfect time with his forward movement.

"Come to me my love." He taunted her, like a wildcat stalking its prey. "I have a need to see the body beneath all your layers of finery. We needn't wait for a priest's blessing to consummate our union. I intend to show you what you stir in me right now."

Her gut lurched. He couldn't mean it.

Oh God where is Gwen?

As he moved closer, the thick copper scent of blood caused her body to convulse with the urge to retch. She looked around, frantic for escape. He had backed her into the room and could overtake her should she attempt to dash for either exit. Perhaps if he knew the truth, he could be reasoned with.

"Gawain, I'm already married." She managed her confession through trembling lips.

Her words hung in the air for what seemed like an eternity.

The wildcat had stalked enough. He pounced on her, knocking her to the floor. Gawain grabbed the sides of her head and slammed her skull onto the stone tile. White hot pain raced down her spine and the room spun in sickening circles.

Oh God.

Slam!

The agony inside her head was unbearable. His fists were full of her hair which she was sure he would rip it out.

233

I'm going to die.

Slam!

I love you, James.

Sounds faded. Blackness drew closer, dulling the pain in her head, the sound of his cursing and the sight of his monstrous face above her. At long last, the void consumed her.

Chapter Twenty

Aileana bent low over a patch of wild strawberries, smiling at her discovery. These would please him. Her basket was almost full of apples and she couldn't wait to get home to start the pie.

Bending and standing had a dizzying effect after a while. She was almost done anyway, just a couple more berries would do the trick. She leaned over and searing pain shot through her temple.

"Help!" She managed to yell while falling to her knees. "Help," she whispered, just before she fainted.

Aileana blinked several times before recognizing where she was. Her quilts were tucked around her and the smell of rabbit stew and burning peat eased her tension. She smiled at her husband when he placed a cool cloth on her head.

"Are you feeling better my love?" he asked.

Aileana looked into his eyes; he had cared for her tirelessly these past months. He loved her so much.

She had no memory of anything before the accident. Gawain had told her of their courtship and how, because of her uncle's greed, she was to be married off to a vicious chief. He said their love for one another prompted them to run away and live here in the forest, far away from her uncle's clutches.

"I'm well. Thank you."

She sat up to see if the throbbing had passed. It had. Gawain watched her before moving away to the table to continue going through some papers he had stacked there.

"I wonder—"

"Aileana, I've told you it's not safe for you to go back there." He cut her off like so many times before. "I know you want to remember, but I fear, even if we were careful, someone would recognize us and you would be forced into the hands of that beast. I simply couldn't bear the thought of him touching you."

The more she recovered, the more determined she was to return to her home and her uncle to gain back her memory. Gawain was ever patient, yet deterred her from it every time.

"I know, I know. I just can't help but think there must be a better way for you to live than stuck here with me all the time. You must love me a great deal to give up all your wealth to live here with me living on so little."

Gawain gave her his best attempt at a smile.

"My dearest, I couldn't imagine anywhere else I would rather be than here with you. Please don't distress yourself as I'm truly content." Gawain moved toward her and patted the top of her head. "I need to replenish our stores. Rest up. We can gather more fruit tomorrow." He gave her one last smile and left the cottage.

Nothing was too much for him. She drew the thick patchwork quilt up to her chin. Her anxiety must be due to her loss of memory and nothing more, for if something were wrong, Gawain would come and discuss it with her and they would work it out together.

She thought of how strained his face looked when he smiled. Damn her uncle for beating him so savagely and fracturing his jaw. He'd endured much and the last thing he needed was her nagging at him.

She took in her surroundings. Their home was small, everything contained in one room with a privy outside behind the weathered structure. It wasn't much, but she tried to improve the gloomy space by adding fresh flowers as often as possible. He must find it hard to cope with his change in fortune so she tried her best to keep him happy. On one point she would be forever guilty. Aileana was incapable of intimacy with him and feared something from the accident had changed in her. He said they had their whole lives to wait and that she should be sure before they were intimate again. Still, it was unfair to him.

A bairn grew in her womb, so it was obvious they'd mated, but she couldn't for the life of her imagine being with him in that way. Though there was no doubt of his kind nature, she questioned her attraction to him. Oddly enough, she couldn't justify her aversion either. Soon, she would see the deed done. He deserved better than that from her.

The sunset cast a red hue inside the small cottage. The light danced on the walls while she settled down to rest up some more. He was right, she could collect fruit tomorrow. Perhaps she would give him more than a pie for dessert. An odd unease crept over her at the thought. She shook it away.

As she drew the quilts around her, all noise passed out of her consciousness except for the babbling stream running behind the cottage. She focused on it and fell into a deep sleep.

Aileana strolled through a meadow coloured by splashes of heather and bluebells. The warm air enveloped her, spreading happiness through her. She heard peals of laughter behind her and turned to see a beautiful little girl running from a handsome man. They were like nothing she had seen before— so perfect.

They ran toward her, laughing, and calling her name. The wee lass's giggle sounded like perfect ringing bells. Her golden hair fell to her waist and danced all around like imaginary playmates.

When they reached Aileana, the little girl jumped into her arms and they swung round and round. She put the little beauty down just as the man pulled her against his hard chest and gave her the most passionate kiss. They joined hands with the little girl and walked together down a stone path toward a beautiful castle surrounded by the loveliest flowers.

The three walked and laughed together as the sky grew gloomy and thunder rumbled in the distance. They ran hard toward the castle, but couldn't get closer. Before long, a downpour caused her grip to loosen on the little girl's hand. Aileana blinked away heavy raindrops, but lost sight of the man and the girl and ran alone. She searched through the driving rain, but couldn't find them anywhere.

After an eternity, Aileana reached the castle and entered the dark, cheerless keep to find many men and women standing in a circle, mourning. Unable to see for whom they wept, she pushed her way past those gathered to see a kindly faced man laid out on a stone slab.

He opened his eyes and spoke to her. "I'm your uncle Aileana. I'm your uncle and I love you, lass."

Aileana screamed and bolted. She exited the castle and ran until she fell to the ground from exhaustion. The rain fell in sheets. She looked up from the cold, muddy earth to see a man approach her on a large white horse. He bent down, picked her up off the ground and tossed her onto the back of his horse. He didn't speak to her and she had to hold on tight so she wouldn't fall off.

They came to a small dark inn where he dragged her from the horse and shoved her inside. The cloaked man paid for a room and pulled her with him up the stairs toward it. He opened the door and pushed her inside as she turned to face him. When he pulled down his hood, she discovered it was the man from the meadow. He didn't look happy and relaxed anymore—he looked dangerous.

"Aileana, where are you? You must help me find you!"

His emphasis on the last two words was so loud he almost shouted it. She was afraid of him and tried to get around him, but he would not let her leave and instead, took a key from his pocket as he left the room. The man locked the door from the outside leaving her there in the cold and dark, all alone and terrified. She yelled at the top of her lungs, but no one would come to help her.

Aileana awoke with a start, gasping for air and bathed in cold sweat. A wave of nausea overtook her, forcing her to dash outside to empty her stomach. She retched by the side of the cottage and prayed Gawain would not witness her illness.

She composed herself and looked up to the sky to measure the time by the moon's height then retreated into cottage to return to her bed, expecting to see Gawain there. He was not. She looked to the heavy chair near the fire he often slept in on nights when she was particularly restless, but he was not there either.

The wood and peat supply was not replenished outside either, meaning he'd not returned. What if her uncle's men had found him? Did they know where he was? Would they soon come for her as well? Her fear grew as she rocked on her bed well into the early morning hours, waiting.

* * *

James was escorted through the stone walls of MacKay House, near the northern most region of Scotland in the village of Tongue, hoping to find Fergus in a generous mood. It had been a long time and much had passed since they'd last seen one another in Edinburgh. Three months. Christ, James couldn't even imagine what his life had been like back then.

"MacIntosh? Is that you? You look like hell, man. Come in, and feed yourself and your men."

James entered the great hall with its ancient, Norse-inspired design and sat at the largest table he'd ever seen. Nothing in the north was small or quaint. As he took his seat, he could see concern on Fergus's face and imagined it was because of James's haggard appearance.

"I owe you my life, but I didn't expect you to come all this was to claim it. What brings you here?"

Fergus didn't waste time on pleasantries. Thank God.

"We arrived late last evening. Your house servant let us in and gave us a warm bed. Your hospitality has already been extended and I thank you for it." James scrubbed his hand over his face. "I don't know where to begin, but let me tell you, much has changed since we last met at Edinburgh Castle."

James told his story. As he talked, he and drank and ate from the plentiful spread at Fergus's table. He couldn't remember when he'd eaten last. The tale he recounted had everyone at the table riveted, it sounded too fantastic, too impossible to be true even to his own ears. His brand new bride had been abducted a second time from right under his nose.

James struggled to tell his tale. The rage in him for having to say those words threatened to overspill like so many times in the last while. He was worn out from attempts at control, but he would do her no good any other way.

When he and Calum had returned to Linlithgow Palace, Aileana had already been taken. They scoured the palace twice and spent the next fortnight searching all of Linlithgow and Edinburgh. He couldn't believe she could disappear without a trace. Somewhere in the deep recesses of his mind, a fleeting thought emerged that she'd gone willingly.

His initial disbelief turned to panic. Although he questioned everyone extensively, he had no doubt Gawain was responsible and cold fear swept over him at the thought of what that man would do with his beloved wife. With her, Gawain possessed James's soul.

James recounted his interrogation with everyone at the palace that morning, including the hateful accusations he had fired at Gwen. He would never forgive himself for the blame he'd laid at her door, even though she had long since done so.

The search, into its thirteenth week, showed no prospect of locating Aileana. Overwhelming feelings of failure and despair warred with his resolve to find her. Sleep evaded him most nights and only came when he could ride no further. Calum forced him to eat, despite his lack of appetite, and he wouldn't have ever gotten this far had it not been for his brother's care.

"I know Gawain has her. I'm certain of it. I believe she is alive and I've come here to implore, beg, demand or whatever necessary for you and your clansmen to take up the search with me. I fear the longer this continues, the colder the trail becomes, and the less likely I'll ever find her."

Fergus nodded.

"You have it. Myself, my men, any resources we can add to your own, are yours." Fergus's brow furrowed. "James you've been keeping your search to larger centres and villages?"

"Aye, it seemed most logical."

"Well, my friend, I'm glad you came here. I believe you've been going about this all wrong. Think about it. When we were involved with Gawain, he took great pains to ensure we were never out in plain view. I think your village and town searches have been wasted. He wouldn't keep her in any location where someone could recognize her. He'd keep her somewhere remote. Somewhere she'd never be detected. Hell, I bet he even buys all his provisions at night."

A glimmer of hope crept into James's heart. There was only one problem.

"Scotland's wilderness, though, is bigger than the whole of its cities, towns and villages put together. Where would we start looking for a remote dwelling?"

"Andrew! Bring me the lowland map!"

The boy jumped up to do his laird's bidding. James remembered the last time he'd seen Andrew and Fergus together. Fergus caught James's glance in the boy's direction and smiled.

"The lad stayed away just long enough for me to get over the shock of losing William. He's a smart one. He also came back just when I needed an extra pair of hands."

"I'm sorry for your loss, Fergus. William was a good man and taken from this world far too soon."

James noticed Fergus glance towards a dark haired woman. She dropped her gaze to her lap and Fergus looked away. She must be William's widow, James mused.

"I thank you for your words, MacIntosh. I will avenge William's death, if it's the last thing I do." Fergus frowned as the lass arose and fled the room.

Andrew returned and the table was cleared. The map was spread over the large surface and Fergus pointed to the thick forest all around that region where Gawain had grown up.

"How do you know that?" James asked.

"The rat likes to talk about himself. I asked a lot of questions, unsure if the answers would ever prove useful. Turns out they might be."

"When can you leave?"

"Today. Get some rest. We'll leave after the midday meal. I have some things to attend to before I go. Andrew, get everyone fit for travel, and tell Alice to pack a lot of food."

James and his men returned to their rooms to take advantage of the additional hours to rest. When he returned to the bed chamber, it was with a lighter heart. For the first time in forever he had any hope.

As he had done so often over the past while, he fell to his knees and whispered to his wife. "I'm coming love. Hold on just a little while longer, Aileana. I promise I'll be there soon."

They arrived at Chattan Castle and he sought out Gwen straight away. He found her pacing in the great hall, wringing her hands. His reports to her were faithful upon his return from his sometimes lengthy searches.

He was pleased he could refer to her now as Lady Gwendolyn. He'd been in high spirits when he returned from the MacKay trial, wanting only to find Aileana and make preparations for them to go home to start their life together. He would never forget his words to Gwen when he realized Aileana was missing from the palace.

They tormented him still.

"You left her in the room with Gawain! Why would you do that? Did you wish her taken again? Maybe you know more than you are letting on! Are you working with him? Did you lead him to her? How else would he know we were here?"

Gwen had bowed her head as he fired accusations at her. Two days later, he returned, eyes burning and weary begging forgiveness for his outburst. Gwen had wanted no apology. She told him he was right and that she should have never left her lady's side not even for a moment. He would accept nothing less than to make up for his behaviour and complete lack of trust.

Over the past three months and with the king's assistance, he elevated her status to lady, gave her charge of Chattan Castle in his absence, and provided regular and frequent updates to her on all aspects of his search. He entered the library to find her gazing out toward the back gardens with her back to him. "Lady Gwendolyn, are you well?"

"I am well, my lord. What news have you?"

James smiled. "Good news, hopefully. MacKay and his clansmen have joined in the search and given us information that may prove useful. Tomorrow we make our way to a forested area near the town in which Gawain was raised. Fergus believes he may be holed up in a small dwelling near there.

"I seek you out to ask if you will join us. It has been three months and I have no idea what condition she will be in when we find her."

Gwen's eyebrows lifted.

"Aye. I believe we are that close," he said. "I believe that's where he has her. It makes the most sense. Will you come with us?"

"Aye my lord, of course I will come with you. Thank you, it means a great deal."

James smiled again. They'd grown comfortable and dependent on one another in Aileana's absence and he'd developed a sisterly regard toward her.

"My brother is here. As is Fergus Mackay and some of his men, I thought you'd want to know."

He gave her a sympathetic smile. His brother had feelings for her and when they were together they both appeared strained. He watched Gwen square her shoulders as she gave him a curt nod.

"The evening meal should be ready shortly, my lord. I shall ensure extra places are set."

They left the library together. As they were about to separate, he toward the solar and she toward the kitchens, they met Calum and Fergus.

Gwen spoke first to Fergus. "My lord, I welcome you to

Chattan Castle and thank you for your assistance in searching for its mistress. Laird MacIntosh informs me you may have useful information. We shall be forever in your debt if it be so."

"I am at your service," he said. That was Fergus Mackay: a formidable foe or a devout friend. The man had no in between.

She turned toward Calum. James noticed she did not meet his brother's eyes.

"My lord, I trust your travels find you well. The evening meal will be served soon. I will have one of the kitchen maids come and find you when it is time."

Gwen turned to leave before he could respond which left Calum staring after her.

"Dammit, man," Fergus said. "You act as if you've never seen a beautiful woman before. Stop staring before you embarrass yourself."

James stifled the urge to laugh at Fergus's comment and noted Gwen turned back to look at Calum. Their eyes locked for a moment and what passed between them was filled with unmistakable longing. His heart constricted.

At dawn the next morning the party set out for Peebleshire on horseback. Gwen admitted to James travelling this way was like a dream to her. She said it made her feel alive. James hadn't wanted the carriage to slow them and was relieved when Gwen agreed to ride instead.

At Chattan Castle, he chose a young grey mare for Gwen he had only purchased two days prior to the trip to Edinburgh and now understood to whom she should belong. It became yet another gift from James to Gwen, one accepted without hesitation. They shared a silent moment of mutual respect, affection, and hope for the return of the woman they both loved beyond measure.

James himself was in better spirits since being reunited with

Arion. Fergus had returned him to James before they left MacKay House and teased when James stroked the horse's snout. "Would you like to be alone?"

James remembered the comment and it made him smile as he stroked Arion's thick neck. He mounted the magnificent animal and broke into a heavy gallop long before the rest had even mounted.

The party rode hard southward and followed various well worn roadways. Some were in good condition while others were no more than a footpath through thick brush. James stayed ahead of everyone else. It was difficult enough to hold his focus and he couldn't abide idle chatter.

Late on the second day, though they made good time, he realized they wouldn't make it to Peebles before days 'end so needed an overnight stop. They located an inn and settled in for the evening meal.

Most of Fergus's and James's men went to question the patrons of the local taverns while James, Fergus, Calum and Gwen shared a much needed meal in the small, cozy room. After a while, one of Fergus's men returned and was rather anxious.

"You'd better come hear this," he said. "Colin has gotten himself into a bit of a ruckus with a man who claims to have seen Gawain."

James was on his feet and out the door with Fergus following tight behind. When they located Fergus's clansman, Colin, the man he'd been speaking with had already slipped away. Colin recounted the information he'd acquired and another spring of hope burst inside James. The man had remembered someone of Gawain's description. It was the thin frame and twisted mouth that pegged him. James's fist twitched in memory of the encounter. The connection was enough. He couldn't afford to waste one precious moment.

When James returned to the inn, he discovered Gwen and Calum embracing. Might the storm have passed between them? James hoped so. He cleared his throat. The interruption brought a flush to Gwen's cheeks. Aye, they had turned a corner.

"I have some information placing Gawain in Peebles just after Aileana was taken." It sounded fantastic to his ears even as he spoke the words. "I ride tonight and I would like you both to ride with me."

Calum turned to look at James the moment he'd mentioned Gawain's name. "Of course we'll go with you." Calum turned back to Gwen, took her face in his hands and kissed her.

James had to turn away lest someone see the sadness that swept over him. Imagining Aileana so close threatened his focus. But what if she wasn't? This was the nearest they'd come to a lead since she'd disappeared.

He never experienced pain like he had that day. After their night together and their lovemaking that morning, he was a king with the world at his feet, never mind an earl's title. Nothing, no pleasure of possession or previous experience, could match the joy that flooded him when he was with her.

A part of him knew she was still alive, but he still imagined the horrors she would have endured with Gawain. James pushed those terrible thoughts away like so many times before. He was close to finding her at last. He forced himself to believe it.

Gawain had been there. The man had described him well enough and indicated he travelled alone which would be make sense considering he would have kept her out of sight. Of all the places they'd searched during these last months, no one ever remembered seeing him before. There was promise.

James readied Arion, thankful he'd had at least a two hour rest. He would have to ensure they use the horses as little as possible the next day which shouldn't be a problem since most of Peebles could be searched on foot. He dared to hope he would find someone in that town who had seen Gawain. The tavern owner assured them the road to the town was good. James intended to see it with his own eyes by daybreak.

Fergus was tight to his heels and declared his intention to fight side by side with him if necessary. Who knew what they would find once they reached Peebles? James was grateful Fergus was determined to be a part of whatever they found.

He thought of Calum and Gwen. Their kiss brought fresh images of Aileana to his mind. He needed to find her and God help Gawain Chattan if she was harmed.

Their timing was perfect. Just as the first grey streaked across the sky, Peebles came into view. James stopped on the edge of town to determine which direction to go. He dismounted and walked through the main street stopping in front of a tavern with a low light in the window and a sign indicating there were rooms available. It was not his usual type of establishment, but something told him it was a good place to start.

Before James entered the place, he tied up his horse and looked around. He could feel something, some pull he couldn't explain - she was near, there was no doubt about it.

Chapter Twenty-One

When Aileana's eyes fluttered open, she discovered him staring, so close he startled her.

"Where were you last night?" she asked. "I woke to find you gone. I thought you might have been taken!" He didn't look pleased by her onslaught of questions.

"My love, do not distress yourself," he said. "I often go into the town late at night to make contact with the men who are keeping an eye out for your uncle. You sleep so sound, you've never noticed my trip each sennight. I dare not travel there in the daytime in case I am seen."

He left her alone at night? She wasn't sure she was happy about being here on her own, unprotected. Why hadn't he told her this before?

"Do you really think he'll find us here?"

"I'm not willing to take any chances in that regard," he said.

Gawain moved to the stove and a pot containing what smelled like pottage. She clutched the quilts as she tried to reason out his secrecy.

When he turned around, she caught a dangerous flash in his eyes and his sideways grin. As she watched him, uneasiness settled into the pit of her stomach. She was not satisfied with this whole situation, but she couldn't put her finger on why.

She arose from her bed and moved to the small clothes chest in the corner, taking out fresh undergarments and a clean woollen dress. She couldn't bathe or change in front of him because of that same nagging feeling preventing her from intimacy with him.

"I believe I shall bathe this morning. Will you stoke the fire for me?"

Gawain nodded and moved about the cottage as if unaware of her discomfort. Aileana collected her clothes and made her way outside and toward the back to where a rough path led to a stream which formed into a small pool. It was perfect for one person to wash in. *Or two lovers.* Where had that thought come from? She didn't imagine herself and Gawain there together. Who then?

Her previous night's dream floated into her thoughts. The man seemed so familiar. She was safe and happy with him, but who was he? The kiss they'd shared was natural and sent fresh excitement through her. Was he someone she once knew? A shiver ran down her back as a slight breeze brought her back to the present. The chill encouraged her to rinse and dress.

When she returned to the cottage, Gawain was no longer there. She assumed he was collecting more wood. The fire she'd requested crackled and spread warmth which enveloped her. She moved to the hearth to begin the task of finger-combing out her long hair all the while staring into the fire.

Slow moving images formed in her mind. Through the mist a horse thundered toward her, but she couldn't see the rider. A casket contained the body of a dead man, the same as in her dream the previous night. She saw him from another time, holding a little girl's hand who cried. A woman dressed in servant's clothes came out of the mist. Her face was kind and ever smiling with dark hair and hazel eyes. They laughed together.

She sat near the fire, transfixed, until it was almost gone. She had so many questions. If Gawain would perhaps describe her uncle and others she might place some of the faces. She had an overwhelming feeling her uncle was the man she saw in the casket, yet they ran from him. If her uncle was dead, what then? Could they go home?

Aileana braided her hair. She was desperate for answers and went looking for Gawain. She was familiar with the area and would locate him without trouble. These questions couldn't wait and the answers might be able to help her piece together the broken fragments of her memory.

A small thrill rushed through her when she thought of the remote possibility that these were actual memories and not some muddled fantasy. She would not dwell too much on the handsome man from her dream. How unfortunate if he was real and she a married woman?

Bright green above from the canopy created by the dense forest and dark brown earth below, Aileana explored the entire area. She found the place where they collected firewood and followed a path they used to collect berries. She searched every part of the wood she was familiar with, but was unable to find him anywhere.

Upon retreating toward the cottage, she heard voices. Aileana scanned the area and noticed two men in the distance through the trees. She didn't know if she should make herself known or not. Her thoughts returned to Gawain's dangerous expression earlier that day which brought back the uncomfortable feeling in the pit of her stomach. Her instincts told her to keep quiet, but her curiosity was intense. She crept closer, doing her best to remain unseen and hid behind the large trees. As she inched toward Gawain and the stranger, she overheard part of the conversation.

"And your man is certain, the MacIntosh and the MacKay

travel south together?" Gawain asked.

Aileana sized up the man to whom the question was put. He was larger than Gawain and his rotten, toothy smile made him appear unfriendly; almost menacing. The hairs on the back of her neck stood up as she watched them and listened for his answer.

"Aye, I'm certain. I don't know what changed the direction of his search. We thought he'd given up when he headed north but it turns out he went straight to the MacKay. The next day they all headed out with a large party headed due south. With the roads he's taking, by our accounts he'll be in the Peebles any time now."

"And your source, it's reliable?"

"As reliable as any message carrier can be. If you're leaving, I'd do so now."

"And go where?" Gawain asked. "If he's got MacKay on his side that means he has more resources. He already has a healthy spread of the King's Guard keeping an eye out in the larger centres. As I see it, as long as I'm travelling with her, I'll be found."

"What'll you do with her?"

"You leave that to me. I grow tired of her questions and whining. I'm sure I can find a hole big enough to bury her in."

Gawain and the man shared a sickening laugh as Aileana put her hand over her mouth to stop from gasping out loud.

"Well you had better bury her deep. I'm surprised he's still searching for her after three months and hasn't lost interest. Will you need help with her?"

"No, this is something I will take much pleasure in doing myself. You better make yourself scarce for the next little while. When I'm finished here, I plan to go further south myself. I'll see to it her body is never found. As for me well, I have many places I can go where they'll never find me."

"Farewell, Gawain Chattan."

The two men clapped each other on the shoulder before parting. Gawain walked a few steps and stopped, looking in her direction. As he scanned the area, she did not breathe or move. A deer stepped onto the path just ahead of him, causing him to shrug his shoulders and continue on his way.

Aileana remained undetected and when they were both long gone, she crept over to where they stood to find a faint path leading in opposite directions. One way led back to the cottage, which was the path Gawain had taken. The other must lead to Peebles. She took a mental note of where the path was before moving away from it to find someplace safe to think.

She reviewed the conversation between the two men. Gawain was planning to murder her, but why? Why when he claimed to have rescued her? Wasn't she better off returning to her uncle? Had Gawain lied to her? How much of it was untrue? She buried her head in her hands in frustration. If only she could remember something.

Aileana's thoughts shifted and turned and more than once she almost grasped something important. Her uncle - he was the key to the whole puzzle. Was he after her? Or was he, as her dream suggested, already dead?

"MacIntosh."

Aileana heard herself say the name out loud knowing it meant something to her. Was the man in her dream the MacIntosh? Was he the man Gawain said her uncle was going to marry her off to? Aileana's head started to pound from the dozens of unanswered questions.

There was one question, however, she needed answered. Where would she go? The town they mentioned was the only place she could think of. She didn't know the way and prayed to God the path she had chosen would take her there.

The sun was high in the sky which meant she had plenty of

daylight left. She moved towards the path and heard something faint. A voice. She gave a moment's pause and heard it again. It was louder this time and unmistakable.

Gawain was calling her name!

Aileana located the path and ran as fast as she could go in the opposite direction away from him. She ran until she could no longer feel her legs. The path went on forever with little to distinguish one part from another.

Just how deep into the woods had they been?

As the sun set, she happened upon a clearing and noticed horses tied up near a building on the other side of it. She paused behind a large oak tree to catch her breath. Her lungs burned, but her drive to be as far away from Gawain as possible kept her focused ahead. Looking around, she walked toward the building under the cover of the trees, hoping someone might help her.

Once on the other side she could see more of the town a little further along. Gawain could just as easily take the same path to the town. She needed to find a good hiding spot to figure out what to do.

She scanned the town as best as she could from the trees until she spied a tavern. An upstairs room was a perfect place to hide. Aileana cursed. It might have been a great idea if she had any coin. She was about to go to the tavern anyway and appeal to the owner when the man Gawain had been conversing with came out through the door.

She hid behind a small building to ensure she couldn't be seen and in doing so discovered an elderly woman who had been watching her from behind her home.

The woman approached her with her palms facing out.

"Hush lassie, that one there is bad and no mistake," the woman said. "If 'tis a hiding spot you need I can help you." She motioned her head in the direction behind her. "Quietly lass, follow me."

She had no alternative but to follow this strange woman. The two walked behind a couple more houses before ducking inside a smaller one. The old woman ushered Aileana into a sitting room and motioned her to a well-worn chair.

"Now lassie, I know fear when I see it. You're safe in this place, my Iain and I will make sure of it. These are dangerous times dear. You know you shouldn't be about on your own don't you? My name is Shauna Campbell. You could start by telling me yours."

Her words caught in her throat at the mention of the name Iain. An image flashed across her mind, not just one but many, dozens of the same man. The man in the coffin, Aileana could see him in all sorts of places, each time looking at her and smiling, always smiling. Her uncle's name was Iain! She loved him and he wouldn't hurt her for the world.

"Are you all right, love? You look as though you've seen a ghost."

"I—I'm sorry. You're kind to help me. My name is Aileana. I'm sorry that's all I can tell you."

"I understand dear, you don't have to tell me all your secrets. It's just that you looked so afraid outside. Tell me dear, are you in trouble?"

"Yes, I mean no, I mean, I don't know."

"Well that's a start isn't it?"

"You don't understand. I know my name is Aileana because he's been calling me that. I have no idea what I was called before that. I fell, or at least that's what he told me. I don't actually know what happened. I woke up in a cottage just back there in the wood and he told me we hid from my uncle but I keep dreaming about him and in my dreams he's a kind man."

"Love, you're going to have to slow down. I want you to stay right here. I'm going to go fetch my Iain and we'll try to help you with this."

Aileana was afraid to be left alone. This woman could expose her. She had no idea who to trust.

"Ahhh I see what you're thinking." The old woman touched her shoulder. "Listen well, dear. You're safe here, as safe as any dwelling in this town except the one I saw you watching. I'll be back in a quick minute. Do you ken?"

Aileana nodded, what choice did she have? While Shauna was gone, she explored her surroundings. The humble dwelling was comfortable and welcoming, and under different circumstances she could feel at ease here. She looked around the room with its humble decorations. What did her home look like?

"There she is. And a fantastic tale she's telling to be sure," Shauna said.

An elderly and hobbling Iain shuffled into the room and sat next to her. After sizing up his new guest he grabbed a knitted quilt and placed it over her shoulders.

"You'd better stoke the fire, love. I think she's got herself a good chill out there today. Now dear, why don't you start from the beginning and tell us everything you can remember."

True gentleness rested in his eyes. It was easy to take them both at their word as she recounted all she could remember or was told by Gawain.

Quite some time later after much discussion, they led her to a small undecorated chamber with a bed. She settled down onto it and drifted off. Her dreams were filled with images of her uncle, a kind man who was dead and unable to save her from the clutches of Gawain Chattan.

Aileana awoke some time later to the most delicious smell. Rising from her bed, she made her way out into the main section of the small house. Shauna and Iain were there waiting for her with a full spread of eggs, cured boar, warm fresh loaf, and hot mead. Aileana was famished.

"Well come on dear, you look like you could use a good meal on those bones."

It was like she hadn't eaten in months. The morning meal smelled so good. She heaped mounds of food onto her plate and noticed Iain nodding to his wife.

"What? What is it? Has something happened?"

"Hush, lass, let me collect my thoughts before I begin. I went to see the sheriff earlier this morning to ask some advice on how to help you. I recounted your tale as well as my memory would serve. He stopped me mid sentence and I didn't know what to make of it. He told me that James MacIntosh is here in Peebles and had just left him. Turns out he and his party travelled all night to get here."

Aileana shook her head. Who was James MacIntosh?

"Yes I see. I'm getting ahead of myself. Where do I start? The story you told me was different so I want to get this right. Laird MacIntosh was betrothed to an Aileana Chattan through an arrangement between the man and her Uncle Iain. It seems the uncle died and his last wish was for the lass to be married to that chief. They were married at Linlithgow Palace in Edinburgh three months ago. He, the MacIntosh, appeared at a trial for Fergus MacKay at Edinburgh Castle and when he returned to the palace where they'd been staying, he learned his wife had been taken.

"The man was convinced she'd been taken by Gawain Chattan, a distant cousin of hers who expected to inherit the uncle's estate and marry her. This part may come as a shock, lass, if the rest of it has not. It turns out, the MacIntosh had good cause to be sure this Gawain had captured her because he'd done it before, but she had come away from that first time unscathed."

Aileana's hands moved to her face. She stroked her forehead and covered her mouth as she listened. If true, it meant everything Gawain had said was a lie. Which tale should she believe?

"I told the sheriff your story. We compared yours and the one he was told and we think you must be this Aileana Chattan, lately married to James MacIntosh, Earl of Moray and chief of his clan no less. The sheriff said he'd like to come here to speak with you himself. He'll make his own judgment whether or not to hand you over to anyone. He wanted me to assure you of that, lass, you'll not be forced to go with this or any other man if you choose not to."

Her head was about to burst. It was too much for her to take in without any memories to confirm if any of it was true. She put her head in her hands and sobbed.

"I don't know what to think, or what it is I must do."

She must place considerable weight on what she overheard Gawain plotting, though. It was enough for her to run away from him, but who was this other man? The MacIntosh? What did she know of him? Could he be telling the sheriff a made up tale meant to draw her out?

"Come lass, let's get you cleaned up. You'll have a visitor here in an hour and we need you looking decent," Shauna said.

One part of Iain's account struck her. "Iain? I've one question."

"Aye, what was it?"

"Where is he? This Laird MacIntosh, where is he right now?"

Iain glanced at his wife for a moment before answering.

"He's at an inn across the way. Don't worry though, he doesn't know you're here. The sheriff assured me no one would hear about you until he had the opportunity to see you for himself."

The room spun around her. Shauna led her into the back room so she could lie down again for a bit. While she lay there, she thought about the story. She tried to remember something, anything, but instead her head pound harder.

Shauna left the room and returned a short time later with a simple but beautiful cream coloured gown. She helped Aileana up and out of her tattered woollen dress and fit her into it.

"My daughter, you see is a wonderful seamstress. This was a gown she'd made a long time ago and must have forgotten it when she packed up to move into her own home with her new husband. Now there's a fine gentleman if I ever saw one, you know one time—"

Shauna prattled on about her daughter and as she did so the image formed of a young woman working on the most exquisite blue gown. She strained to picture the full image of it and realized it was a wedding dress, the most beautiful one Aileana had ever seen.

"Dear, are you all right?"

"Oh, yes, I'm fine thank you. I sometimes drift off like that. I don't know if I'm imagining something or remembering something."

She was excited by the new image, but frustrated that she was unconnected to it.

Shauna paused as she tried to fit the dress around Aileana's frame.

"Oh dear, I can only imagine what that must feel like. There, you're all ready except this stubborn clasp at the back. It doesn't seem to want to close up. And here I thought you were the exact same size as my daughter."

The floor rushed up to meet Aileana. She was in a large room surrounded by servants busying themselves, In the centre of the room, stood a woman in a stunning dress. The seamstress made small adjustments before turning the woman in the dress toward the mirror. Aileana saw her reflection and gasped.

She came to with a start and a concerned Iain and Shauna

hovering over her.

"I don't think she's fit to see anyone. I'll go and send him away."

"No, wait, don't leave. I promise I'm fine. I want to meet him."

Iain sputtered a bit, but didn't disagree. He left the small bedroom to sit with the sheriff.

"How often do you faint dear?"

"Not a lot, only when I get a real flash or an image of someone."

"Hmmm. And you get sick?"

Aileana nodded.

"And how long have you known you're pregnant?"

"Awhile."

She had realized a while ago. She somehow knew through instinct now that the babe didn't belong to Gawain. A fleeting sense to her then, it was a relief to her now. She couldn't process it any further than that. Who the father of this child was at this point was still a mystery.

"I see. That certainly complicates things doesn't it?"

The two women proceed to the sitting room. Aileana was surprised by the sight of the man to whom she was introduced as the sheriff of Peebles. Malcolm MacDougal did not have the imposing countenance of a sheriff. He was quite stout and when he stood for introductions Aileana found he was no taller than she.

"Good morning to you, lass. My name is MacDougal. I'm pleased to make your acquaintance. Please sit and tell me everything you remember. Don't tell me about any dreams you may have had. I just want to hear about anything you're certain of."

She did as she was asked and told of waking in a cottage with blood soaked cloths on her head, of Gawain's care, and her early vertigo when moving about. Aileana told him every detail she could remember right down to how often they'd picked berries and cooked.

When she was done, MacDougal didn't speak right away, but when he did it was with caution.

"You've a vivid memory but it only goes back to a certain point. Gawain told you that you fell from a horse and that's how you hurt your head?"

"Aye."

"Well, you had a serious bump of some sort. And you don't know how long you were unconscious?" he asked.

"No, I'm sorry I don't. But I remember him saying he was relieved when I finally woke."

"Now that we've established what we know, let's talk a little about what we do not. Have you dreamt or had visions of certain people?"

"Oh aye! There are three people in particular I've been dreaming about. One, I believe, was my Uncle Iain. I've seen him in a coffin which leads me to believe he may be deceased."

MacDougal said nothing so Aileana continued.

"I also dreamt about a woman with dark hair and hazel eyes wearing servant's clothes. She appears friendly, but I cannot tell any more of her."

"Aye. Go on."

"And there's a man. He's not old or young. And he appears to know me well."

Her cheeks grew warm and she lowered her head.

"Please describe him for me."

"Well, he's tall. He has brown hair and green eyes and he's quite handsome. He wears a brooch centreed with a wild cat and surrounded with rubies. In my dream he kisses me like we're lovers."

No one acknowledged her embarrassment.

MacDougal arose from his seat and moved to the window. He paused there for a few minutes before turning to Aileana.

"I must admit, in all my years I've never encountered a situation quite like this. Up until you described James MacIntosh, I was about to say you should consider taking some time before meeting him. However, I am now quite convinced of his account and can do no more here than to urge you to see him."

Aileana's belly flooded with tremors. Did he just confirm that James MacIntosh was the man in her dreams? That meant they *were* married and she *was* taken! What had Gawain done to her to make her forget so much?

Meeting her husband was nerve racking and the absurdity of it was not lost on her. She knew she must see him and asked those present if they would come with her and they agreed.

"So 'tis Lady MacIntosh we should call you is it? Well, Lady MacIntosh I have a suggestion and if you are in agreement with it, I believe it might make this unusual circumstance a little easier."

Iain suggested MacDougal go and tell MacIntosh she was safe, but more importantly that she may not know him. They all agreed it was a good idea and the sheriff left at once.

The three sat without speaking as they awaited his return. Aileana tried hard to maintain some composure despite her fragile emotional state. What should she say to this man? She assessed he at least wanted her back since he had been looking for her, but she was desperate to find out what the nature of their marriage had been. Was theirs a cordial relationship, did they share any common interests, how well did they know one another—were they in love? Before she could assume answers to any of those questions, MacDougal returned.

"He knows. It was all I could do to convince him not to tear over here. Aileana, your husband is waiting for you."

Chapter Twenty-Two

Fergus and Calum had to restrain James from MacDougal. The man's face was ashen. James wanted to squeeze the words from his lips for they would not come fast enough. His mind could only register two words. Aileana. Found.

"You'll do more harm to her! I say man, you must listen to me!" MacDougal said; his tone insistent.

MacDougal shifted his attention to Gwen. "Are you with these men? Can you talk some sense into this one?" he said, motioning toward a fuming James.

"Aye, stranger I can try, but you must first explain why he wants to see your insides spilled upon the floor."

"My name is MacDougal, I'm the local sheriff. A man came to me early this morning with your story. I've come here to tell him that I believe I have found the woman you seek."

Gwen approached him and grasped his shoulders. "Well, why didn't you say? Come now, where is she? Why isn't she with you? Come on man speak!" Gwen shook the man hard enough to make his teeth chatter.

James experienced a small satisfaction at the sound.

Calum released his hold on James and went to Gwen. He grasped her arms and turned her to face him. "She has been found, but she is damaged. We may have to go slowly with her.

She's confirmed to MacDougal here that she has been with Gawain these past three months. She appears unable to remember anything from before her time with him, though. She's safe and is with a couple who found her just yesterday. It seems she was running away from Gawain. If we all tear off to where she is, who knows what it may do to her? She has shown some signs of remembering, but it may be a while before she regains her former self, if she ever does."

Hearing the news again from his brother's lips made James want to hit something. Gwen moved toward him with tears in her eyes and embraced him.

"She has been found and that's all that matters. Do you hear me? She has been found!"

He heard her and returned the embrace, though he couldn't speak and his eyes stung.

Gwen released James and forced him to look into her eyes. "This is why you brought me here, remember? I can help with this. We can all face this together."

James nodded and Gwen faced MacDougal again. Her voice trembled. "You say she cannot remember anything from before her time with Gawain. What has she told you about her time with him? It would be good of you to tell us." Gwen pointed her thumb towards James. "Don't you think it best if he hears it here before she arrives? Believe me, if Gawain has harmed Aileana it will be better if she doesn't see her husband's reaction."

MacDougal swallowed.

"It appears, apart from whatever injury befell her initially, he's not laid a hand on her. She appears in good health. She said this Gawain told her they were married and running from her uncle who was going to marry her off to some barbarian. I can't imagine who he meant."

James grunted.

"We've a physician here in town, but I'm certain this is not his specialty. You may want to consider some of the surgeons in Edinburgh, however, I shall summon him straight away, in any case. Shall I retrieve her?"

James looked to Gwen and nodded his approval. He still could not speak.

"Aye," Gwen said for him.

Malcolm MacDougal heaved a sigh of relief before he left the inn. James paced, Calum wrapped his arms around Gwen and they waited.

"I think we should all at least sit down so we don't frighten the wits out of the poor woman when she arrives," Fergus said. Calum raised his eyebrows.

"What?" Fergus raised his hands in the air.

Gwen smiled. "I have a better idea. We should let James have the first few moments alone with Aileana before we all descend upon her."

James smiled at her in thanks. Calum, Gwen and Fergus left the room. The silence allowed him to absorb the information he'd received. In all his imaginings, he never considered she would not know him and had great difficulty understanding what it would mean. Even without the memories, would their attraction to each other still exist?

* * *

Aileana opened the door and stepped inside, followed by Iain, Shauna, and MacDougal. She looked all around as she moved into the dark tavern. Her eyes took a few moments to accustom to the difference in lighting.

Then she saw him.

She recognized him and gasped when she locked eyes with this stranger she must call husband. Her first impression sent sharp tingles down her spine as she realized it was the same handsome man from her dreams. She was drawn to him. He didn't move, allowing her to take all the steps.

As she drew closer, she could see the physical signs of fatigue. He looked much older than in her dreams. Before she could help herself, she reached her hand up to touch his face and viewed the lines and scratchy beard. She searched every last inch of it before looking into his eyes. She couldn't blink or move and her breath caught in her throat. An image floated up of them dancing together. She raised her hand. He did the same and pressed his palm against hers.

They stood like that for long moments. They belonged together. He was her husband.

"My name is Aileana. I believe I am your wife."

Aileana's whispered declaration caused James's breath to rush out through his teeth. He scooped her up into his arms and swung her around in a crushing embrace. They laughed together at his outburst.

He put her back down and smiled. His eyes held neither cruelty nor deceit. All would be well. She remembered enough to be with him and if they had to start all over, well she would be satisfied. She watched his eyes mist until light tears trickled down his face.

"I can't believe you're here," he whispered. "I don't care if you don't remember everything. We can start from the beginning if you like. I'll even court you again if you wish."

His smile was infectious prompting her to laugh out loud at his suggestion. This man could charm any woman.

"May I ask you a question?" She was a little wary about asking, but if she was going to trust him, how he answered would be helpful. "Were we, I mean, are we in love?"

His answer was simple and prompt. "Yes. Very much so."

She smiled and he embraced her again and held her tight. Here, she was safe.

In the other room an impatient voice called out. "Can we come in?"

James laughed again. "Aileana, there are others here anxious to see you. Are you well enough?"

She was so happy at that moment she was certain she would have agreed to just about anything. "Of course," she said.

Three people entered the room. A giant hulk of a man moved to her first and introduced himself as Fergus MacKay. Something about the look of him was familiar, yet she was unable to place it. Barbarian? No.

A second man appeared and introduced himself as James's brother, Calum. He embraced her much longer than James appeared comfortable with and broke them apart. "Hug your own woman," James said.

James's comment brought a chuckle from both Calum and the woman standing behind him. The third figure from her tormented dreams moved into view.

"I've seen you. I mean, I've dreamt about you. Are we well acquainted?"

The woman nodded, tears filling her eyes. As they spilled onto her cheeks, she rushed into Aileana's arms. To her surprise, Aileana embraced her back.

"I am Gwen MacGregor, my lady. Your maid and dearest friend," she whispered. "I've missed you so much." Gwen sobbed into her hair.

Aileana pulled back from the embrace and looked at all the eyes fastened on her. She caught a flash of Fergus's brooch pin and focused hard on it.

The room went dark.

She was in a small crofter's cottage with several men and one wearing a similar pin. She was tied to a chair and a man placed a woollen blanket over her.

She awoke sometime later in a warm, soft bed covered with many blankets and James sitting beside her and speaking to another man she didn't recognize. Her eyelids were too heavy to keep open so she closed them again.

"The shock of seeing everyone at the same time was too much, but I assure you she appears in full health. The bairn appears to be growing fine as well and that may add to the fainting."

"A babe?" James's voice cracked.

"You weren't aware of her pregnancy?"

"Can you tell? I mean, do you know how long she's been with child?"

"I can't say exactly, but I would suspect about three months."

Boots hit the floor and moved across the room. Aileana opened her eyes a crack as Gwen entered. The mattress dipped as the woman sat on the bed and stroked her hair. The motion was soothing.

"How is she? How is she really?"

"Well, as I just informed her husband, besides being pregnant, I would say her body is perfectly normal."

Aileana's eyes opened a little seeking James. His fists were clenched and his teeth bared. He looked like hell.

"Three months. You don't have to ask, I'm guessing you didn't know either. The lass has been through an enormous ordeal to be sure, but I see no reason why she won't make a full recovery in time. It appears by all your accounts she may have only recently begun remembering events and people. That's because she's had no exposure to anything which could trigger her memory. Now that she has all of you in her life again, it should only be a matter of time before most of it comes back."

"How much time do you think it will take?" Gwen asked. James still said nothing.

"There's no way to know that. It could be months or years. Some parts of her memory may never come back, but as I said, her prospects are good."

The physician left the room and she fell back into a deep sleep. When she woke again the sky was much darker and James was nestled into her.

"Do you want me to sit up?" he asked.

"No, you're warm, please stay."

"Aileana, I know you don't remember much of our time together but you remember me right?"

"Aye, I think so. I dreamed of you. I dreamed you kissed me and we walked with our daughter. Where is she? She's so beautiful and I want to see her."

His brows drew together.

"My love we don't have any children. A babe grows in your belly. Maybe it is of that child you've dreamed."

There was sadness in his expression and she anticipated what he was thinking.

"Gawain never touched me. Not once. I don't know why he didn't bed me, nor do I care as I am glad he didn't. He convinced me I was his wife and if he'd insisted, I couldn't have refused him. I knew I didn't want him, especially after I started dreaming about you. The child growing in my belly is yours."

She wiped her tears away as she told him all about her time with Gawain. She wanted him to know every detail, but she needed him to know that she had not been invaded by another man.

"Hush, love, you don't owe me any explanation. You're not to blame for anything that happened. 'Tis I who was careless. But I will make you a promise. I shall never be careless with you ever again. You, our child and our future children will always be protected. This I vow to you."

"I trust you." She poured conviction in those words. She trusted him. Everything made more sense when he was near.

She inhaled and caught his scent of leather and her insides flipped over. Though she did not remember all of their time together, she *knew* him or rather, her body did.

"Will you kiss me?" she asked.

He raised his eyebrows. "Aileana, you don't have to do this. We don't have to do anything until you're ready."

"I know, but I need to know something and the only way I can find out is if you kiss me."

He moved his face to just inches above hers, turned and brushed his lips against hers. Aileana's lips parted as she responded to his touch. He pressed his warm mouth onto hers and wrapped both arms around her, pulling her closer.

She curled her hands around his neck and sank her fingers into his hair as she pulled him even deeper into the kiss. She had to find out if it was the same. When his tongue stroked hers, all doubt fled. James MacIntosh was her dream, her fantasy, and her husband.

She awoke alone the following morning, remembering his arms around her all through the previous night. She frowned, not wanting to be away from him even for a few minutes.

Aileana dressed and descended the staircase toward the tables in the tavern. When she arrived, she discovered several men including James, Calum, Fergus and MacDougal together with several clansmen and members of the King's Guard engaged in heated discussion and hovering over some sort of drawing spread out on one of the tables.

"I say we re-trace her steps, it makes the most sense and is the only way we can hope to find any clue as to which direction he may have gone," James said, pounding his fist on the table.

She froze in place as she comprehended the context of his statement. James intended to seek out Gawain. Her heart thumped hard in her chest as the room spun all around her, Aileana took a step forward to protest, but her words would not be voiced.

"The old lady said Aileana had reacted when she saw the man, and later told the couple she had seen him conversing with Gawain. We must find him also. He may know where Gawain would go."

"James." She couldn't say another word. Her fear consumed her. She was about to faint. He must have sensed it too because he caught her before she fell.

"Aileana, you look unwell, you shouldn't be up. Here, let me help you back to your bed."

"No! You're planning to go after him aren't you? You're planning to confront him and after that, God knows what."

She feared Gawain's unpredictable, violent nature, but she also feared being separated from James.

Calum stepped toward them. "Aileana, he must be found, he'll not stop coming for you and he cannot be permitted to get close to you again. If it's confrontation you're worried about, we intend to find him and escort him to Edinburgh to stand trial. We have no intention of harming him any further than necessary to secure him."

Her gaze never left James's face—she saw a different possibility there.

He was a man of integrity and different from Gawain in every way. If he were to kill someone in the heat of battle that would be something he could live with. But, if he were to seek out a man for the sole purpose of harming him, no matter the provocation, that would be something he would never get over. James could not be responsible for Gawain's death, for it would always sit between them. She might not have memories of his life, but she was certain she knew this man better than she knew herself.

"Laird MacKay?"

Fergus displayed mild surprise.

"Lady MacIntosh."

"Is it not true that you owe my husband a life debt?" She sensed James's unease. James would never claim the debt Fergus owed him. She would claim if for them both.

"Aileana, no." James said.

"It's the only way."

"Yes, my lady, it is true," Fergus said. "Your husband saved my life and those of my clansmen. I owe him a life debt, possibly more than one."

Fergus appeared to understand what she asked. James did too but wore an expression of defiance.

"I don't want you to leave me," she said.

James released her and ran his fingers through his hair in frustration. His eyes narrowed and pained, he shook his head and stormed out of the tavern.

Aileana had no words to offer any of them, she wanted Gawain found, aye, but she wanted to protect her husband as well. James was not a killer and she would not allow him to become one. She wasn't concerned about the level of violence any of the other men might use since they didn't have the same motivation.

Fergus returned to the map and the table. He studied all the roadways leading into and out of the town. He confessed he could not see the path Aileana had described but at least knew where it led. When he had gained all he could from the map, he spoke to Aileana.

"I'll find him and make you safe again," Fergus said.

Aileana couldn't thank him. She was torn between putting everyone else in danger for her own safety and knowing Gawain's blood could not be on James's hands.

Fergus nodded to her. He gave explicit instructions as to where they should search. Only MacDougal remained without a task.

"You know this town better than any of us," Fergus said. "Speak with the Campbell couple. Find out what they know about the man Aileana saw speaking with Gawain. If you identify him, find some men here in town and secure him. I'll want to speak with him myself when I return."

Fergus offered Aileana one last look of assurance and left the tavern.

Chapter Twenty-Three

Fergus divided the men into two parties. They headed southwest, then spread out to cover about a mile and a half of terrain. He had assigned Neil Stephenson as leader of the other group, trusting in his ability for stealth better than anyone else.

Aileana's description of the path leading toward the cottage was fairly accurate. Fergus found it with little difficulty and by midday saw the cottage in the distance. Fergus drew his broadsword and crept toward it.

He listened.

Trees rustled, a brook babbled and somewhere close a raven cawed. More than a day had passed since Aileana had escaped and Gawain must have fled by now. No smoke wafted from the chimney and the door was closed.

From what Fergus remembered, this man slithered in and out of places undetected unless you looked hard. He would find him, though. That rodent would get what he deserved.

The debt he owed MacIntosh was great indeed. Were it not for the man's involvement, he'd have spent more than a fortnight in the king's dungeon. Perhaps he'd never see Nessia again. A troubling thought. He'd see her again soon enough and when he did, she'd know she could rely on him to secure a good future. He would do right by her for his brother's sake—

even if it meant marrying her to another. His feelings for her would not serve her best interests. He glanced sideways at her brother, Colin. The man had proven his worth. She'd be proud of him.

Fergus's men surrounded the dwelling. He approached the door and lifted the wooden latch, careful not to make a sound. At first the door proved to be more stubborn and creaked with every inch Fergus demanded of it. Halfway open, it stopped resisting and noiselessly swung open the rest of the way. He peered inside. The place appeared empty.

His shoulders relaxed just as a soft creaking sounded behind him. Fergus turned to see Gawain flying through the air toward him with his blade aimed at Fergus's heart. He had only a split second to react and managed to divert the deadly attack just enough, but still received a deep gash on his left shoulder.

Son of a whore!

Gawain's body struck Fergus and the impact unsettled both for but a second. Gawain steadied himself and lunged at him again with his blade this time aiming at Fergus's throat. Fergus was faster this time and swung his sword down, knocking Gawain's hand away before he could make contact.

The man didn't appear to recognize the immense difference in their size. Gawain swung forward a third time, this time slicing Fergus's right arm, but still could not dislodge his sword. Warm liquid spread down Fergus's arms. When was the last time he'd been cut?

He'd had enough playing around. Fergus's left fist crashed into Gawain's face sending him sailing through the air and landing the smaller man on the ground just outside the cottage.

"Stay down, lad, or you will die!"

Gawain's eyes were wild and he appeared beyond reasonable thought. The daft man didn't take Fergus's advice and leapt forward one more time with his blade again aimed at Fergus's heart. The distance between them allowed Fergus time to counter the attack and his sword came down with a fierce blow on Gawain's right wrist. The loud crack was followed by his blade clattering to the ground.

Gawain let out a tortured howl, fell to his knees cradling his wounded limb.

"Stay down or you will die!"

Gawain's face twisted as he pulled another blade from a strap on his leg and plunged it toward Fergus who stepped out of the way this time.

Fergus had lost all interest in any further fight. The pathetic sight of the man was sickening. He didn't deserve death, after all the grief he had caused, he deserved to live with it.

"Bind him. Tight!"

Fergus stepped back from the scene for a moment. He looked down to see blood dripping from both sides of him and was rattled by the damage this man had caused him. He leaned against the cottage as his head spun, his body sliding until he sat with his back against the wall and closed his eyes. He'd been in battle many times before and had received never more than a scratch or two. How was it possible this whelp turned out to be so lethal?

When he opened his eyes again, Gawain was secured and one of his men examined the gashes on his shoulders.

"You look unwell," Colin said. "We need to get moving before we lose our light."

"Aye, let's go. I want to be rid of this business and off home."

"Any particular reason you're in such a rush?"

Fergus grinned. "Lowland air makes me sick."

"Sick indeed. Perhaps you are homesick for a certain black-haired lass."

"Your sister has nothing to do with my anxiousness to return home." He had no intention of discussing Nessia with her brother, or anyone else for that matter.

Colin put his hands up in surrender. "Oh aye, Fergus, I believe ye. No need to be defensive."

Colin helped Fergus up and onto his horse to begin the trek back to Peebles. Gawain was tied to a crude litter and carried by two men. He moaned and mumbled all sorts of nonsense. After a few hours of this, combined with Fergus's fatigue, Fergus had endured enough.

"Someone shut him up!"

No one moved to carry out the demand, he was after all, tied to a wooden plank.

"You can do it you know." Gawain spoke his only sane words of the day. "You can kill me. It's what I deserve."

Gawain's sober statement caught Fergus off guard. What he said was true, Fergus could kill him and no one would question it. This was why Aileana hadn't wanted James involved in this capture and she had been right, James wouldn't have resisted. What would Nessia think if Fergus killed a defenceless man?

Fergus stepped toward Gawain and his men stepped out of the way. They knew he was capable of snapping the man's neck like a pheasant bone.

"You don't deserve death," Fergus said. "You deserve no less than to live with what you've done and the knowledge that James and Aileana MacIntosh will live a long and happy life at Chattan Castle."

"Tell Aileana I'm sorry." A tear slid down Gawain's cheek.

* * *

James sat at a table with his head hung low while Aileana paced. He was angry with her still, but she had made the right decision. If she had to live with the consequences of his hurt pride then so be it. The thought of being apart from him made her chest constrict.

Aileana had made a choice. She could either endure his anger or endure his imprisonment. She had made the right choice. Of that she had no doubt.

Fergus swung the door wide, dripping crimson splatters as he entered the tavern and interrupted her inner musing.

"Fergus! Oh! Gwen, get some cloths and water! Hurry!"

Aileana grasped his arms and guided him toward the fire. Once Fergus was seated, Aileana removed his shredded shirt and assessed his wounds. Gwen returned with the items she had requested and Aileana set about cleaning the angry gashes.

"You'd better go get the healer" she said to Gwen. "He's lost much blood and is in need of stitching."

As she examined Fergus's arms, James paced behind them. The day had been torturous for everyone, but she spent hers wondering if James would ever forgive her for denying him his vengeance.

"We found him," Fergus said. "He's secure and here in the town prison."

The weight of many sleepless nights lifted from her body. She turned to James, who would still not meet her gaze, but instead stood frozen staring at the back of Fergus's head. He had not spoken to her since that morning and she found herself searching for the right words to say to him. Fergus found them for her.

"James, you would have killed him. You would have had to. He begged to die."

Aileana watched the conflicted emotions cross James's face before turning back to Fergus and whispering 'thank you' over and over. She was racked with guilt from having asked him to go instead of James.

James was by her side as she finished dressing Fergus's wound. She gave the man a much needed drink of ale and helped him stretch his long legs onto a stool and covered him with a blanket. Fergus was better off sleeping where he was than risk stumbling on the stairs.

James's expression was filled with pain. He shifted his weight and frowned at her. Fine. Let him lament his wounded pride. Gawain was caught and James would not swing for it. That knowledge was enough for her and she would make it enough for him too.

James remained silent, but eventually met his wife's eyes. He nodded once and Aileana rushed into his arms. For a long while they held one another. His forgiveness was worth more than a king's ransom.

The next day, Aileana watched from the tavern window as a wedding procession make its way through the town. Three days had passed since she had been found and she was impatient with her slowly returning memory. She'd recalled bits and pieces of James and Gwen but not as much of Calum. It was enough for her to decide that everyone's lives had been held up long enough because of her, especially with Gawain no longer a threat.

She wanted to go home.

James had insisted they not travel just yet, and she longed for distraction from the intensity building between them. She'd earned his forgiveness and without an immediate threat to her safety, discovered a desire for him without measure. Unfortunately, he was not willing to give in to it. He said it wasn't right.

He wanted her to remember their intimacy before they resumed that part of their relationship, but she experienced an undeniable desire surging through her every time he came near. Wasn't that important too? She'd been denied long enough.

As the bride and groom passed, Aileana stole a glance at James and caught him staring at her. For one brief moment they were the only two in the world.

Many of the men involved in her search left after Gawain was captured, anxious to return to their responsibilities at home. The ones who stayed were those most loyal to Fergus and James. Among those to leave was Colin. His sister, Nessia, Aileana learned, was the widow of the late William MacKay.

"Will you give your sister a message for me lad?" Fergus asked him.

"Of course I will Fergus. You just need to tell me what it is."

Fergus smiled.

"Tell her all is well and I'll return shortly."

Colin grinned at Fergus as he went to do as he was asked.

"Is she the pretty, black-haired lass who couldn't tear her eyes away from you the entire time we were at MacKay House?" James asked.

"She what?"

James laughed and walked away from him. Fergus looked as though he was about to follow and force an explanation, but James had moved into Aileana's embrace for protection. James and Fergus behaved like comrades—brothers.

Aileana looked back toward the street and sighed. James sat beside her and kissed her head while brushing a lock of hair from her face.

"What is it?"

"I keep thinking about a wedding."

"Go on," he said.

"There was a dance?"

"Aye, we danced."

"Take 'er upstairs?"

Her whispered words brought a huge smile to James's face.

"That's right, love. On the night of our betrothal ceremony. One of my clansmen yelled those words."

Aileana was pleased with herself. This memory was special

for with it there was no doubt it was real. All the others had been foggy, but this one was crystal clear.

"You know, in your condition, you shouldn't be out of bed too long." His deep voice rumbled in her ear, sending thrilling shivers down her neck. "I believe I can make a reasonable excuse for us to retire early."

Aileana raised her eyebrows.

"I still think we should give it some more time before we are intimate, but you can always check to see if my kisses are still like they were in your dream."

James nuzzled Aileana's neck as he spoke those words. She was disappointed he still would not make love to her, but was satisfied to be in his arms.

James and Aileana retired to their chamber. He removed her clothing his own and crawled into bed next to her. The heat coming from his body was intoxicating and she sought to absorb more.

"Aileana, what are you doing?" James asked.

She snuggled closer. "Getting warm."

"Aileana, don't," he said as she pressed her firm breasts against him. He looked so serious and worried that she relented and pulled her body back a little from his. Lying together in each other's arms would have to suffice. For now.

"Tell me about our courtship," she said, hoping he would welcome the distraction. She was right. His resulting smile thrilled her. God that man's smile was intoxicating.

"Well, you couldn't keep your hands off me, like now, and I had to relent and marry you," he said.

"That's not possible!"

"It is true, I swear. You were all over me and kissed me whenever you could find the opportunity. You were quite scandalous in your wanton behaviour, Lady MacIntosh. I believe I saved you from a most embarrassing reputation. It was a sacrifice, but I would not see a lady dishonoured."

"Oh indeed! Would not see a lady dishonoured would you? Well aren't you the chivalrous gentleman?"

"Aye, I am. You know I was a virgin on our wedding night," he said, but the gleam in his eye suggested there wasn't likely much truth in his statement.

She cast her eyes downward. What if she never recovered her memories?

"What is it?" James asked.

The concern in his eyes made her heart twist.

"I want to remember," Aileana said.

James tightened his hold on her and she lost herself in his embrace. The scent of his skin, the feel of his hard body, even the steady thud of his heartbeat calmed her.

"Well, maybe I wasn't exactly a virgin," James said.

When Aileana looked back at him it took a split second before they both burst into a gale of laughter. James spent the rest of the night recounting every moment they had shared together, answering questions until they both fell into a deep sleep entwined in one another's arms.

* * *

James intended to make the journey back to Inverness-shire a slow one. He would not consider putting Aileana or their child at further risk for one moment. When they left Peebles, it would be to travel to Edinburgh for a night or two before proceeding further north. James was bent on ensuring Gawain would remain imprisoned this time and planned on pulling a favour from the king. Gawain Chattan would never see the light of day again if James could help it.

His thoughts shifted to the king. As it turned out, the MacDonald's were indeed responsible for the attack on the MacKenzie clan. They had devised a plot with the Sutherlands to do the deed, but it grew more complicated from there. James had learned while the king had been imprisoned in England, Alexander MacDonald had gained much support in the north. It was even suggested that years earlier, opportunities had arisen to return James Stewart to his rightful place as monarch and the Duke of Albany and MacDonald had interfered. In the end, MacDonald had fronted a good deal of the ransom. Who could guess why he later turned on the king?

King James had unravelled the Duke's involvement and the MacDonald's had been quick to provide their reason for targeting MacKay as the villains. MacDonald's younger sister, Elizabeth it turned out, was Fergus's widow.

The only part of the plot that he still wasn't clear was the MacKenzie as the target for the attack. Also, while it was true the MacKay-Sutherland mutual hatred was legendary, how had the MacDonald managed to secure Artair Sutherland's allegiance?

James's head swam with questions. In the end, it didn't matter how the plot had evolved. What mattered was that his friend Fergus had been acquitted, Gawain was locked away for a long time, and he and Aileana could go on with their lives together. His biggest worry was how well she would readjust to her former life.

James had secured a carriage for their travel and watched her rocking body, curled up across from him. Her hair cascaded down across her body like a golden blanket. He longed to touch her again, but he would not take advantage of her that way. Aye, he wanted her so much it was painful, but he wanted all of her, not the just part that only somewhat remembered him. He needed her to remember their love first.

Six months ago, he would have bedded just about any woman on their first acquaintance if she were willing. His Aileana had released him from that unfulfilling life. She had saved him, loved him. He was determined to spend the rest of his life spoiling her far worse than her uncle had. Cherished girl, indeed. His precious wife would never want for anything.

Chapter Twenty-Four

Chattan Castle, near Inverness, Scotland, August 1430

Aileana laughed at the commotion Sheena caused. She understood the woman's wishes and demands, but was surprised at James's reaction. Aileana had been home for a fortnight. Her memories of her intimacies with James had returned, though she hadn't found one spare moment with him to let him know.

She'd arrived at Chattan Castle to her beloved aunt bursting with questions and suggestions. James had taken immediate exception to her behaviour stating it wasn't good for the natural return of Aileana's memory to have so many thoughts pushed at her.

"Pig's poo! The lass needs to be reminded of all the things she's forgotten and then she'll remember!"

James and Sheena had battled it out and came to a mild compromise to go easy. When James wasn't around, however, Sheena produced an old doll or garment from Aileana's childhood.

Aileana was not as affected by all of that as much as she was affected by her home. She had remembered various bits and pieces of her life and was satisfied, for the time being, at the

286

pace of her returning memory.

A sennight ago Aunt Sheena had made a suggestion that even James admitted was sound. She suggested he and Aileana exchange their wedding vows again, hopefully sparking the right kind of memories.

James said he would marry Aileana every day for the rest of her life if it would help her and so he agreed. Aileana needed a little more convincing, though, so James tried to bribe her with a surprise. He'd kept her waiting for ages in their bedroom and made her close her eyes before he entered with it.

When Aileana opened them, the beautiful wedding gown from her visions lay across her bed. She gasped and asked him where he'd found it.

"We were married at Linlithgow Palace, you see, and the young seamstress there made this for you at the queen's request. When I left she insisted I take it with me. It is yours after all."

Aileana walked toward the exquisite gown and grazed her fingers along its luxurious fabric.

"It's not that delicate, believe me," James said in a husky voice.

Aileana pulled him towards her and sealed her mouth over his. James's hands went around her waist and pulled her body close. He hardened against her, causing her insides to coil in anticipation.

"I know I want you. I don't want to wait any longer," she said.

"Please don't. We've been over this. I will not make love to you until you remember. I would feel like I was taking advantage of you and I won't do that. Please understand."

Aileana did understand, she loved him all the more for it, but it didn't change the intensity of desire that flowed through her body every time he was near.

Watching Sheena and James fuss over where the flowers should be placed on the table, Aileana knew she loved them both more than she ever had, or at least more than she ever remembered.

Gwen collected her to dress. They linked arms and walked to Aileana's room to begin the process of putting her into the gown.

"I remember helping you the first time," Gwen said.

"So do I."

"What?"

"I said so do I. I remembered this morning. Yesterday I remembered my wedding night and this morning I remembered preparing for it. Please don't tell Aunt Sheena her plan worked. We'll never hear the end of it."

"So why are you still going through with this? You and James can, you know, disappear and be a married couple again."

Aileana had remembered enough of her previous relationship with Gwen to be comfortable with her usual candour. Both women benefited from it.

"If you could relive the happiest day of your life again just one more time after losing it entirely, wouldn't you?"

"Well, what did your husband say when you told him you'd remembered?"

"He doesn't know. I shall consider it a wedding gift to him."

Gwen smiled at her friend as she continued to help Aileana into the dress.

The women finished their task and proceeded to the chapel near the side of the castle. Gwen walked in first, as maid-of-honour for her dearest friend she positioned herself to the right of the clergy to make room for Aileana.

Many faces passed before Aileana's eyes, memories of people congratulating them on their betrothal, listening to them as they told of raiders nearby and sitting at a feast in a lavish palace miles away.

Aileana saw so much in her mind's eye as she walked up the aisle toward her husband. At last, only one face, the one in front of her—her past, her present and her future. James placed his hands on hers and they exchanged vows.

As they walked back to the castle to where the feast and all her guests waited, James whispered in her ear.

"Thank you for marrying me again."

"Thank you for my dress. And especially for having the buttons stitched back on the bodice."

James stopped and stared into her eyes. She beamed at him.

"There's no way you could know that unless you remembered it."

"I also remember how the buttons were removed in the first place," she said. "I remember taking the dress from you the next morning and what followed. I've been deprived of those, and any new memories like them, for far too long. If it's all the same to you, I'd like my husband back please. All of him."

James and Aileana linked arms and entered the dining hall to address their guests. Perhaps they could skip the meal. She was hungry, but not for food. Sheena intercepted them and insisted they be seated before James had a moment to speak. The food was served and any chance they may have had to sneak away was delayed.

She was polite, but her body was taut with anticipation. When the music started, Aileana knew her chance to escape with her husband was near. They moved to the dance area, took position and moved together. One form made of two bodies. Free flowing heat move from his hand to hers. This was no memory and it turned her blood to fire.

When the dance ended, a wonderful soul in the back cheerfully called out, "Take 'er upstairs!"

James didn't hesitate. He scooped Aileana up in his arms.

"I believe I shall!" His declaration was loud enough for all to hear.

The crowd applauded.

James removed his wife from the staring eyes, up the stairs and to the master chamber formerly occupied by Aileana's uncle and decorated for her and her husband; the Laird and Lady of Clan MacIntosh.

James walked through the doorway and kicked it shut with his foot. He carried her toward the bed and set Aileana on her feet, turning her around to begin the process once again of removing her from her gown. James was about half way through unfastening the tiny buttons when Aileana lost patience.

"Oh, for Heaven sake! Just rip it off!"

He sucked in a breath. "But my love, the servant who made it worked so hard on it. We do her a disservice if we destroy it."

His teasing served to increase her urgency. Reaching around, she grasped the top of the bodice on either side and pulled hard. Satin buttons flew to and fro across the room. She slid out of the rest of her clothing and focused on removing his.

The sight of his naked body stirred her passion to great depths. She was self conscious because her breasts were fuller and her belly slightly rounded from the bairn she carried. James's expression smouldered as he drank in every inch of her. He finished removing his clothes in one sweep and gathered her up to carry her to the bed.

He kissed her jaw, moving down her neck to her breasts, his mouth skimming her heated flesh. He seemed to want to go slow, but she would have none of it. Her body writhed under his, urging his heat closer.

"Will we hurt the babe?" he asked.

"Certainly not. But if you're worried, Gwen told me I can ride you."

James coughed and gasped.

"Ride me?"

Though his words sounded shocked, Aileana watched his body's eager response. His hands were already moving to grasp her hips.

"Aye, ride you like a horse."

He chuckled and kissed her hard on the mouth. She loved the way he touched her new curves. She would never love any man like she loved this one. She might never remember all the moments they'd shared, but she was satisfied that she remembered enough for them to move forward and make new memories.

They moved together as he entered her, clinging to one another as if they were the last people on earth. Their unleashed passion wasn't satisfied until many hours later.

They lay together as the sun rose, gazing into each other's eyes. A tear slid down her cheek.

"What is it?" James asked.

"I want to meet her."

"Who?"

"Our daughter, the little girl in my dream, I want to meet her."

"I'm sure we will." As he spoke his hand moved over her belly.

"But what if this is a boy?"

"Hmmm. Let me think. What could we possibly do if we have one child and want to have more?"

She smiled. "Aye, but how many more?"

"Well, if you insist, we will make love and have babies until you get the little girl in your dream."

"Do you promise?"

"I promise. We can start right now if you like."

She was shocked he was ready again considering the night they'd shared.

"But I'm already pregnant."

"Well we have to be sure we're doing it right for when you're not pregnant, don't we?"

She grinned and climbed on top of him.

"Can I ride you again?"

James's body jerked in response.

"You can do anything you want with me," he said. His voice was husky and thick.

"Do you promise?"

"I promise to love you as long as the sun rises and sets."

Later still, she woke to find him staring at her. She shifted her head to view him better and grinned. "My lord, is something amiss?"

"There was."

"Oh, and what was that?"

"Me."

"I don't understand."

"I was so blind when your uncle first approached me. I thought the answer to my future lay with the king, but instead I have been given a kingdom by a wee lass with golden hair who is as strong as any chief I've ever known."

"James."

"I expect you by my side, Aileana." His smile disappeared. "And I look forward to hearing your thoughts and sharing my responsibilities with you. My parents had a special partnership. I've always wanted that, but never knew such another woman could exist. Until I met you."

ABOUT KATE ROBBINS

Kate Robbins writes historical romance novels out of pure escapism and a love for all things Scottish, not to mention a life-long enjoyment of reading romance. Her journey into storytelling began with a short screenplay she wrote, directed, and produced which was screened at the 2003 Nickel Film Festival in St. John's, Newfoundland. She has also written and directed several stage plays for youth.

Kate loves the research process and delving into secondary sources in order to give readers the most authentic historical romance possible. She has travelled to Scotland and has visited the sites described in her Highland Chiefs series.

Bound to the Highlander is the first of three books set during the early fifteenth century during the reign of James Stewart, first of his name.

Kate is the pen name of Debbie Robbins who lives in St. John's, Newfoundland, Canada with her hubby, the man-beast, and her two awesome boys, the man-cubs.

GET IN TOUCH WITH KATE ROBBINS

Kate Robbins
(http://katerobbinsauthor.com)

Facebook
(https://www.facebook.com/pages/Kate-Robbins-Author/150717751758382)

Twitter
(https://twitter.com/KateRobWriter)

Goodreads
(http://www.goodreads.com/user/show/9566304-kate-robbins)

Tirgearr Publishing
(http://www.tirpub.com/krobbins)

Thank you for reading Bound to the Highlander

Please log into Tirgearr Publishing
(www.tirgearrpublishing.com)
and Kate Robbins' website for upcoming releases.

Keep your eyes open for Promised to the Highlander, book
two in the Highland Chief's Series.

Cover Art: Amanda Stephanie
Editor: Maudeen Wachsmith
Proofreader: R.L. McCoy

More from Kate Robbins

Promised To The Highlander
Highland Chiefs Series, book two

Nessia Stephenson's world was safe until a threat from a neighbouring clan forces her to accept a betrothal to a man whose family can offer her the protection she needs. The real threat lies in her intense attraction to the man who arranged the match—the clan's chief and her intended's brother, Fergus MacKay.

When powerful warlord Fergus MacKay arranges a marriage for his younger brother, William, he has no idea the price will be his own heart. Fergus is captivated by the wildly beautiful Nessia, a woman he can never have.

When the feud between the MacKay and Sutherland clans escalates, Nessia, William, and Fergus all must make sacrifices for their future. Longing and loss, honour and duty. How can love triumph under such desperate circumstances?

Enemy Of The Highlander

Highland Chiefs Series, book three

Two years ago Freya MacKay walked away from the only man she would ever love, her family's bitter enemy, knowing her clan would never accept their love. A fragile alliance has been forged and now he has returned to warn of a terrible threat. Freya MacKay is torn between the familiar surge of passion he evokes and her promise to wed another man.

Ronan Sutherland has lost everything to a cruel uncle who will lay the entire north Highlands to waste if he is not stopped. There is only one who can help—but seeking alliance with his former enemy, Fergus MacKay, means encountering the woman who left him two years ago, breaking his heart.

A bitter feud keeps their clans at one another's throats and it seems nothing will stop one from destroying the other. Will Ronan ever forgive Freya for leaving him? Can he trust her again? Or will the decades of hatred and deceit between their families prevail?

92106256R00169

Made in the USA
Middletown, DE
05 October 2018